VICTIM'S CHOICE

❏   ❏   ❏

VICTIM'S CHOICE

❑ ❑ ❑

Michael McClister

THOMAS
DUNNE
BOOKS

St. Martin's Press ≈ New York

The author wishes to acknowledge as a valuable source in the writing of this novel the nonfiction work *Homicide: A Year on the Killing Streets* by David Simon, copyright 1991, published by Ballantine Books.

THOMAS DUNNE BOOKS.
An imprint of St. Martin's Press.

Library of Congress Cataloging-in-Publication Data

McClister, Michael.
    Victim's choice / Michael McClister.—1st ed.
        p.   cm.
    ISBN 0-312-20618-6
    I. Title.
    PS3563.C34157V53   1999   99-21986
    813'.54—dc21   CIP

First Edition: July 1999

10   9   8   7   6   5   4   3   2   1

ONE

❑   ❑   ❑

WHERE IS A cop when you need one? I had been trying to
get arrested for twenty minutes.

I had swiped at handbags and briefcases and cursed everyone going in and out of the building. I had rushed at pedestrians and flipped off two rubberneckers in an open
convertible. I had pounded on the *USA Today* machine with
both fists.

Finally I decided to hit somebody. A slender redhead was
edging around me—I shoved her into the revolving door. As
she fell her mouth dropped open but only a sad gurgle came
out. She fumbled her bag toward me but I slapped it away
with a snarl. I whirled. A dozen men, frozen in a half-circle
of fear. None of them seemed to recognize me. I charged; they
gave way. *Cowards!* A tall pear-shaped man stumbled and
went down heavily. *Don't croak you silly ass!* I was sweat-
soaked, my old workclothes clinging damply. I reversed
course back toward the building. There was movement behind
me, reflected in the high windows. *Finally!*

The first uniform was a female, too plump for her blues,
her eyes hidden behind mirrored aviators that glittered in the
sun. She was mouthing something, her left arm extended toward me, the other hand riding the big Beretta. As I relaxed
to surrender the two studs hit me from behind.

"Stay down, asshole! Don't move!" she screamed.

1

"Down!" The studs wrenched me into the cuffs. "Easy!" I yelled back, as if they were in on it, and they hit me again. *Twenty minutes! I could have slaughtered dozens.*

At Police Headquarters I refused to talk. They found nothing in my pockets. The chubby female marched me upstairs and stuck me in the Fishbowl, the holding tank with its faded pink walls from the days when soft colors were deemed to soothe savage breasts and beasts; California bullshit. The Fishbowl was empty but I knew there were eyes behind the one-way window. I sat and stood, sat and stood, shivering as the perspiration dried. My arms ached from the cuffs. Finally one of the typewriter cops summoned me with a fat finger to his desk in the squad room, which was busy this morning. When I wouldn't talk he shrugged and kept typing as if I had. The female officer, her eyes still hidden by the mirrors, read from her notebook in a bored drone. They gave me a John Doe booking for assault and public disturbance, as I expected. Eight counts.

McDade spotted me first. He was pouring coffee from one of the permanently-stained carafes on the four-burner Mr. Coffee. He looked up and caught me trying to reaffix the mustache, my hands free for a moment after fingerprinting. The wig was loose too. I could feel the gray peeking from beneath the black.

"What . . . Joe! Is that you? Jesus, is that you, Joe!"

I froze. The ever-rumpled McDade hurried over as fast as homicide detectives ever hurry. He was a little roundshouldered and a little flabby, but as he moved you could see traces of linebacker. I looked down. He had me.

McDade grabbed the sheet and scanned it, then nodded the uniforms aside and steered me down the corridor toward Patterson's office, sloshing coffee all the way. Headquarters was swarming; as we sailed past the Wall of Honor, I saw most of the brass. Every voice was too loud. Two detectives recog-

2

nized me and gaped in amazement. The wig was halfway off now, the mustache gone.

Without knocking, McDade pushed open the door marked Homicide Commander and waved me inside. As always, it was like stepping from noir into Technicolor. Soft glow of lamplight; polished cherry desk; green leather upholstery; watercolors on three walls. On the fourth wall were Captain Avery Patterson's diplomas and citations, grouped around a stark white-on-black placard: We Work for God. Patterson wasn't there.

McDade, breathing raggedly, unlocked the cuffs and motioned me to the hard chair. He raised and lowered the coffee mug without drinking. Then the door crashed open and Captain Avery Patterson himself swept in. Square jaw, square shoulders in tailored gray, but red-faced this morning despite the yearlong tan. He stood beside his highbacked judge's chair and skimmed the arrest sheet. McDade was behind me, close.

The Captain leaned on the desk with both fists. His furious eyes lasered into mine. The famous Look.

"Are you drunk, Joe? Or using? What the fuck's happening here?"

The hallway was quiet; I felt many ears straining.

"Joe, what the fuck? Eight assaults! Goddamn, of all days! Talk to me!"

I was oddly relaxed. "I'm not drunk, Captain. You know me."

"Do I? Do I know you, Joe?" I lowered my gaze as the Look bored in. Patterson's knuckles were white against the gleaming desktop. With an angry motion he flicked the sheet toward McDade, who caught it in the air.

"Jesus, Joe, what the fuck? You just lose it or something?"

"Yeah, I just lost it or something. I guess."

"You guess? You guess? Steve, I got to get back out there—throw him in a fucking cell." But he didn't move.

3

From behind me McDade said, "Joe, you wanna lawyer? You wanna *exercise your constitutional rights*? Maybe you better."

"But we can't help you if you do," Patterson said, folding his arms across his chest.

I was offended. *Use this on the homeboys, Captain. You can't bluff me.*

"Joe, goddamnit, were you *trying* to get arrested?" Steve McDade asked.

I turned to look at him. "Sure. Of course."

"Of course!" Patterson snapped. "Of course! You were gonna kill him?"

I nodded, my eyes challenging his now. The detectives eye-talked the way cops do and gulped bushels of air, as if they'd been underwater. I was panting too. Patterson went to the door, jerked it open and shooed away the eavesdroppers. He closed the door gently and returned to the big desk.

"Joe, Joe," he whispered. The Look was gone now. "What were you thinking, you've been through hell, worse than hell. . . ."

"He stabbed Buzz twenty-one times, Captain. Twenty-one times! You didn't tell me that, Captain Patterson. You didn't tell me that, Sergeant McDade." My voice was as cold as death.

"Joe," Steve McDade said gently.

Avery Patterson eased into his highbacked chair and looked at me from far away.

"That animal raped Belle and strangled her, and when Buzz tried to save her, he stabbed him twenty-one times. Maybe she was still alive, maybe she saw it." Inside I was raging but my voice stayed steady.

"It came out at the trial, Joe."

"I didn't go to the trial! I didn't go to the goddamn trial— you know that! I depended on you guys to tell me *like you said you would.*"

4

"We thought—"

"Bullshit, Captain! I've got other friends around here, I got the story. Real friends."

For a long moment all of us were silent. Then McDade said, "What made you think you could disguise yourself with a wig and a mustache and that fruitpicker's outfit and raise enough hell to get arrested, and then get locked up somewhere near Boogie Brown, who's isolated like all child molesters—*as you know, you've covered this place*—then if you *could* get to him be able to put him down? Five ten, one sixty tops, grayheaded, forty years old—against a stone killer. Goddamn, Joe, tell us you're on something."

"I'm on something, Sergeant McDade. I'm on a mission. And Boogie Brown's not isolated twenty-four seven, I found that out. Your jail's not all that . . . I could have gotten to him. When he least expected it." I locked eyes with Steve this time. "It took your crack cops twenty minutes to get there. Twenty fucking minutes." I began to tremble. Soon I was heaving, my head in my hands.

"Jesus, Joe," Patterson sighed. "What a day for this."

I heard the door open and close as Patterson left. After a moment I felt Steve McDade's hand on my shoulder. The only sound was my sobs.

TWO

I SPENT ONLY four hours behind bars. They gave me a private cell and allowed my inamorata Elly Briggs to join me. Even in her realtor's clothes, wet-eyed, trembling, Elly was alluring. I called her the Countess. We fell together on the steel cot and necked like the illicit lovers we had once been. The jailer watched sourly from the corridor.

Everyone rallied to my side—I was stunned. Steve McDade sent two uniforms to herd my victims to the Headquarters pressroom, then paraded me before them in handcuffs for an emotional mea culpa. I insisted on the handcuffs. No one pressed charges. The redhead I had thrown into the revolving door ignored my fruitpicker's rags and hugged me for the cameras. Nice bazongas.

Then Steve made me face my fellow reporters. It was odd, answering questions instead of asking them. I had a reputation for asking the tough ones, which was why Channel Nine had the best ratings. But today my competitors lobbed me softballs; even they understood.

In the rallying-to-my-side department, Channel Nine went over the top, sending out the Boss himself, Station Manager Logan Murphy, who hadn't looked into a camera in twenty years. But his reserves of confidence were immense, and he hustled outside to catch the late-afternoon light and did eight minutes live. I couldn't have done better.

"This is more than a news story to us at Channel Nine," Logan Murphy declared solemnly as he ambled across Courthouse Square, the sun playing warmly off the old fountain. "It's a family story, because Joe Colby is part of our family. And this family sticks together." I felt a twinge, and I thought I was beyond twinges.

Then they split the screen—Logan on the left, StairMaster-fit in his navy blazer; and, on the right, the file footage that ravaged me every time.

". . . Joe's wife, Connie, died of breast cancer two years ago, and the family thought it would never recover, but Joe and Buzz and Belle managed to keep going. Somehow. And just as they were rebuilding their lives, an unspeakable crime, a crime so savage, so inhuman . . . a handyman whom Joe Colby befriended . . . a paroled ex-convict he gave a job to . . . raped and murdered Joe's daughter, Belle. Belle the ballet dancer. Belle the straight-A student. Belle who at bedtime sat alone with her mother's picture and talked about her day. Raped and strangled by Bougainvillea Brown, known on our mean streets as Boogie Brown, a violent career criminal with arrests dating back to childhood. Annabelle Colby was ten years old."

Elly reached for my hand and held it tightly. We were huddled on the leather sofa in Captain Patterson's office, watching on the fancy Sony with some of the murder cops. As Logan Murphy itemized my horrors on television, the familiar blazing chill whipped and raged inside me. It was my permanent invisible scar: the icefire. The detectives peeked at me behind their hands.

". . . and when Buzz Colby came home and surprised this monster in his savage crime, and tried to save his sister, Boogie Brown stabbed him to death, slashed the life out of a twelve-year-old-boy who wore his baseball cap backwards and wanted to be a doctor to save cancer patients like his mother, stabbed him twenty-one-times. . . ."

8

On the right half of the screen Buzz's young pallbearers, their black baseball caps backward, struggled with his casket on the steps of the church; then came the grim deacons gripping Belle's with both hands, as if it were heavier than it could have been. Then I saw myself on the screen, head down, friends holding each arm as we followed in the cortege, my face suddenly lifting to the sky and wailing as the icefire had swept through me.

"These murders occurred a year ago, but Joe Colby learned the gruesome details only recently. He could not bear to attend the trial, which ended in a hung jury . . ."

The right screen dissolved to Boogie Brown in the courtroom, fraudulent in banker's pinstripes, jotting notes on a yellow pad, offering Life Savers to his lawyers. Then his entourage outside the courthouse, jiving and dancing after the mistrial, finger-shooting the prosecutor as he descended the long steps. Again I felt the icefire, a fixture within me now. I could summon it.

". . . and this morning he tried to get arrested by disturbing the peace—so he could get inside the jail and confront Boogie Brown and somehow avenge his children. His colleagues at Channel Nine understand why Joe Colby's victims outside the Wellborn Building this morning didn't press charges. Joe has apologized to everyone and promised to get help to deal with his rage and to learn—"

McDade came in. I stood up with an effort. "Steve, I can't . . ." I waved vaguely. "Can Elly take me home?"

Steve walked us down the private stairway and outside to Elly's stodgy Buick with the real-estate stuff spread over the back seat. I shook Steve's hand for the third or fourth time.

"I'm sorry, Steve, that's all I can think of to say. I guess I went crazy. I'm—"

"You picked a helluva day, Joe."

9

Elly and I got in. She started the engine and I lowered my window. "What's up, Steve?"

"Caught a double Kodak this morning. Haven't released it yet."

I let out a low whistle. *Kodak* was cop talk for high-profile murder. It meant constant pressure from the mayor, the brass, reporters like me. A *double Kodak* was sheer hell.

"Who, Steve?" I asked.

Steve glanced behind him, then leaned toward me.

"Two very prominent women, Joe, shot this morning. Judge Lodge's wife and Marvin Isaacson's wife. Same shooter. Worst we've had . . . since your children, Joe."

Elly was moaning "*Oh no no no.*" I started to get out of the car but sagged back. "No—my God—Maggie Lodge? Where was—Isaacson's wife too?"

"Judge Lodge and Isaacson were at the courthouse. The women were at home. We don't know what we got, Joe—except a double Kodak. Off the record."

"Jesus, my stupid . . . I'm sorry, Steve. Jesus, of all days."

Behind us brakes squealed and a horn sounded. The police garage was busy.

"Joe, what you tried to do today was get revenge. In your lunatic way. But somebody *did* get revenge today—against a lawyer and a judge."

"By shooting their *wives*?"

Elly slumped against the door, weeping softly. I reached for her hand.

Steve whispered, "They were *executed*, Joe. *Executed*. And it was directed at the system—at a judge and a criminal lawyer. There were notes left on the bodies."

"Notes?"

"Off the record, Joe. We're not releasing this yet."

"Then don't tell me, Steve. I don't want to get blamed when somebody leaks it."

10

Steve braced himself against the car with both hands. He looked very tired.

" 'To Judge John Lodge: Now you know how it feels.' 'To Marvin Isaacson: Now you know how it feels.' Both notes were signed 'Avengers.' "

"Avengers? *Now you know how it feels? Avengers?* Who—what is this, Steve?"

Another horn blared nearby and I jumped. The veteran homicide detective straightened up, drumming his fingers on the roof of the car. "It means you won't even make the front page, Joe. Take care of him, Countess." He turned and was gone.

Elly drove hurriedly to a pay phone so I could call Logan Murphy at the station. He had just returned from the courthouse.

"Boss, you've had your hands full with my stupid caper, and I appreciate everything you said on the air, you were great—but first we got business. There's been a double murder. . . . how the hell did you know, Logan? McDade just told me."

"My sources, Joe." I could hear Logan's grin.

"Well goddamnit, Boss, your sources must be the shooters."

Logan laughed wickedly. "Go ye forth and get laid and tell the Countess to keep screwing you till you're sane again." He hung up with another laugh. The Boss was back on the front lines and loving it.

Soon Elly and I were nestled under goose down sipping chilled vodka from the bottle we kept in the freezer. She said, "I was so scared when they took me to your cell. I've been scared all day."

"I know. I was scared too. I'm still coming down."

"How did McDade know I'm the Countess?"

"I don't know, I guess he heard me say it."

11

"He thinks I was in on it."

"No, no. It doesn't matter—they got a double Kodak on their hands."

She pressed her warmth against me and kissed my face, my neck, my nipples. Then her tongue traced my body slowly and found its target.

"You're not scared now," she said. I pushed into her face.

Later she whispered, "Did they think you were crazy, trying to get thrown in jail to attack somebody who's already there?"

"They said Boogie's isolated like all child molesters, and I said bullshit. They know it's bullshit—I could've gotten to him."

She snapped on the light. "If they had really locked you up . . . could you have killed him?"

"We'll never know," I said.

But I knew.

THREE

❏ ❏ ❏

*H E **WORRIES ABOUT** the name.*

Avengers.

*Ancient British TV show, who would remember it? He cer-
tainly remembered Emma Peel in her boots, sexier in black
and white than today's hot buttered bimbos in fifty-two-inch
Pussyvision.*

*Or the Jewish assassins who hunted down Nazis after the
war. Executioners, called themselves the Avengers.*

He had invented other names: The Retaliators. The Sword.
The Justice Department. *Which would resonate in the head-
lines? It was too late to change, anyway. Avengers. First
thought best thought.*

*He sits in a straightbacked chair behind a battered wooden
desk, staring at a sheet of paper curling out of the portable
typewriter before him. The drone of the old generator seems
louder than usual. The room is damp and cold, the light cold
and dull.*

*He inhales deeply and exhales slowly, a trick he has learned
to counter anxiety. The trick does not work for long. He jams
his hands under his thighs.*

*His eyes fall upon two padded envelopes stacked on the cor-
ner of the desk. Each contains a videotape. One is addressed
to* The Honorable John C. Lodge, United States Court House;
the other to Marvin M. Isaacson, Attorney at Law. *Just push*

Play, Your Honor. Just push Play, Counselor Isaacson in your ponytail. See how they run, gentlemen, see how they hurl the bright flowers, see how they fall. No stay of execution today, Minimum John, Your Fucking Honor. No stay of execution today, Counselor Ponytail. Now you know how it feels!

He thinks he hears a distant sound, then realizes it is only the generator. Any noise is unusual. Once he had heard a tractor, some hayseed lost in his own shortcut. He remembered the farmer's astonishment when he stepped from the dense trees into the tractor's path and signaled the way out. The only security lapse. Never again.

He rereads the letter he has typed on the old Olympia.

Dear Joe Colby:
We sympathize with your desire to avenge your children. We will execute Boogie Brown if you validate his death warrant by leaving your exterior house lights burning throughout the daylight hours of Thursday, May 19. To decline this offer, do nothing. Observe strict silence.

He types Avengers *at the bottom and folds the letter easily despite the rubber gloves.*

He checks the typed envelope. Kolby with a K? Probably not. First thought best thought. He adds the zip code in black ink, printing the numbers from back to front with the wrong hand. He inserts a photograph. Finally, using a sponge and a few drops of bottled water, he seals the envelope and affixes the stamp.

The next morning he drops the videos into separate mailboxes and the letter into the mailbox in front of Police Headquarters. A sergeant hurries by headed for roll call.

"Good morning, Officer," the Avenger says.

"Morning, ma'am."

FOUR

❏   ❏   ❏

THE MURDER POLICE, bent over their desks and phones, threw me tense looks when I came in. The double Kodak had cast a grim spell over Homicide. I paced outside the Fishbowl until I heard my name.

"Goddamnit, Joe, we're busy," Patterson growled as he motioned me into his office. A new watercolor leaned against the credenza behind the cherry desk. Haitian; lots of color.

As I took the hard chair, he said, "Assault anybody today?" He smiled but there was something behind it. "You okay?"

"I think so, I'm still embarrassed. I made an appointment with el shrinko. Can we get Steve in too, Captain?"

He shifted into the Look.

"Just us three. It'll be worth it."

He stepped outside and yelled for McDade, who appeared within seconds with the usual disarranged shirt and steaming mug of coffee. Steve closed the door and took a seat on the sofa behind me. Patterson slumped hard in the judge's chair and swiveled his feet up.

"Go."

I took out the plastic bag containing the letter, envelope and photograph and laid it gently in front of Patterson. He scanned the letter, then wheeled his chair back so McDade could lean in. A speed-reader, Steve devoured everything in a glance.

I said, "That's a photograph of my mother. I've never seen it. I described it to my sister over the phone and she's never seen it."

"It's a threat," Steve said.

"No shit."

"Where's your mother, Joe?" Steve said.

"My sister took her . . . somewhere. I don't know." I locked my hands behind my head to conceal my jitters.

"Tommorrow's the nineteenth, Joe. Your outside lights going to be on? To validate Boogie's death warrant?"

"Sure, of course. Would I be here? I thought about it."

Patterson stood up energetically. "Joe, you did right coming to us. You're getting smart." He handed the plastic bag to McDade. "DNA under the stamp, everything. And total secrecy."

McDade sailed away, the rumpled linebacker who looked younger than I did though we had graduated together. The smartest cop in the territory. And Avery Patterson was no slouch.

"Joe, could anyone have seen you coming over here?"

"No, I don't see how. An intern drove me over in the an, straight into the garage. No one could have seen me. Does my letter look like the others—the notes on the bodies?"

Patterson, jotting something in his leatherbound notebook, ignored my question. He wrote with a maroon Waterman like a CEO. Which he was.

"When did this arrive?"

"This morning's mail, about eleven. I thought it was a sick joke, we got some people at the station. . . . Then Mom's picture fell out. I'm still shaking."

Without looking up he said, "You got any ideas?"

"No, none. Last year we did a series on extremists, some real nutcases like Burl Devine, but we never came across any Avengers."

"Why the handwritten zip code, you think? Everything else is typed."

I shrugged. "Maybe he had to look it up in the post office."

Patterson stared out the window. The heavy drapes were open today, the sun streaming in. I was perspiring.

I said quietly, "Should I be afraid, Captain?"

He paused before answering and I watched his eyes. Not even a Homicide Commander can control his eyes all the time.

"We prepare for the worst, Joe. Very seldom does the worst occur. But, as you know better than anybody . . ."

Steve McDade returned, fresh coffee in hand. "Looks like the first two, Joe." He peered at me over the rim of the mug. "Off the record."

"We'll give you protection, Joe," Patterson said.

"What about the DNA? Did you get DNA from the others?" I asked, too loudly.

"Off the record," Patterson said.

"Sure, off the record. But two women were killed and now I've been threatened, I think I'm entitled to know something."

Patterson nodded. "Just so we understand each other, Joe. Everything's off the record."

"Sure, of course! Fuck the record! Just tell me something!"

"No DNA."

"No DNA," I said derisively. "Off the record."

I looked from one face to the other. Detectives' faces now, flat and hard with dead eyes that had seen everything; cops' faces, not friends'.

I jumped up and began pacing. "What exactly does protection mean?"

Steve said, "Maybe you should bunk somewhere else for a while, Joe. That big old place of yours . . ."

"Big perimeter," Patterson said.

I stopped pacing and looked at them incredulously. "Hiding, is that what protection means? Hiding? *Running?*"

Patterson tilted back in the big chair, affecting nonchalance, but his voice had an edge. "Not running. Not hiding. Being prudent."

"*Prudent,*" I sneered.

"We'll protect you, Joe," Patterson said. "But you can make it easier. Doesn't that make sense?"

"Of course, of course it does," I said. "I don't know, I'm really getting scared. Who are these people?"

"They're organized and bloodthirsty and very dangerous," Patterson said. "They posed as flower deliverymen when the wives . . . there were fresh flowers all around, florist's paper. Had to be at least two of them, one person couldn't handle all those flowers, a big weapon and a video camera."

"A video camera? A *video camera?*"

"Off the record, Joe. They taped the murders. Sent videos to Lodge and Isaacson."

"Like . . . snuff videos?"

"We're not releasing this at all. Judge Lodge and Isaacson are wiped out. Devastated."

"Jesus," I whispered, "who are these monsters?" We fell silent. The only sounds were the hums and whirs of the building. I understood why Patterson was keeping the videos secret. The cops always held things back to authenticate confessions and snitches.

McDade said, "We had some cops, flirted with this shit. Remember that Eastwood movie, *Magnum Force*? Renegade cops fed up with the system, with bad guys getting off on technicalities. Imposed their own justice, like vigilantes. This phrase 'if you validate his death warrant' . . . some cops rent that movie all the time and get drunk—"

"Burl Devine," I said, taking another walk across the room. I was breathing audibly. I sat down in a green leather chair.

Now Steve stood up and began pacing. "British TV series, *The Avengers*, Patrick MacNee and Diana Rigg. She played

Emma Peel, very sexy, black boots. Cultish following, A&E has reruns. Sean Connery did the movie." He sighed vacantly. "Seems like a stretch. Wasn't about revenge anyway."

Patterson was listening alertly. Like everyone else, he paid attention to Steve McDade's musings. More than a few cases had been put down because the paunchy caffeine addict in the rumpled shirt let his great mind and memory "spazier" around, as he called it. The Irishman who sprinkled in Yiddish—his wife was Jewish. Commander Patterson trusted Steve's memory more than the case files, and his spaziering more than trace evidence. So did I.

Patterson looked almost plaintively at Steve. "Goddamn I hope cops aren't in this."

"Burl Devine," I said for the third time, giving them my hardest look.

"Burl Devine," Steve said. "The crackpot's crackpot."

"Crazy as a shithouse rat," Avery Patterson said.

"Burl gives shithouse rats a bad name," I said. "Crackpots too. When Burl was on the force . . . well, you know better than I do. After the mistrial he told me Boogie Brown should be tortured by Apaches."

"You know Burl has four balls," Steve said. "Speaking of torture."

"Four balls . . . as in testicles?"

"As in anatomical anomaly. Rasputin had four balls, called him the Mad Monk. You'd be crazy too, testosterone overload."

"So some poor bastard is wandering around nutless? Burl got his?"

"Had a choice, rather have two johnsons."

"*Two*? We'd all be in cages, two."

"Jesus, I hope he warns his fellators. Fellatrixes. Caution, normal load one quart. This makes *I won't come in your mouth* a felony."

We were laughing hard, too hard.

"Joe," Avery Patterson said, leaning toward me with the friendly version of the Look, "what time you get home from the station?"

"Midnight, Monday through Friday. Sometimes later, we have a taste."

"I'll have a man at your house every night from midnight till you go to work the next day. What about the station?"

"We got as much security as you do. Full-time, not rent-a-cops."

"I'll talk to your head of security. Is Elly living with you?"

"Sometimes. A lot."

"Change your routine, Joe. Mix it up. Take Elly away on weekends. And make sure your mother—"

I nodded vigorously. "I understand."

The phone rang and Patterson answered. He eyetalked with Steve, who hustled me out of the office, closing the door behind us. The corridor was empty.

"Joe, how they hit Boogie? Hypothetical, you take their deal, you leave the lights on tomorrow. Now Avengers got to dust a tough guy *who is in jail.* Isolated like all pedophiles. How?"

"Don't kid yourself about that isolation shit, Steve. I guarantee you I could've gotten to Boogie—one of your ex-jailbirds told me how." I expected him to ask who but he didn't. His mind was spaziering double-time.

I said, "Maybe they have another inmate lined up. Maybe a gang-banger. An assassin behind bars."

Steve frowned and shook his head.

"Or a cop," I said quietly.

The frown became a furious glare.

I threw up a hand. "I know, I know. Off the goddamn record."

FIVE

CONFIDING IN THE cops had made me nervous. I wanted to skip Group and curl up with the Countess, vodka on the side. But sooner or later I had to face the Crime Victims Support Group as its most spectacular failure. I had already missed too many meetings. Showtime.

I arrived late but my pal Ned Cromartie, wearing his sinister eyepatch, was waiting for me in the YMCA parking lot. We called Ned "the crossing guard"—he always came early to escort people inside. The Y was in a marginal area, and we'd made sick jokes about getting mugged on the way to a Victims meeting. I couldn't see a bulge under Ned's blazer but I knew the Glock was there.

Ned pumped my hand and stammered what he'd told me on the phone: "Don't w-worry, Joe—they've all g-got false m-m-mustaches." Ned's stammering increased with tension; tonight he seemed as anxious as I was. As we entered the old brick building and climbed the smooth wooden stairs, the smell of chlorine hit me harder than usual. I felt nauseous. And when Ned pulled open the frosted-glass door to the drab meeting room, I had to force myself to step inside. But I managed, and they stood and applauded. I couldn't hold back the tears.

The first to greet me was Juanita Daley, a stately black woman in her forties wearing a long wine-red dress and enormous hoop earrings. "Joe, dear dear Joe," she murmured, embracing me unaffectedly. "God bless you, Joe, God bless you." She stepped back, still gripping my shoulders. "Joe, I wish you would've got in there. Yes, oh yes, Joe."

There were two cliques in Victims—the Savages and the Turn-the-Other-Cheekers. I was a Savage, and Juanita Daley was Mother Savage. Twelve years earlier, her eighteen-year-old daughter Debbie had been raped and smothered to death by a tattooed white sadist named Franklin Delano Hollowell. Arrest, trial, conviction, death sentence—but three times the execution had been stayed, thanks to Hollowell's lawyer Marvin Isaacson and U.S. District Judge John Lodge. In Group we had debated Juanita's yearning to witness the execution. All of us Savages approved: It would bring closure, The Cheekers wailed: Revenge cannot bring closure. Juanita had listened to everyone, then declared that nothing short of her own death could keep her away from Central Prison on the appointed midnight. And she had been there, in a white gown with Debbie's picture pinned over her heart. But with sixty seconds to go, Minimum John Lodge issued another stay of execution, and Franklin Delano Hollowell eluded the eighteen hundred volts yet again. I hadn't seen Juanita since.

"Joe, I looked him in the eye but he couldn't look *me* in the eye. Not even in his final hour. When they strapped him in, Joe, I thought it was going to be over. This feeling came over me, peaceful, like you get from Valium or a joint. But then the call came, he could look at me then. He gave me the finger, Joe."

Everyone was crowding around, and Juanita's voice soared. "Those poor women, God rest their souls, we must have a moment of silence tonight. God rest their souls. But I must say this: I don't wish no innocent people killed, God knows I'm the *last* . . . but as long as two innocent people *were* killed, I'm just as glad Minimum John and that filthy Isaacson has to

22

suffer. Just as glad! Just as glad! Wonder what the judge and the lawyer think now about the death penalty, wonder do they want the death penalty now!" She turned to me and her voice fell to a whisper. "Joe, I still wake up at four-fifteen every morning, every morning of the world." I drew her close. That was the hour the police had come.

We had never begun a meeting with such naked emotion. Ended some. We ignored the circle of folding chairs where the apple-cheeked facilitator waited uncertainly, balancing a stack of multicolored pages on her lap. Both Savages and Cheekers clamored for the details of my escapade—the wig, the mustache, the sham assaults on the sidewalk, the pear-shaped man collapsing in a heap and my horror that he had croaked, shoving the bosomy redhead into the revolving door and slapping her handbag away, the tubby policewoman with the mirrored glasses distracting me from the front so the two studs could nail me from behind. *No, there was no I.D. in my pockets; yes, they fingerprinted me; yes, the disguise faltered just as McDade came for coffee, I couldn't repair it in time.* They groaned at my bad luck.

"People understand, Joe! People understand! They love you!"

"They wish you'd made it!"

"*We* love you, Joe!"

"Damn that McDade, put that boy on decaf!"

Soon the Savages and even a few Cheekers were confessing their own dark fantasies of vengeance. All of them were victims of violent crime, and, like Juanita Daley and me, most of them had been victimized a second time by the system. All their pent-up furies poured forth, and for two hours we drank coffee and laughed and cried and embraced uproariously. It was raw catharsis; therapy noir. And Ned was right—they all had false mustaches.

Finally Juanita rose in her long red dress and spread her

arms like an evangelist. "People who say we're wrong don't know. These *bleeding hearts*! Revenge ain't wrong, revenge ain't unnatural. It's the most *natural* thing I ever felt! *Pretending* it's wrong is what's unnatural."

We were drained. The new facilitator, an earnest young psychologist named Deirdre whom I'd never met before, had wisely packed up her colored pages and left early. She had never been a victim, never lost anyone to a human predator, possessed no credentials for therapy noir. And recognized it, which impressed us all.

As we were breaking up I got Juanita alone.

"There's something crazy happening, Juanita—there's a group called Avengers—they killed Maggie Lodge and Ruth Isaacson! And left notes behind! And listen to this—they sent *me* a note saying they would *execute Boogie Brown*—and he's in jail!"

She stood very still, her soft eyes wide and unblinking. She seemed on the edge of laughter or tears.

Finally she said, "Joe, I got a note, too. From Avengers. They offered to execute Hollowell. And he's on Death Row."

"What did the police say?"

She coughed a few times and pursed her lips. "I didn't tell the police, Joe. Avengers said not to."

We stood silently, looking at each other.

"Did you tell the police?" she asked.

I nodded hesitantly. "I wasn't supposed to but I did." I looked around. We were the only ones left.

"I should have, Joe, I know I should have. Should have been a *good citizen*. But didn't you have just a little feeling of saying yes, just saying go ahead, the justice system won't give me any justice, you give me some justice. It's been twelve years, Joe, for me. Twelve years. And the so-called justice system ain't punished Boogie Brown either. *Mistrial!*"

We walked out silently, Juanita's big shoulder bag thumping against her hip. As she unlocked her red Firebird, she chuckled humorlessly. "You tried to break *into* jail, Joe. Maybe Avengers don't have to."

SIX

❏   ❏   ❏

AFTER MY REVERSE jailbreak and public humiliation, Logan Murphy yanked me off all newscasts for a "cooling-off" period. I fumed, but he was right. Then one day he popped into my office with a sly grin, boomed, "Showtime, Joe," and took me to the Press Club for lunch.

As we passed through the archway into the main dining room, I got several thumbs-up salutes and plenty of waves. Only the bluenoses snubbed me. Rudy, the maître d', pumped my hand and pointedly ushered us through the center of the vast room, weaving among the white tablecloths, to Logan's corner table. I shook several hands en route, and Rudy even held my chair. I felt something in my throat.

"See?" Logan said.

Another twinge. "Boss, I still don't know how to thank you for sticking with me. I embarrassed you and the station . . . you've been more than compassionate . . ." I looked at Logan, my eyes wet now. "Thanks, Boss."

I had said all this before, but not as warmly. Logan waved it off with a CEO's toss of the hand.

We ordered drinks. Logan grinned roguishly as he always did when a taste was on the way. But he had another reason to smile.

"Joe, we've gotten more mail on you than anything we ever ran, *including* the governor's bimbos and the bishop's boy-

27

friends. You're hot! *Hot* hot! *Tor*-rid! So—dum-da-dum-dum—*Crime and Punishment with Joe Colby*—weekly exposé of the justice system—the *injustice* system—none of this half-assed chase-the-cops-with-a-camera horseshit, none of this bor-ing analysis-paralysis by some criminologist twit—in-your-face *advocacy*, by God! *For* the good guys and *fuck* the bad guys! The purists will call it trash TV. Fuck the purists too!"

Logan was talking too loudly. "Many ears," I muttered. The waiter arrived with our manhattans.

"Fuck many ears!" Logan whispered venomously. We clinked glasses. "It's perfect, Joe—gory details and a Pulitzer too!" Logan straightened abruptly as uncertainty struck. His backbone was a barometer.

"Joe, Joe, forgive me, I get carried *away*. I should have asked, Do you *like* the concept? Do you *want* to try it? I try to feel what you've been through, Joe, but I *can't, I can't*. I can sympathize but not empathize. But *Crime and Punishment* is the perfect way for you to strike back—avenge Buzz and Belle by exposing the system! You have unique credentials—you're a great reporter and a victim too!"

Logan was gesticulating and getting louder again. The eavesdroppers were straining every nerve.

"I love it, Logan," I whispered. "I'll always be haunted by this . . . ache for revenge. It seems so wrong in your head but so right in your heart. *Crime and Punishment*—can Dostoyevsky sue?"

"We'll make the little Russki bugger proud," Logan crowed. He signaled our waiter, who scurried over. "A bottle of Bollinger's, my man, if you please! Joe, we must celebrate. The first day of the rest of our lives. Breaking new ground and *kick . . . ing . . . their . . . ass.*"

The Channel Two contingent, our strongest competitor,

was leaving; they would not sit by and watch Number One in the Ratings throwing down toasts.

I leaned conspiratorially across the corner of the table. "I've got the first show, Boss."

"You *do* like it." The sly grin had turned positively evil.

"My glands say yes. I only listen to my glands now. Sometimes I get this feeling inside, like a cold fire. . . ." I gestured apologetically.

Logan was all sympathy or empathy again. "I know, I know. I mean I *don't* know, but I *know*." Through the evil grin he whispered, "What's the first *Crime and Punishment*?"

The waiter arrived with the Bolly. He filled our glasses, set the bottle in a silver bucket on a silver stand, and retired. I checked again for eavesdroppers. We were safe.

"I got a letter offering to *execute Boogie Brown*. From some group called *Avengers*. They warned me not to tell the cops but I did. Listen to this, there was a note from Avengers on Ruth Isaacson's body. 'To Marvin Isaacson: Now you know how it feels. Avengers.' There was a note on Maggie Lodge's body. 'To John Lodge: Now you know how it feels. Avengers.' "

"Avengers! Goddamn, Joe, my sources . . . goddamn! *Now you know how it feels*! Holy holy!"

"You remember Juanita Daley—the Hollowell case, he raped and smothered her daughter. The redneck with the tattoos. I saw her at Group last night. She got a note from Avengers offering to *execute* Franklin Delano Hollowell."

"Execute Hollowell—holy holy—Isaacson's his lawyer . . . and Lodge stopped the execution!"

"Stayed it three times. There's more, Boss, you won't believe it—Isaacson and Minimum John got *videos* of the murders. *Snuff tapes* of their wives being killed. They're both suicidal."

"Snuff tapes? Jesus, no wonder . . ." He reached for the bottle but froze halfway. "*Execute* Boogie Brown? How? He's in the city jail—the jail you tried to break into."

Classical Boss. Show me how.

"We didn't get that far. The note said to turn on my house lights on a certain day. *To validate Boogie Brown's death warrant.* And don't tell the cops, but I told them."

"And Juanita Daley got one? Offering to execute Hollowell?"

I nodded.

"How in hell would they pull *that* off? Boogie Brown's easy compared to Hollowell—he's on Death Row. How could they execute somebody who's already on Death Row waiting to be executed?"

I shrugged and spread my hands. "I don't know, Boss. It's crazy."

"It's Pulitzer country is what it is! Holy Holy Holy Mother of Television." He went for the bottle again but straightened up, frowning. "Can we report this, Joe?"

"Not yet, but they can't hold it forever. I'll work on 'em."

This time Logan made it and refilled our glasses. "Sure, work on 'em. Hell, we're all on the same side."

We drank some champagne. I had to restrain myself from gulping it down. *Crime and Punishment with Joe Colby!*

"They threatened my mother, Logan. They sent me her picture."

"Your mother? Wait a minute, Joe—"

"Avengers don't know I went to the cops. I don't *think* they know, unless Avengers are cops themselves. Patterson's giving me protection—an officer at my house all night."

"Holy holy—what a show!"

Something nagged at me to quiet down, but I bubbled on.

"I got another one, Logan. Ned Cromartie, an old friend in my Victims group. Years ago he was mugged—they cut his nuts, they cut his eye, he has to wear a patch. Now he prowls the streets at night with a gun. Trying to *lure* a mugger."

"The same mugger?" Logan whispered.

"Ideally. He ain't particular."

"Holy holy holy goddamn!"

He poured more Bolly, overfilling both glasses. "I feel like toasting all afternoon," he said.

We clinked glasses again. "To *Crime and Punishment*," I said. "Especially punishment!"

A silent minute passed for the first time in two hours. We were marginally drunk. The other tables were empty now.

Logan folded his arms on the table and leaned forward. "Joe, I've got a possible show, too. My sources say the cops have panicked, they can't handle a double Kodak, so they're bringing in a hired gun. Some supercop—Elmo Finn."

My skin prickled. Elmo Finn—I knew the name from somewhere.

"So you want to do a show with this Elmo Finn, whoever the fuck he is?"

"Sure. Supercop, why not? Just an idea, Joe, it's your call. Your show. These Avengers said they'd kill your mother?"

"They sent me a photograph I'd never seen."

"Jesus, be careful."

"I'm gonna buy a gun."

"Goddamn, Joe, a gun? I'll get you a second bodyguard. Third, fourth. A gun, holy holy."

I felt another twinge. Logan.

"Can't have a night watchman forever, Boss. I want some firepower."

He peered at me through the fog. "You gonna buy a gun legally?"

"Sure, legally. I'm through with illegal, I ain't too good at it."

"Let's do a show? How to buy a gun. How to use a gun.

How to protect your house and family from predators."

"Now we got four shows, Boss. Not bad for one lunch."

"Not bad indeed!" Logan roared, hoisting the dripping bottle from the silver bucket. "Pulitzer country, fine holy vintage in Pulitzer country!"

SEVEN

❏　　❏　　❏

THE MUSCULAR YOUNG *black man crosses his legs to frustrate the toddler climbing onto his lap. He ignores the boy's whimpers, concentrating on his two visitors. He lights a cigarette and exhales short bursts of smoke.*
　"Made some coffee, you ladies want some."
　The taller visitor settles an oversized shoulder bag on the round table. "Sure, always."
　"Staff of life," the other says.
　The young man turns in his chair, gets the aluminum pot from the stove and pours coffee into three mismatched cups. He sets the pot on the table and leans back, his hands in his lap. "Don't have no milk."
　The taller visitor makes a gesture. "May as well get started. Like we said there's things we hope you can help us with." The visitor reaches into the oversized bag.
　"I can help you, I can sure help you. Those—wha—no—wha—"
　It is over quickly. The noise is louder than they expected. The tall visitor takes a long knife from the shoulder bag and drops to the floor. The other gathers certain items and stuffs them into the bag. They work rapidly and efficiently. There is no sound from the boy. Soon they are outside, turning on the doorstep and pretending to say good-bye, walking away unhurriedly, as they have practiced.

Forty-five minutes later he walks the route he has walked hundreds of times: around the building, into the trees, along the overgrown trail that only he and she know. Does he hear a noise? He stops; nothing. He is soaked with perspiration. Again he remembers the dumbstruck farmer gaping from the high round seat out of the idling John Deere, suspicions forming on his lips. What had impelled him to step out in front of the goddamn tractor, materializing like an apparition from the trees? He forces the image from his mind.

He crunches through the S-turn that would throw off pursuers, abandons the trail for an unseen path and continues for thirty paces. Again he stops and listens. Only the usual night sounds. He shifts the heavy bag from one shoulder to the other. Crouching now because of branches that he feels rather than sees, he maneuvers down the steep bank to the tiny clearing that cannot be seen from above even in daylight. In the pitch black he feels expertly for the key and noiselessly inserts it in the lock. When he is inside he engages the generator and the cold lights begin to throb hoarsely toward full illumination. He checks his watch: fourteen minutes. Acceptable for a dark night, magnificent for this dark night!

He sits in the straightbacked chair behind the old desk where the Olympia is poised, a sheet of paper rolled in. As the light improves, his eyes dart around the room—from the stack of leatherbound books on the rickety side-table to the freestanding metal shelves along the concrete wall, slightly lopsided from their overload, to the bulky black comforter on the quilted mattress on the floor. She had wanted a bed but he said no.

Suddenly he realizes the shoulder bag is still outside. He retrieves it hurriedly and drops it with a clang on the worktable. He must clean the weapon. He gets a bottle of beer from the cooler and returns to the straight chair. The evening has unfolded just as he visualized, scene by scene, like a movie in

*his head. Like a movie he has seen before. He cannot resist a
smile: déjà vu all over again.*

*Unable to relax, he yanks the sheet of paper from the type-
writer, accidentally tearing it in half. His hands tremble as he
fits the pieces together. He locks his hands beneath his thighs
and reads. No changes. First thought best thought.*

*He fidgets his hands into the rubber gloves and rolls in a
fresh sheet. He begins typing at half-speed to still the tremors.*

Dear Joe Colby:

Your new program, "Crime and Punishment," is
of interest to us. We expect "equal time."

You are released from your obligation to observe
strict silence.

Though you rejected our offer to execute Boogie
Brown, we chose to execute his brother—because
defectives like Boogie Brown must be made to feel
what they cause others to feel.

Avengers

*When he finishes the letter he types an envelope; with a drop
of beer he applies the stamp; then, using a felt-tipped pen with
the wrong hand, writing right to left, he begins to add the zip
code.*

*The coded knock reverberates sharply through the room.
The pen flies off-line and he crumples the envelope, then hurries to unlock the door. She enters silently and he relocks the
door. Soon she is naked.*

He embraces her. "The boy. Do you—"

*"Yes. Probably." She is whispering though there is no need
to. "The law of unintended consequences." She leans back to
look at him. "Are you okay?"*

"Of course. Don't you think I'm okay?"

"Yes, yes, of course," she says.

"Shoes and clothes?"

"Goodwill bin. Have you cleaned the Smith?"

"No."

"Dress up again. Clean me."

EIGHT

❑   ❑   ❑

"ROUNDNOSE, HOLLOWPOINT, ROUNDNOSE, hollopoint—mix 'em fifty-fifty. That's the best way to approach your basic predicate felon."

Burl Devine, the ex-police sergeant and anatomical anomaly with four testicles, curled his left fist like a cylinder and jabbed around the circumference with his right index finger, as if he were loading a revolver. We were standing outside the Fishbowl at the Wall of Honor—three rows of black-framed photographs of policemen killed in the line of duty. Burl was dressed like a curator in pinstripes and oxford cloth, his ash-brown hair long and curling up in back. He was fifty and looked forty. I was pushing forty and looked fifty. And felt older.

"See, the roundnose is the stopper, the dumdum is the killer. Dumdum bounces around inside, clippin' organs. The natterin' nabobs are always protestin' dumdums—too *brutal*, too *dangerous*. But they're the safest—won't go clean through and hit some innocent bystander! 'Course they *are* slightly brutal for the target."

Burl made a little bow as if he heard applause. I smiled and edged away a little.

"Hell of an idea, Joe, breakin' into jail. Wish you coulda got in there."

He closed the gap between us, folding his arms and bounc-

37

ing on his toes like a boxer. I moved on a little more but Burl kept pace.

"Two of my partners are on that wall, Joe, top row, third and fourth. I know how it feels to want justice. I couldn't sleep, couldn't eat, couldn't do nothin' till I dusted the fuckin' animals. Stone killers, just like Boogie Brown. The ER nurse looked 'em over and said, 'D-O-A-A-F-D—Dead On Arrival Absolutely Fuckin' Dead.' I love that. 'Course, Internal Affairs bumbled in and said, 'Oh Burl, must've been two shooters, we found dumdums *and* straights.' Had to teach the peckerheads—roundnose, hollowpoint, roundnose, hollowpoint, you want to kill somebody. And I sure wanted to kill somebody." He gave me a genteel curator's smile. "Dead On Arrival Absolutely Fuckin' Dead. IAD sure knew me by my first name."

I laughed sharply. We drifted into the squad room toward the coffee area. "Best place to catch Steve," I said lightly.

"If you want to catch him."

I poured a cup of the strong coffee and sat down on one of the scarred benches. "Burl, we've got a new show—*Crime and Punishment*. Expose the system, down and dirty. I'd like to have you on."

"*Expose the system?*" Burl chuckled silently. "Sure, Joe. You want me as defrocked cop or vigilant sentinel?"

"Vigilant sentinel?"

"My free enterprises, Joe—Sentinel Security, Sentinel Guns, Sentinel Survivalist Camps. Incorporated. And my philosophy—standing watch against the usurpers." Burl moved another step closer and eased from curator into curate. "Joe, the Constitution gives us three boxes. Three boxes. Ballot box. Soapbox. Cartridge box. They've usurped the first two." He straightened to his fullest height. "Sentinels must stand watch."

"Perfect, Burl, that's good. Three boxes. Have to focus on law and order, you know, crime. Can't really get into political stuff."

"Sure, law and order, crime and punishment. Gun control's about law and order."

"Hell yes it is."

I wondered if the cops considered Burl Devine a suspect. Roundnoses. Hollowpoints. Three boxes. Four balls. I studied my coffee cup.

"You here to see McDade, Joe? He's old news now, they're bringin' in the Company."

I looked at him blankly.

"CIA, Joe, ain't you heard? And you're the reporter. Elmo Finn's comin' in to save the day. Formerly employed by the Central Intelligence Agency in Vietnam. Somebody must think these Avengers are VC or somethin'. *Elmo Fuckin' Finn.*"

Burl horselaughed and bounced on his toes. A trace of memory flickered inside me. There was something about Elmo Finn.

Sergeant Steve McDade appeared at the coffee machine carrying the oversized mug with a stick-on label: *Mug.* His teenage daughter Cassie, an industrious prankster, loved to label his things. She had stuck one on the back of his gold shield: *Badge.* And on the butt of his detective special: *Gun.*

"You're on, gentlemen." Steve steered Burl toward an interview room and waved me down the corridor. I told Burl I'd call him.

Patterson's office glowed invitingly from the lamps. The latest watercolor had been wedged in on the long wall. It was spectacular. I took my usual seat in the hard chair.

"We've got a new show, Captain, I wanted you to know about it."

39

"*Crime and Punishment.* Ain't exactly original."

"Goddamnit, I wish my sources over here were as good as yours at Channel Nine."

"Joe, if your show tells our side of the story, we'll give you special access. Favoritism, pure and simple. Only place I'll draw the line is compromising an investigation."

You never know with cops. I had come to beg for some insider trading, and before I could even make my pitch the Homicide Commander had opened the books.

"Joe, when it's all over, maybe you'll do a video, you know, a book, something we can sell. This is a national case. You can be our historian."

"Hell yes, Captain, good idea."

"Can't let you in on everything, of course."

I nodded, still a little stunned.

Patterson squared up a stack of folders on the cherry desk. "Joe, maybe you can help us some."

In the soft lamplight the Look burned toward me. I was on guard; a quid pro quo after all.

"This Avenger thing scares us. Maybe without violating the canons of journalism, whatever those might be, you could interview some people, give us the footage. You might get people to open up in ways we can't. The psychologists want to study body language, verbal patterns, whatever. Behavioral science—Steve calls it B.S., I don't know. But you might get something. . . ."

"Captain, that would make me an agent of the police. Talk about violating canons—"

"You draw the lines, Joe. But you're more than a reporter, you're a victim, too. Like Juanita Daley is a victim. Like Minimum John and Marvin Isaacson are victims. We're fighting for the system here, Joe, the system against the jungle. Buzz and Belle—Joe, their killer was *caught* by the system and he will be *punished* by the system. It's *working*—imperfectly and too slow and all the rest. But if the system goes, everybody becomes an Avenger. And a target." I had never seen Captain Avery Patterson, the well-to-do aesthete in the tailored suits, show such passion. If that's what it was.

"If you'll come on the show, Captain, and say what you just said, I'll do it. Who do you want me to interview?"

"Burl Devine and Juanita Daley for openers."

"Fine," I said. "I just saw Burl outside. Were the bullets that killed the wives hollowpoints or straights?"

Patterson didn't seem to hear me. He folded his hands primly on the desk. "Joe, we're ready to release the snuff videos and some other details. I'll do it on your show."

"All right, all right, perfect! You can write your own questions."

"You write the questions, Joe. Wouldn't want to violate the canons." We almost smiled at each other.

"Off the record, Joe, we're bringing in some help. The best."

"More FBI?"

He shook his head and tilted back in the big chair. "We're bringing in Elmo Finn. Steve and I met him at the fat farm. We were inmates together."

I whistled. "Whoa—I've heard of Elmo Finn. He was CIA."

"Elmo's been a lot of things. Right now he calls himself a consulting detective. Like Sherlock Holmes."

"Sherlock Holmes."

"Elmo ain't exactly modest but he don't have that much to be modest about. Played golf with two presidents."

Another flash of memory. It was coming back.

"What kind of budget does it take to hire the best, Captain? Off the record."

"Zero. Elmo Finn works for reward money only. No catchee, no payee."

"Captain, I'd like to have his first interview."

"I don't see why not, at the proper time. You'll like him, Joe."

"Can we report he's on the case?"

"No. You'll get it first."

"I love favoritism when I am in favor. I just remembered, I think Finn was CIA in Vietnam. He did something wrong— there was some controversy."

Patterson leaned forward and shot me the Look to about the tenth power. "He did a lot in Vietnam but it wasn't wrong."

"After, then. There's something . . . I'd really like to have him on the show."

"You'll get him first, Joe, unless you ask me again."

McDade came through the door in a burst. I jumped.

"Captain, Nasty Brown's been shot dead. Boogie's brother. Avengers left a note."

NINE

THE UNIFORMS HAD secured the murder scene, a rundown frame house with flaking paint and a dying maple in the bare front yard. It sat in a ragged row of similar houses, a few better maintained, a few with grassy plots struggling to survive. Outside the barricade of sawhorses and bright yellow Police Line Do Not Cross tape, a hundred spectators were rubbernecking each new arrival. Official vehicles were double-parked along the narrow street.

I was wearing a criminologist's blue lab coat with a camera case around my neck, fake glasses distorting my eyes, a false mustache draped from my lip and a wide-brimmed canvas hat pulled low. Why had they brought me along, I wondered. As Patterson nosed our drab, unmarked sedan, instantly recognized as a cop car, into a parking place, Steve fussed with my hat.

"Better than that applepicker's crap you wore the other day." He made me remove my watch and ring. "You okay with this?"

"I think. I don't know. I don't like to see innocent people killed, but as long as an innocent person was killed, I'm glad Boogie Brown will suffer. If an animal like him *can* suffer. Maybe I'm part of the jungle too." My voice rose. "I don't know, I don't know what I feel!"

The modest house was aswarm with uniforms and technicians. As we went in, the Channel Two crime reporter stared at us coldly but didn't recognize me. I almost waved at Channel Nine's field reporter, who was interviewing a trio of bystanders while others tried to jostle into the frame. Steve handed me a police-issue notebook and stuck me in the musty front room, away from the kitchen where the body was, but I could see a lot. I heard Patterson sending detectives outside into the crowd. He took it for granted that someone knew something; but would someone say something?

Steve returned with the plastic-bagged note.

Defectives must feel what they cause others to feel. Now Boogie Brown knows how it feels.

                                          Avengers

"Looks like the same typewriter," I said.

He nodded, watching me intently.

I said, "Just had a thought. Maybe when they realized they couldn't get to Boogie in jail, they decided to target his brother."

"But if you didn't turn your house lights on there was no deal. Why'd they kill *anybody* if you didn't *validate the death warrant?*"

"I don't know, Steve. Do you think I did leave my lights on, is that why I'm here in this pissy little blue jacket? You think maybe they wrote me about this too, Sergeant McDade? Look, goddamnit, I wanted to kill Boogie Brown and still do! And still fucking do! But not this . . . jungle. The goddamn lights were off!"

"I know."

"What? How do you know?"

"We sent a car by. Several times, couldn't have missed those lights. They burn brightly in daylight."

44

"How do you know they burn brightly in daylight?"

"We turned them on."

"How?"

"Professional secret."

"Goddamnit, Steve." The icefire washed over me. I was trembling. "What is this, asking me questions you already know the goddamn answer!"

A voice called for Steve but he didn't move. "Joe, I'm a cop. I arrested Boogie Brown, I testified at his trial, I'll testify again, Bucky will prosecute again and we're going to fry his rotten scumbag ass, legally. And I'll be right beside you at Central to watch him cook. But when you, Joe, when you try to get thrown in jail so you can kill him yourself, I got to follow that up too. You know how it works, Joe. The system, not the jungle."

Harry Covington, a black detective who had been Steve's partner before Steve made sergeant, came in, and I dived into my notebook. Harry wasn't interested in me.

"Nobody's talkin' and everybody's lyin'," Harry said. "Nasty Brown was a halfass dealer, just like Boogie. Nobody cares he's dead. No one knows where his mother is. Iris. She wasn't so popular either, knew a few husbands a little too well. Boogie's little boy was hit in the neck. He's at Presbyterian, critical, could have been a stray shot. White van parked outside last night but there were always vans around. Old man down the street thinks he might have seen a strange woman."

"Strange how?" Steve asked.

"White."

Captain Patterson came in, barely glancing at me. I felt invisible. "Six shots fired, no casings, nobody heard nothing."

Harry Covington shook his head. "Nobody *says* they heard nothin'."

Steve said, "How they get inside the house, sittin' around the kitchen table with Nasty Brown, a lowlife drug dealer who'd be suspicious of anybody? Drinkin' coffee, the highest form of socializin'. Then zap zap zap."

Covington consulted his notebook. "Everybody called the little boy Snot Boogie, three years old. Mother is Letitia Carter, about seventeen, she fed him Pepsi in a baby bottle. One of the neighborhood mothers had the kid over one day, Snot ate the fuckin' crayons. Now he's got a bullet wound in the neck, three years old. Goddamn, the underclass is a step up from here."

Harry's words were steel-tipped. He was a proud black man.

"Any hunches?" Steve asked.

"Joe Colby," Harry said. "He tried to get into jail to kill Boogie, maybe gettin' Avengers to dust brother Nasty was the next best thing. Or it's a drug hit *disguised* as Avengers. Whatever it is, it's Godalmighty Old Testament. Nobody ever killed the *relatives* before, except the Colombians. Ruth Isaacson dead, Maggie Lodge dead, Nasty Brown dead, maybe little Snot. Innocent relatives, Godalmighty Old Testament."

I stood apart from the cops, still pretending to make notes. Kimberly Whitten, Harry Covington's current partner and one of two women in Homicide, hurried in. Darkly tanned, tall, sexy without trying. Called herself "PMS on patrol." Always wore a blazer and pants, and everyone said she carried three guns. Best shot in the division. Her notebook was open to a sketch of the kitchen.

"The throat wounds don't look like gunshots to me. More like a knife. There's a gun on the body, twenty-two automatic. Not fired."

Kim eyed me suspiciously. She seemed to expect an explanation of my presence. When nobody volunteered one, she said, "You know about their names? Iris Brown, the mother, was named after a flower so she named her kids after flowers. First son Honeysuckle killed in a drug deal. When the detectives came to tell her, refused to go identify the body. Said, 'Thank God I'm rid of him.' Heard that story three times outside."

Harry Covington nodded as if he'd heard it too.

"Then Bougainvillea, Boogie, who did the Colby kids. Then Nasturtium, Nasty, he's killed at least one person."

"Any girls?" Patterson asked.

"Hyacinth and Pansy. Nobody knows where they are. But get this about little Snot. This wasn't his first bullet—he was *born with bullet wounds in his back*. The mother—Letitia—got hit with a twenty-two when one of Boogie's crack deals soured up. Miracle either one lived."

I was queasy now. Images of Buzz and Belle flooded my mind. The undersized caskets, Belle's ballet shoes on the altar, Buzz's Little League pallbearers with their baseball caps backward. The icefire surged inside me. It had been there all morning. It was always there.

I had to talk to Steve. As the discussion broke up, I signaled and he stayed behind.

"I have to ask you again, Steve, is all this my fault? If my fiasco hadn't been splashed all over the media, Avengers might not—"

He quieted me with a gesture. As his pen flashed in the air I saw a tiny label: *Pen*. Something my Belle might have done one day. I felt warm tears.

"No, absolutely not, Joe. Avengers were in business *before* your fiasco. You know that. Go to the car if you want."

I knew I should leave but the crime scene transfixed me. I could see into a slice of the kitchen—it was like watching a play from a darkened box. The techs were photographing, scraping, dusting, collecting. The coroner's people were standing around, waiting for clearance from the detectives, who were working their way in from the periphery.

The murder cops are impassive at a crime scene. I'd even

heard them crack jokes, one of their defense mechanisms. Corpse after corpse could get to you. The jungle could get to you. So they concentrated on the clinical details, not the depravity; the science of murder was a refuge. And now, instead of pondering the nature of evil and the inhumanity of man, Steve McDade and Avery Patterson and Harry Covington and Kim Whitten were sketching Iris Brown's kitchen, carefully stepping around the overturned chairs, estimating angles of fire, combing for shell casings, debating whether Nasty Brown's throat wounds were inflicted by bullets or a serrated blade. Dispassionately circling in. Working for God.

Finally I went out to the car, edging my way wide to avoid everyone. The noon heat was oppressive, with no rain in sight. I resolved to visit the cemetery this afternoon and lie on the grassy plot reserved for me, and feel the presence of Connie and Buzz and Belle. My refuge.

The rubberneckers had quieted down some. As I reached the police sedan, two small boys darted past me.

"Snot Boogie, Snot Boogie," one yelled.

"Yabba dabba dead," was the answer.

TEN

❏   ❏   ❏

LOGAN MURPHY AND I were drunk. One part Bollinger's, three parts euphoria. The first *Crime and Punishment* had aired at 7:30 and we were modestly proclaiming it a smash.

"To the world's greatest producer," I crowed. "Logan Murphy *rules!*"

Every few minutes we bowed to each other and sloshed more champagne. Logan's normally immaculate office looked like a fraternity basement. The giant mug shots around the walls—television pioneers like Milton Berle and Dave Garroway and Howdy Doody—had been knocked aslant. Logan's electric minifan for cooling the executive brow was turned crossways, and papers were wafting crazily above the credenza. Empty champagne bottles were everywhere.

Janie rushed in, breathless as usual after talking to New York. "Network wants *everything!*" She was almost singing. "Joe, you're on morning show *and* tabloid. Both papers called for a VHS. Channel Two will blow their brains out—three cheers for Avangers. Oh that's terrible! Sober up, Joe, it's only a few hours."

"Holy holy, Janie, Mr. Joe Colby is better drunk than anyone else sober. Have a bubbly. Before we have to start living up to our laurels."

Janie leaned over the vast desk and kissed Logan wetly on the lips. I saw her succulent legs and booty and a wisp of thong panties. Janie randomly dispensed tush and twat shots to passing males but only Logan got beyond the tease.

For the third or fourth time Logan rewound the tape. "We're national after one show! National!" He gave me a huge wink, punched the remote and *Crime and Punishment* bloomed again on the fifty-two-inch screen.

The set was stunning. Stark limbo background, spartan desk and chairs in what Logan called "gunmetal gray," giant rear screen for graphics and remotes. And the logo—*Crime and Punishment* arcing over a smoking Saturday night special manacled in silver handcuffs. No question where we stood. Fuck objectivity and the Fourth Amendment.

Captain Avery Patterson was the perfect opening guest— solid square commander's jaw, salt-and-pepper hair, immaculate CEO's suit and tie, strong sorrowful eyes that saw horror every day and sought to combat it. Our man in the jungle. Working for God.

I tossed puffball questions and Patterson swatted them out of the park: revenge, serial killers, vigilantism, the Hotline, the Reward Fund. And the jungle versus the system.

During a commercial Logan whistled onto the set pumping both fists like pistons. He said the switchboard was already erupting, which charged us up though we didn't need it.

Near the end, I said, "Captain, certain murders are called Kodaks. High profile. Why are some murders more important than others?"

He paused just long enough. "Joe, no murder is more important than any other to the police—only to the media. A Kodak is where the media get in the way with their cameras and questions and make the policeman's job harder. Justice often suffers. And justice deserves better from you and your colleagues." Hoist with my own petard, as expected.

"Are you bringing in outside help? Experts?"

I saw a flash in his eyes that the camera missed. "We're

working with the FBI," he said. "The answer is yes."

I wanted to press on about Elmo Finn but instead lobbed a closing puffball. "Captain Patterson, on your office wall is a sign—We Work for God. What does that mean?"

Grand slam. "We speak for the dead. We speak for victims. We deliver society's retribution against the guilty—that's the way the system works. If the system breaks down, we end up with the jungle. We end up with Avengers. We can't let the system break down."

Logan, still ear to ear, clicked off the VCR. "Keep an eye on your mail, Mr. World's Greatest Reporter—maybe your next guest will be an Avenger!"

A message from Avengers demanding "equal time" had arrived the day before. I tried to show it to Logan before delivering it to the cops. He wouldn't even touch the plastic bag.

"*Equal time*, Joe, they want to read their goddamn manifesto or something."

"They'll send a video, Boss—we know they have a camera. They're not going to show up at the studio to be interviewed, for Christ's sake."

"Can't be sure, Avengers don't do nothin' nobody expects. Let's have another taste and watch Captain We Work for God one more time."

The phones ran fifteen to one in favor of the Homicide Commander. The next morning I made my first national TV appearance. Four minutes of fame, eleven more to come. The network anchors were spellbound as I recited Avengers' chilling message: "Now you know how it feels." Of course, they dug into my personal history, too—Connie's cancer, Buzz and Belle, breaking into jail. I cried only once. They cut me off when I tried to describe the icefire inside me. Network television had no time for the deep stuff—just yabba dabba dead.

ELEVEN

❏   ❏   ❏

"THE GUILLOTINE WAS *invented to make executions more humane," he says as they curl together on the damp quilted mattress. "More humane. Everything's relative."*

She shivers and burrows into him.

He says, "When they picked up Ruth Isaacson her head almost fell off."

"I wish you had raped her first."

He strokes her breasts, then squeezes them together and lowers his mouth to both nipples. Soon they are moaning and she presses his head tighter against her.

"I'm still sensitive," she whispers. "No don't stop."

They make love feverishly as they had the first time. For them sex is always a tempest. Later she says, "God, if it weren't for you."

"I don't see how you do it. On this day."

"Don't call it this day. *Call it what it is."*

"I don't see how you do it. On your anniversary."

From head to toe they press against each other for warmth. Neither reaches for the comforter bunched at their feet.

She nuzzles closer. "This is the first year I haven't driven by. Thirteen years. Some day I'll go in."

"And say what?"

"Well I probably won't say, Look, I used to live here and a man with a lot of tattoos named Franklin Delano Hollowell*

dragged me into that back bedroom and tied me down and raped me for six hours and then tried to kill me and do you mind if I just take a look, it's the anniversary."

He kisses her hair. "Do you wish you'd reported it?"

"I wish I'd cut off his dick and made him eat it."

She sits up and gathers her clothes. "At the luncheon today I told someone about my anniversary. A woman I didn't even know, I just met her. She held my hand and said, 'Mine was in April.'"

"Hollowell will get the death penalty. You know that. All Isaacson can do is keep the state from executing him. But Frank Hollowell will be executed. You want to drive by?"

"I have to."

"I could go with you."

"No."

When she is gone he sits in the cold metallic light reading the index cards. He trusts his instinct; first thought best thought. Suddenly he flings the cards to the ceiling. Pure randomness, he thinks, laughing out loud. No thought best thought. He picks up the topmost card and laughs again. How will they explain this? A fine puzzle, none of the pieces fit! Every piece a puzzle! And laughs again.

He walks to the row of crowded shelves behind the battered wooden desk. He opens a square metal box and counts the hundred-dollar bills inside; twenty-four thousand dollars; enough. He surveys his tools: the long-lens Nikon, the paratrooper's carbine, the Smith forty and thirty-eight and Beretta twenty-five, the baffled suppressor and customized brasscatcher he drove twelve hundred miles to buy, the line of olive-drab ammunition boxes with thousands of rounds, the hunting knife with the serrated blade, the machete with the built-up grip, the makeup cases, the wigs and lingerie and uniforms, the nameplates and license tags and badges, the cartop signs—Dining Express, Meals On Wheels, Pizza Pony. He studies the index card and chuckles. Why not? First thought best thought. Free pizza.

TWELVE

❏   ❏   ❏

"YOU'RE OUR CELEBRITY, Joe," Juanita Daley oozed over the phone in our monthly ritual. Mother Savage was flattering me into coming early to Group to have coffee with the first-timers. As always, I said yes. When I drove into the YMCA parking lot, Ned Cromartie, our crossing guard with the visible black eyepatch and the concealed semiautomatic, was already waiting to shepherd the flock inside.

"As long as somebody ended up d-dead, Joe, I'm glad B-B-Boogie Brown has to suffer." He hugged me like a brother. "Isaacson, M-Minimum John and B-B-Boogie Brown. Birds of a f-feather must suffer t-t-together." Ned's hand shot up and I gave him a high-five.

Juanita had set up a half-circle of chairs in the back of the meeting room beneath a faded poster of Reverend Bob Richards in mid-pole vault. The aroma of her strong chicory-laced coffee rivaled the chlorine. There was a tray of fresh pastries and chinaware and silver spoons.

The newcomers fussed and fawned over me, praising *Crime and Punishment* and embarrassing me with autograph requests. No one mentioned my arrest and exposure. Juanita, in a flowing rainbow dress that looked African, beamed beside me like an agent.

Then she shooed us into chairs for the storytelling. Juanita's coffees were like an A.A. meeting with One Step: You Are

Not Alone. She never invited a Turn-the-Other-Cheeker to speak, only us Savages. I went first and held up better than usual, making it dry-eyed through Belle's rape and strangulation and Buzz's twenty-one stab wounds. I faltered a little at the icefire. Juanita got me some water and held my hand as I finished.

John Ewell, the unlikeliest Savage, had slipped in during my story. Tall and thin, wearing scholarly horn-rims and his usual black suit, John balanced a cup and plate on his sharp knees but barely sampled the contents. Instead he chainsmoked, bending forward to tap the ashes into a paper cup on the floor. When Juanita introduced him, John Ewell trained his eyes on a spot above our heads and in a soft voice told his story.

Two weeks before their wedding, a second marriage for both, John and his fiancée Gwen were driving home after dinner and mall-browsing—a big night for them. They were rhapsodizing about their upcoming honeymoon on Kauai and planning to curl up with the brochures and a pot of hot chocolate when a fifty-five-pound cemetery vase crashed through the windshield on the passenger side, shattering Gwen's skull. The car ended up atop the median, with John Ewell frantically waving down motorists. The seventeen-year-old boy who had pushed the vase from the overpass drove by several times to taunt John Ewell. "Hey hey bombs away! Hey hey bombs away!"

Gwen never regained consciousness. Every night in room 311 of Presbyterian Hospital, John Ewell sits beside the bed holding her hand and watching the slow silent drip of the IV. Sometimes he reads aloud about kayaking and helicopter rides and the volcanoes of Kauai. Sometimes he thinks she squeezes his hand though the doctors dismiss it. The seventeen-year-old is free on bond awaiting trial for manslaughter. His attorney, Marvin Isaacson, insists that no matter what the verdict, state law requires his client to be set free when he turns twenty-one.

John's bony hands worked nervously above the clattering cup and plate on his knees. "If someone had to die, I'm glad Marvin Isaacson has to suffer."

Then Ned Cromartie, his eyepatch slightly off-kilter, hurried in. John Ewell handed his plate to Juanita and huddled with Ned, who slipped the Glock into John's pocket. John left to fill in as crossing guard.

Juanita said, "All of us suffer every day of our lives, just like you, and the pain will never go away. Time does not heal everything. This is Ned. Ned is our godfather." Juanita had been a Victim longer than any of us, but she always called Ned the godfather. In his black eyepatch he looked like one.

Six years earlier, at dusk on a fine spring day, Ned had been robbed at knifepoint in a downtown parking garage. Four black brain-dead teenage sociopaths. Ned handed over everything without protest—wallet, watch, ring, keys. They took the spoils, then mutilated Ned Cromartie for their pleasure. A medic in Vietnam because he didn't want to harm another human being, Ned lost an eye, most of his testicles and all of his pacifism. There were two witnesses but neither would testify. No arrests. After three operations and a long convalescence, Ned began roaming mean streets at night wearing the eyepatch and his U.S. Army field jacket, the Glock auto in his pocket and a five-shot backup on his ankle. Aching to lure a mugger.

To minimize his stuttering, Ned spoke in a lifeless monotone. He told of the surgery, the therapists, the drugs; how he couldn't make love to Julia for two years; how he could never father children; how the eyepatch still threw him off balance. The only thing he left out was that he still walks those streets.

Juanita hugged him exuberantly, then hugged me and each

of the new members in turn. One of them looked familiar. He was about thirty, with a buzz cut and the trim, tight build of an athlete—and an earnest expression that bothered me. He came straight over to Ned and me with his hand outstretched. "Tad Sullivan. My brother was gunned down standing on a curb, waiting for the light to change. Gangbangers just drove up and blasted away, totally random, they didn't even know him. I remember how small the bullethole looked—like a cigarette hole. Every day my mom stood on that street corner with a sign—Please Help Me Find the Killers of My Son. My dad started going to funerals every day, people he didn't even know. Still does."

I had never met him, but I knew Tad Sullivan's voice—stoic, distant, bloodless—the voice that speaks the unspeakable. It was our voice. You learned to quell the blood, the icefire. You could be talking about the weather.

He said, "Funny, we thought Mom was crazy, standing out there with her sign, but some calls came in. Now the police know who did it but nobody'll testify." Tad Sullivan's universal monotone trailed softer. "My dad says life is different when the worst that could ever happen has already happened."

John Ewell ushered in the last of the stragglers and the full session began. Deirdre, the chubby young psychologist, rushed into a spiel on "inner wellsprings," about which each of us knew more than she ever would. Ned and I watched the circle of faces for the first glazeover—we had a regular bet. Then the door opened and Marvin Isaacson came in. He was wearing scuffed slippers and a dark suit with no tie and took small shuffling steps. His face was mottled with red blotches, his ponytail askew. A matronly woman accompanied him, holding his arm. A few paces inside the door he stopped and looked around uncertainly. Deirdre hurried over and helped him to a chair in the circle. He sat with his head half-bowed, his hands folded meekly in his lap.

Deirdre resumed her rat-a-tat therapy without introducing the newcomer, as if his presence were routine. Juanita Daley, a half-dozen chairs from Isaacson, her face an ebony fist beneath swept-back raven hair, looked straight ahead for a minute or two, her lips pursing, then turned and glared unrelentingly at the lawyer who for twelve years had shielded her daughter's murderer. She craned her head toward him dramatically, her long rainbow dress spilling around her. Finally Isaacson rolled his head toward hers, gazing back numbly.

Like dry thunder Juanita's brutal whisper crackled. *"Now you know how it feels. Now you know how it feels. Now you know how it feels."* There were cries of alarm and disapproval and then a few of support. Deirdre bounded up nervously to demand order and a vast hairtrigger silence descended.

Isaacson tried to stare back but there was no fire. He could not challenge Juanita Daley, whose snarl was as merciless as a death mask. I suddenly remembered the lifeless face of my own lifeless Belle, her gentle features so disfigured by horror that when the coroner lifted the sheet I said, "No, that's not my daughter, that's not Belle," and turned away. Steve McDade had prodded me back, whispering something, and I looked again into the face of God transfigured by evil, as the icefire consumed me. My innocent daughter was inhuman in death, feral, rabid, tearing at Boogie Brown with her teeth.

Isaacson managed to stand and his companion rushed over. He shuffled out on her arm, a little faster than before. Deirdre was weeping, unable to continue. Through her own tears Juanita embraced me as the Savages gathered around. Most of the Other-Cheekers hurried out.

"Oh, Joe, I am what I am, Joe."

"Juanita, Juanita," John Ewell said, bending forward awkwardly. "We know. We understand."

"We're the only ones who d-d-do know." Ned Cromartie

protected his eyepatch with one hand and pulled Juanita close with the other.

"Don't feel guilty, anybody," Tad Sullivan, the athletic young newcomer, insisted. He squared up to face us like a drill sergeant. "Don't feel guilty. We are what we are."

It hadn't taken Tad Sullivan long to join the Savages. Ned was right—they all had false mustaches.

THIRTEEN

❑   ❑   ❑

THE WORKING-CLASS NEIGHBORHOOD *is as dead this morning as on his four trial runs—parents working, kids in school, no traffic. He has established four Abort signals. None is present. His instinct says proceed. First thought best thought.*

He swings the hatchback into the narrow driveway dotted with patches of gravel and trots to the door. There is no bell, no screen door. After insistent knocking a teenage boy answers. Behind him a dog whips and snaps.

"Any Pattons live around here? We got an order."

The teenager shakes his head and begins closing the door.

"You want a free pizza? Somebody screwed this up. Pepperoni and sausage."

As the teenage stares uncertainly the Avenger thrusts the flat box toward him and pushes into the house, smoothly extracting something from beneath the box. The dog, a lean, shorthaired mongrel, snarls and dances. With an easy motion the Avenger swings the big automatic down and shoots the dog. The noise is muffled but in the cramped hallway the smell of cordite is intense. A funnel of blue smoke drifts in the air.

"Suck the gun. Suck it! Suck the gun!"

Soon they drive away in the hatchback. The boy slumps in the front passenger seat, his arms bound behind him, his head lolling brokenly from side to side, his lips bleeding, his eyes red and wild. The front of his oversized jeans is damply stained.

They ride for an hour without speaking; the only sounds are the boy's whimperings and moans. They stop once, on the fringes of a parking lot, where she gets in. As they continue, the road surface deteriorates; the final miles are very rough. The boy's pleadings intensify until she strikes him from the back seat.

Finally the car stops and they get out. The boy falls to his knees and cringes. The Avenger stands over him.

"Look up Duane! Up! Up there! Just sitting up there! You recognize it don't you Duane! Hey hey Duane bombs away! Hey hey bombs away!"

The boy tries to scrabble sideways. The Avenger shoots him in the leg and drags him to a prepared position. The Avenger begins to climb as she lifts the automatic and trains it on the figure of the frothing prostrate boy.

FOURTEEN

❏　　❏　　❏

ON THE WELL-WORN stairs to Homicide I caught up with Harry Covington, the suave black detective whose wardrobe was almost a match for Patterson's. Harry looked tired—all the murder cops looked tired these days.

"Slow down, Joe, we're early," Harry said. As we passed the Fishbowl he rolled his eyes. "Man, what a monster you created." The Fishbowl was teeming—police cadets schlepping fat canvas bags off dollies, civilian aides at worktables slitting stacks of envelopes. Processing the fan mail of Captain Avery (We Work for God) Patterson, Homicide Commander, TV star and the fickle public's latest hero.

"One came in from Australia, Joe. Australia! Cap loves it—I just wish he'd admit it."

In Patterson's office still another new watercolor rested against the wall under We Work for God. Mailbags were piled in the corner. Steve McDade drained his mug labeled *Mug*, flashed us a raised index finger and hurried out for a refill. Harry and I were alone.

"They're bringing in a genius, I guess you heard." Harry clasped his hands in mock thanksgiving.

"The great Elmo Finn, who compares himself to Sherlock Holmes. From what I've heard, this guy could cause more problems than he solves."

"He's a fuckin' killer, Joe, don't you remember a few years

back, this cowboy detective tracks down some carjacker and fuckin' *executes* him, like the Wild West or somethin'. In Boston I think. Well, the cowboy detective was Elmo Finn and he got off scot-free—nobody didn't even prosecute—like the fix was already in. And now Cap's bringin' the cowboy detective down here to catch Avengers and he's the biggest fuckin' avenger of 'em all!"

The memory came exploding back. Elmo Finn . . . controversial ex-CIA agent . . . fianceé kidnapped, raped and murdered by carjacker . . . carjacker found dead . . .

"Goddamn FBI's enough of a headache," Harry muttered, "now they bring in some prima donna wild man who don't know the city, don't know the people, don't know nothin'— so we'll have to hold his hand and by God he'll get all the credit when we put 'em down! Another fuckin' genius, man, we got all those we need."

We were laughing about out-of-town geniuses when Steve returned with a full coffeepot and a stack of cups. Avery Patterson, who was even getting fan mail at Channel Nine, trailed in wearing the usual tailored three-piece suit and settled into his highbacked chair. As Steve poured coffee, the Commander riffled through a stack of pink phone messages. Without looking up, he said, "I hear Isaacson showed up the other night."

Harry winked at me. "Juanita told me."

Juanita told him. Suddenly I remembered that Harry Covington was the detective who had put down Franklin Delano Hollowell after the rape and murder of Debbie Daley . . . and that Marvin Isaacson had filed a complaint against Harry for police brutality.

Patterson wanted a blow-by-blow account of Group, including the names of those who supported Juanita and those who opposed her. I gave them an edited version slanted toward the Savages.

"Juanita's a wonderful person," I said. "Isaacson's put her through hell for twelve years. She's got—"

"We know," Steve said. "Did Minimum John show up?"

"No," Harry said.

The door opened and Three-Gun Kim Whitten, Harry's sexy partner, stepped in. Black blazer and tight khakis today; not much room to hide the third gun. When she saw me, she froze.

"Sorry, Avery—"

Patterson motioned her to stay. "Joe's on our side. Journalistic canons be damned." I smiled obligatorily.

There were suspicions about Kim and Avery Patterson. She was single, he was divorced. They laughed too readily at each other's bons mots. She called him *Avery*, not *Captain*. And Kim Whitten had managed to vault a long line of aspirants to snare the gold detective's shield. "Pussy pull" was a frequent bitter whisper among the passed-over officers.

She said, "The kid named Duane Hickman who dropped the cemetery urn on John Ewell's fiancée—Avengers dropped an urn on him. About ten times."

"Jesus, I just saw John Ewell. Dead?" I must have sounded stupid. Ten times.

"Dead on arrival absolutely fuckin' dead. Officers found something odd in his effects. Ned Cromartie's American Express card."

FIFTEEN

❑　　❑　　❑

LOGAN MURPHY AND I were drinking, but not champagne. Instead of joining me on the sofa as he usually did, Logan was playing big boss behind the vast oval desk, imported, ten grand. Plumped up like a potentate. *Manifesting authority* or whatever the hell they call it in the plush seminars at White Sulphur Springs. I sat upright on the edge of the sofa, drinking doubles at a singles rate.

"Goddamn planning doesn't mean goddamn *set in concrete*," he groused for the third or fourth time. "Television means *right now*, riding the goddamn wave!"

"Goddamn right!" I sneered.

"Goddamn right it's goddamn right!"

I spun to the bar and sloshed in a triple, but I wasn't as steamed as I pretended. Logan was right.

"Joe, surely you understand," he whined as if I would never understand, "we just broadcast our second *Crime and Punishment* with a fucking crackpot while Channel Two preempts network for the biblical stoning of a seventeen-year-old redneck. Goddamn Old Testament's being reenacted right under our noses and we run Commander Fucking . . . Nutbeam!"

I bit my lip at the fusion of *nutcake* and *moonbeam*, two of Logan's pet pejoratives.

"What was all that horseshit, anyway—three boxes and going off the grid and burning his driver's license and shooting

67

it out with L.A. street gangs in black helicopters to stop the New World Order—people were rolling in the aisles! This is supposed to be a serious show."

"Boss, the cops wanted him on—because Commander Fucking Nutbeam may be commander of fucking Avengers!"

"Burl Devine couldn't command a two-car parade!"

"Hell he couldn't. Man has four balls."

Logan froze, his eyes turning playful. "Four balls. Commander Morphadite."

"No, Commander Murphy, just your basic testosterone overload. You're thinking of the basic hermaphrodite, who has both pussy and pecker, which basically doubles his or her chances of getting a date Saturday night."

Logan was roaring now. His earlier outburst had been partly show, like mine. We knew each other. He chanted,

There was a young man from Racine

I joined in,

Who invented a fucking machine
Both concave and convex
It could serve either sex
Entertaining itself in between.

Just like that we abandoned our posturing. I walked over and reached across the oval acreage to shake hands. "Sorry, Boss."

"Onward, onward, Commander Colby. I still can't figure who the hell orders pizza at ten-thirty in the morning? *Can* you order pizza at ten-thirty in the morning?"

"Only a mutant like Duane Hickman."

We rehashed how Avengers had snatched seventeen-year-old Duane Hickman from his parents' house with some kind of pizza delivery ruse . . . how they spirited him to a remote railway trestle, tied him beneath it and dropped a cemetery urn on him until he was dead . . . how they tacked their trademark note to a girder: "Now he knows how it feels" . . . how a detective searching Hickman's room found Ned Cromartie's old American Express card that was stolen in a mugging years ago . . . how Hickman was a poor white redneck, Ned's muggers were poor ghetto blacks and the credit card had never been used.

"Go figure," Logan mused. "Have to wait till you interview an Avenger to find out."

"They'll never expose themselves to me, Boss, I'm telling you. They'll mail it in."

"Who you like next week?"

"Marvin Isaacson."

"Holy holy. Can you handle it, Joe, Boogie Brown's lawyer?"

"Got to handle it—Isaacson's the thread. Avengers killed his wife Ruth; they killed Maggie Lodge, the wife of Isaacson's pal, the judge; they killed the teenager, Duane Hickman, who was one of Isaacson's clients; and they killed Nasty Brown, the brother of Boogie, another Isaacson client. Marvin Isaacson's the common denominator to all of this. I can handle it. I think."

"Holy holy—that's a hell of a program, Joe. The Isaacson connection."

I nodded. "Did Network come up with anything on Elmo Finn?"

"They're working on it. Very mysterious, this Elmo Finn. Maybe he was some kind of avenger himself, maybe not. Maybe he was a CIA assassin, maybe not. Maybe he's the real Sherlock Holmes, maybe not. Nobody's neutral."

After two nightcaps I went home, driving meticulously with the windows open. Elly was still at work so I fixed a drink and sat in the dark. Elly's late showings always reminded me of how we met. Connie and I wanted to move closer to town, and Elly had shown me several houses. The houses were blah but *she* took my breath away. Boardroom power suit with short skirt and long firm legs. Pixieish black hair that she combed with a toss of the head. Flawless Mediterranean skin and C-cups that she not so much flaunted as insinuated. She walked in long, confident strides and I loved following her sculpted tush up the walkways. I had never cheated on Connie, but lust at first sight and fresh empty bedrooms were too much. "You're better looking than on TV," she said after the first house. "You're better looking than the newspaper ad," I said after the second. At the third house we didn't get out of the bedroom for two hours.

I was still drinking in the dark when she clumped in wearing a dowdy suit that couldn't hide the curves. The Countess.

"The buyers from hell." She kissed me lightly on the forehead and I reciprocated heavily on the lips.

"Are you drunk? I need a double. They're selling these on the street." She dropped a bumper sticker on my lap and switched on a lamp.

Me & Avengers Don't Dial 911.

We took a communal shower and raced to bed naked and damp, attended by a chilled bottle of Stolichnaya. Soon we had dried and warmed and wrestled into our favorite soixante-neuf, and we worked each other expertly toward release, then away, then back, again and again, at last dying the little death together.

We had more vodka. Elly whispered, "Did you and Connie do this?"

"Twice a day. You know we didn't. Sex with Connie had to be Junior League approved."

"When did she know? When did she *really* know?"

"She never said anything, not even in the hospital. Just that last note with the crayon: 'Elly take care of Joe and my Bs.' I couldn't even make it out, all the chemo." Guilt began stabbing away again, as familiar as the icefire. If Connie and I had remained passionate, I might have devoured her breasts as lustily as I did Elly's, and discovered the tumor myself.

I poured more vodka for both of us. The clear, semifrozen liquid oozed into the glasses like syrup.

"Does her father ever call?" she asked. "Just to see about you?"

"We haven't spoken since the kids' funeral. He still blames me for everything. They say he doesn't even teach his precious English Lit anymore, just wanders around the campus at all hours."

"Should you go see him?"

"Fuck him."

Clutching our vodkas, we lay spoonlike for a while. Then Elly said, "What can this Elmo Finn do that Steve McDade can't do?"

"Nothing. But everybody loves an expert as long as they're from out of town."

"I saw the show. Does anybody really think a nut like Burl Devine is an Avenger?"

"Well, he has four balls."

"Four balls? How?"

"Act of God."

"Hallelujah. I wish you had four balls—you'd be horny all the time."

"You have to have a license to be hornier than I am. Juanita Daley hugged me the other night and I got turned on. At a Victims meeting! We were all crying. What a set."

"You want some of that? Hot chocolate?"

"Would you mind?"

She pinched me in a certain way. I took it as a Yes.

SIXTEEN

❑ ❑ ❑

TWENTY MILES FROM the railroad trestle beneath which Duane Hickman was found pulverized by a fifty-five-pound cemetery urn, a frail, hardfaced woman in her forties walked into a county jail and thumbed out ten one-hundred dollar bills. She was there to bail out her abusive boyfriend, whom she had turned in in the first place. To the deputies it was a familiar domestic pattern: the fight, the arrest, the remorse, the reconciliation. The woman kissed and fondled her paramour all the way to her car; then, as he fastened his seat belt with a cocky grin, shot him dead with a rusty pistol. She went back into the jail and turned *herself* in, thanking Avengers for giving her the courage "to do what had to be done." Two female lawyers were defending her pro bono publico.

In center city a chronic drunk driver with a revoked license shot through a red light and crashed into another car, killing its two occupants. Later that night a person or persons unknown slipped into his hospital room and smothered him to death with a pillow. No one saw a thing.

A murderer who had been acquitted after claiming eleven separate personalities was found dead with eleven bullet wounds. His lawyer was in hiding after a sniper narrowly missed.

"Copycats," Steve McDade said bitterly. "All nightmares coming true."

"The jungle encroacheth," I said. We were in Patterson's office, the heavy curtains drawn, cozy lamplight bathing the room—a surreal setting for Steve McDade's inventory of horrors. I was a true insider now; Steve had shown me how to sneak in from the basement so the other reporters wouldn't know.

Harry Covington came in and dropped a bumper sticker on Patterson's desk: *Me & Avengers Don't Dial 911.* "Seen these, Cap?"

Patterson sighed heavily. "Talk about the jungle."

"We got some jungle cops, Avery," Kim Whitten said, swinging her legs crossed and giving me a twinge. "Cops who just don't give a shit that Marvin Isaacson and Minimum John got a taste of the jungle, or that Boogie Brown got a taste. And they wish Joe had gotten away with his banana-boat scheme and they sure to God don't care about a redneck skell like Duane Hickman getting urned to death—"

"Shit!" Harry Covington exclaimed as he stood at the window. He clapped his hands sharply, like a coach. "Is this what we've come to? Cops who don't give a shit? Cops who don't care?" He wrenched his ID from his inside pocket. "See this, this is the detective's shield, I took an oath to get this! We all took an oath! Shit!" He flung the gold shield toward the wall where it struck the Haitian market scene.

Kim jumped up and clutched Harry's arm. "Harry, Jesus, partner, *I* don't accept it—I'm just reporting what I hear." She looked earnestly into his eyes. "I took the oath, too, partner."

He hugged her. "Kim, they could be cops."

Two sharp knocks. The door swung open and a man entered. Everyone froze. He looked younger than I expected, and more tanned.

"Elmo, baby," Steve said. They shook hands warmly. A grinning Patterson sprang to his feet, hand outstretched, waiting his turn. Harry Covington, who had derided Elmo Finn, queued up with bright eyes. Kim too. Hardboiled homicide cops dancing the fawnorama. When Finn got to me I jumped up too.

"Joe, you look just like you do on television."

"So do you."

Finn was fairly tall, about six one. I expected the angular face and Apache cheekbones, but not the intense gray eyes, gunmetal gray like our studio set, but with flecks of fire. He wore a brown herringbone jacket and gray trousers, a TV-blue shirt with a solid navy tie. Carried a battered tan briefcase with a laptop compartment. Could have been a professor or a playwright. Or a poet or a preacher or a pimp. Or a partridge in a pear tree. But he said he was Sherlock Holmes. And Patterson said he was a hero. And some said he was an avenger.

"I'd like to have you on the show," I said.

"Sure. It's a great show, the whole country's seen it. The dark side of the moon of due process. Soon as these guys let me emerge from the thicket."

"That's fairly poetic for a consulting detective, Elmo, they'll run a sperm count on you around here."

"Kim conducts those," Patterson said. We burst out in laughs and gibes.

"Someone has to do it!" Kim squealed.

"Might as well get it over with," Finn said, taking Kim's hand. "Catch you tomorrow, Commander." General hilarity. I sat down to watch the murder police cavort with their expert from out of town. What a scene for *Crime and Punishment*.

When the commotion died down, I said to Elmo Finn, "What's a consulting detective?"

He smiled. "What you put on a business card late at night in a saloon."

75

"Real late," Kim said.

"You guys met at the fat farm?"

"Duke University," Finn said. "I was a mere observer. These guys were the lardos."

"Oh my God!" Patterson said. "Remember this guy, Steve, had to wear sweat suits all the time. The Sansabelt Kid! Mo, you got to put Michael Hamilton in your will, you'd be in the circus by now."

Finn said, "I wonder who bought a map of Durham and plotted the shortest route to every frozen yogurt—"

"Oh no! I wonder who deduced that walking *to and from a golf cart* was a cardiovascular exercise!" Patterson said.

"That's right!" Steve said. "We played this course where the carts had to stay on the paths, stay off the fairways. So Finn draws a diagram to show how far his ball would be from every cart path because of his hook, the ball always going left and the paths always going down the right side to accommodate the slicers, and how much actual walking was involved, cart to ball to cart. We were in hysterics, even Doc Hamilton."

"Why didn't you just walk all the way?" Kim said.

"Had to play thirty-six, Sperm Queen," Patterson said with a wink, which Kim returned.

"You've kept it off, Mo," Steve said, "you and Avery both. I'm the backslider and enjoyed every calorie."

" 'O that this too too solid flesh would melt,' " Finn chanted.

"I told you!" Steve said. "I told you we'd get a dose of Shakespeare in the first five minutes."

" 'Methinks you doth protest too much,' " Finn retorted, his hands flung wide, the gray eyes dancing.

"It's worse than we thought," Harry says.

"Stop him before he quotes again!"

High humor—I longed for a hidden camera. Finally they

took seats and Patterson gestured for Finn to take over. I expected someone to genuflect.

"Great memo, Mr. Consulting Detective," Kim said.

"The last refuge of the consultant. The memorandum."

"Doesn't hurt to write things down occasionally," Patterson said piously. "I learn what I really think when I write."

"No wonder your memos are so short," Harry said. They were off again. There were precious few moments when Captain Avery Patterson could be laughed at with impunity. We didn't laugh long.

From his briefcase Finn took a sawed-off golf club—it had no clubhead, just the rubberized grip plus a foot or so of steel shaft with a jagged end. I envisioned a berserk Elmo Finn wrapping the full club around a tree after hooking a shot into the trees. Spouting Shakespearean curses. Storming to his golf cart for exercise. At the window Finn made slow-motion swings—I thought of Captain Queeg rolling the steel balls.

Finn's fire-flecked gray eyes swept our faces. "Correct me. Avengers driving a white van appear at Maggie Lodge's doorstep nine-fifteen A.M. with armfuls of flowers in florist's paper, shoot her five times with a forty-caliber while videotaping it, no brass, typed note on the body. Ten minutes later at Ruth Isaacson's, another giant bouquet, they get inside the kitchen, five more gunshots on video, same note, still no brass."

"At least two Avengers," Harry blurted, "but maybe more."

Everything was off the record, but I was taking notes. "Maybe you'll do a video, a book, something we can sell," Patterson had said. With a start I realized that Finn was working without notes.

"Six days later Avengers sit down with Nasty Brown, low-level drug dealer, drinking coffee at his kitchen table. Six shots, Nasty dead, Snot Boogie wounded, no brass, another typed note. A week later one shot fired at Duane Hickman's house, killing the dog. Another fired into Hickman's leg, probably at the trestle.

"So. Four dead, one wounded, eighteen shots fired, seventeen of them in four residential neighborhoods—and no one saw or heard a goddamn thing. Except shaky IDs of a white van, a white woman and a pizza delivery hatchback."

The cops were nodding, consulting their notebooks. Steve McDade perched on the sofa like a sycophant, his legs bouncing furiously. Finn's keen eyes scanned us again as he swished the half-club back and forth.

"Kim, you were right—Nasty Brown's throat wounds were caused by one bullet and many thrusts of a serrated blade. FBI says Avengers' notes were typed on an Olympia portable manual typewriter circa 1950 on twenty-four-pound paper that is forty to fifty years old, curled some from moisture, maybe sitting on a basement shelf all these years. Envelopes pretty old too. Avengers very careful—no prints, no hair, no footprints, no tire tracks. They don't even lick the stamps, they know about DNA. One of 'em drinks beer."

I stopped scribbling for a moment and studied Elmo Finn. Network had sent us quite a file: First in his class at the Virginia Military Institute . . . declined a Rhodes scholarship in order to go to Vietnam . . . active in the Phoenix Program, the largest covert operation in CIA history. Suspected of avenging his financée's murder. A self-styled "consulting detective" whose clients included the FBI, several state police forces, three foreign governments. Wealthy, charged no fee, worked for reward money only. Habitually quoted Shakespeare, amusing some and annoying others. Born prematurely on a cruise ship after his mother had tangoed the night away.

One of Finn's old cases intrigued me. He had tracked down a serial killer, then discovered in a series of chummy jailhouse interviews that the murderer got stoned before each killing, hence felt an aversion to what he was about to do, hence knew his acts were wrong, hence was sane, hence could be tried, convicted and condemned to death. And was. Of course the slime is still alive and well and filing appeals and has gained ten pounds on that good Death-Row Cuisine.

"A few thoughts. Does the old man who may have seen a white woman at Nasty Brown's remember if she was carrying a large bag or wearing gloves or both? Have we thoroughly traced Nasty's movements that day—did he meet any strangers? Why were there three saucers and only one cup?"

Finn gripped and regripped the half-club, carefully knitting his fingers together. Swish, swish. He was merely summarizing. Everybody knew all this.

"We got more to do on Nasty Brown," Harry said. "His circle don't exactly like to talk to us."

"Avengers managed to look like they *belonged* wherever they were," Finn said. " 'One may smile, and smile, and be a villain.' Was the Lodges' housekeeper normally off that day?"

"Very convenient coincidence," Steve said.

"No coincidence," Kim said. "They knew."

Finn nodded agreement. "Let's expand the radius for florists and nurseries—those flowers came from somewhere. Cemeteries—that urn came from somewhere. Gunsmiths and dealers and shooting clubs. Ranges. Plinking."

"We checked Pizza Pony," Harry said. "They say no cartop signs are missing but I don't think they'd know."

Finn continued, "An automatic can be silenced but leaves shells. Revolver can't be silenced but leaves no shells. Which problem do they want—noise or brass? Brass. They *have* to keep the noise down. Don't want to leave casings to help ballistics, can't hang around to police up, so they add a brass-catcher. This weapon is bulky, fifteen inches or so. Hard to conceal."

Steve was beaming as if Finn had just solved the case. I had never seen his toady side.

"Did the suspicious Nasty Brown welcome two strangers to his kitchen table? Or *were* they strangers? And good enough to avoid touching anything except the cups, which they took with them?"

Frowns and stares all around.

"Hickman was shot in the leg?" I asked. "I only heard about the urn."

"We're holding that back," Steve said.

Finn turned his gunmetal eyes on me. "Joe, you know John Ewell. He says he didn't get Avengers' letter until the very day Hickman was killed. Snail mail. We rescued the envelope before it reached the landfill—"

"Whoa!" I said.

"Nice work if you can get it. Like sperm counting. Postmark was unreadable so we don't know if Ewell's lying."

They were waiting for me to say something so I milked the silence a little. Then I said, "John Ewell is a solid citizen but I don't think he's grieving for Duane Hickman. Go out to Presbyterian Hospital, Room 311, John's there every night holding Gwen's hand. Reading to her about Hawaii, watching the IV drip. She's a vegetable."

"Hell, Hickman's parents aren't even grieving," Harry said.

Finn rested the golf club on the window ledge. He had removed his jacket earlier and now loosened his tie.

"What about the pattern?" he said. "First, Juanita Daley gets an offer from Avengers to kill *Hollowell* . . . lies about it for days . . . then *Hollowell's lawyer's wife* and the *judge's wife* are killed. Joe gets an offer to kill *Boogie* . . . ignores it . . . then Boogie's *brother* is killed. John Ewell gets an offer to kill *Hickman* . . . says he ignored it . . . and this time the actual target, Hickman, is killed. 'Though this be madness, yet there is method in it.' Joe, is John Ewell . . . obsessed?"

I felt the icefire flaring and fought to suppress it. "We're all obsessed to some degree—we're all trying to find *closure*. That's the buzzword, *closure*. But I'll never get through a day without seeing my children on those slabs. And Juanita will never get through a day without seeing Debbie in her coffin. And John Ewell holds Gwen's hand every night and sees those tubes . . . yes, he's obsessed, you guys may know all about—"

The phone rang. Patterson answered, listened for a moment and hung up sharply.

"Isaacson's here. Apparently Boogie Brown tried to kill himself in his cell this afternoon. How the fuck does Isaacson know this before I do?"

Steve was first out the door. Everyone followed except Harry Covington, who stooped to pick up his gold shield from the floor.

"Boogie attempting *suicide* while he's on *suicide watch* . . ."

"This is some Isaacson trick," I said.

"That could be, Joe. That could absolutely be."

"Harry, what about this Sherlock Shakespeare. Is he for real?"

He shrugged. "He was CIA, Joe. Cap loves him, Steve loves him, I ain't convinced. You know the first thing he asked me on the phone? When are the birthdays of the two wives who were killed. The birthdays! Who gives a shit?"

"I'm going to interview him, Harry. Anything you can give me, if he's getting in the way, you know, these fucking prima donnas . . ."

"He wants to set up community meetings to discuss Avengers, get the public involved. Hold hands."

"Sounds like horseshit."

"We can waste a lot of time on horseshit like that."

"Hell yes, Harry. Just keep me posted, you know, I'll help however I can."

"Sure, Joe. Confidentially."

"Sure, totally."

Patterson's phone rang again. Harry walked over and answered it.

"Homicide Commander's office."

He listened for a few seconds.

"I'll tell Cap," he said softly, hanging up. He shivered his shoulders inside his well-cut jacket and made an infinitesimal adjustment to his necktie. He stared at the window as if he could see through the heavy drapes.

"Boogie Brown's little boy. Little Snot. He didn't make it."

We stood frozen in silence. I didn't know what to say.

"Born with bullet holes in his back." Harry's voice was a whisper.

"Does he know?" I said. "This could explain the suicide."

"Or," Harry said, his hands flitting to the necktie again, "it could be a pretext for . . . Joe, I just don't believe Boogie Brown attempted suicide; he's been on suicide watch . . . if cops are involved in this–"

A look crossed his handsome black face, as if he had just realized that I might not care what happened to Boogie Brown, or who did it.

SEVENTEEN

❏   ❏   ❏

NED CROMARTIE WAS frantic. "Got to see you, Joe—n-
n-now! Can't talk on the phone."

He picked me up at the station in his black Explorer. He
sat rigidly upright in the high cab, a two-fisted death-grip on
the wheel, and accelerated out of the horseshoe drive into busy
traffic. Ned was a lousy driver at best—the eyepatch.

"Easy, Ned! Jesus." I hurried with the seat belt. "What the
hell's up?"

His mouth was working before anything came out. "Suicide
attempt my ass! B-B-Boogie Brown? Avengers!"

"Hanging by strips of clothing in his cell, it does sound
fishy. But they say it's happened before."

"Avengers!"

"Or cops, Ned. But Avengers may be cops."

"Who c-cops? Who says?"

I fished out a cigarette, my hands trembling a little as I
worked the lighter.

"The brass is worried. There's a black detective, Harry
Covington. I hear he's a suspect—he's the one who arrested
Frank Hollowell, he despises Marvin Isaacson for defending
Hollowell and he dates Juanita Daley."

"Fucks those t-t-titties, does he? God!" Ned shot me a
quick, crooked smile. His hands were white on the steering
wheel.

"And there's Burl Devine. Ex-cop."

"N-Nutbeam!"

"Card-carrying," I chuckled. Ned turned onto a two-lane street and got caught in traffic. I was thankful.

"They're looking at Group, too, Ned. Juanita's linked to Hollowell, I'm linked to Boogie Brown, John Ewell's linked to Duane Hickman. We're all linked to Isaacson. Even you, Ned, they found your American Express card in Duane Hickman's shoebox, which I'll never understand."

He pulled out to pass but braked abruptly and swerved back. "Joe, listen to this, this is why I called you! They found a f-fingerprint on my American Express card! After all these years! S-Some slime named Darnell Throp, they call him Three-Finger Th-Thorp, he's doin' time at C-Central for manslaughter. Sergeant McDade sh-showed me his p-picture—he's the one who stabbed me. No question, he's the one. McDade said he probably s-sold the c-credit card on the street and somehow Hickman ended up with it."

"Goddamn, Ned, only three fingers and he still left a fingerprint?"

"F-fuck you, Joe. I want to contact Avengers!"

"Contact Avengers? To assassinate Three-Finger Thorp?"

"S-s-stick a knife in his eye, s-stick a knife in his b-b-balls. If he dies . . ."

"Eye for an eye, nut for a nut."

"Fuck you, Joe!"

"You don't need Avengers, Ned—any gangbanger can set up a prison hit."

"Then why didn't *you* call a g-g-gangbanger instead of trying to b-break into jail?"

"Because I wanted to watch Boogie Brown die."

He made another turn and accelerated. "I never knew who they were, Joe. Now I do—at least one of the b-bastards."

Ned's voice throbbed with emotion and determination—just as it had when I tried to talk him out of his armed night-walks. He told me to fuck off then, too.

"Why are you telling me this, Ned? If you're serious you should keep quiet."

"Because you won't t-turn me in, Joe."

"I won't turn you in."

"I know you w-won't. I know that. Guess what the new g-g-guy at Group asked me, Sullivan, the one whose dad goes to f-f-funerals all the time. How to contact Avengers. We d-discussed it."

"So?"

"C-Classified ad."

I couldn't help laughing. "Classified ad? What would you say—Help Wanted, Assassin with Good Maximum Security Prison Contacts. Avengers Phone Home. Goddamn, Ned, how would they even know to *look* for a classified ad?"

His face reddened. "There's another way. Say it on your s-s-show."

I looked at him incredulously. His eyes shone with fear but with something else, too. I was speechless.

" '*There are reports that p-p-people want to hire Avengers*' . . . something like that. Let Avengers know someone's looking for them. To do b-b-business."

"Elmo Finn will love that."

"You could say you've gotten anonymous c-calls! You get a lot of calls, Joe, right?"

"Then what, Ned?"

"They'll c-contact you somehow, you r-r-refer them to me, you're done."

"And you hire them to get Three-Finger Thorp."

"S-stab him in the eye and the b-balls."

"Ned, Ned, all their activity has been *outside* prison. They *talk* about dusting people inside but they haven't." I was talk-

85

ing like the cops and the perps. Before Boogie Brown I didn't even know what *dusting* meant.

"They got to B-Boogie Brown. *Suicide!* They can do wh-whatever . . ."

Ned stopped at a market to get a soda. I stayed in the Explorer, confused and alarmed—I didn't know Ned Cromartie at all. I was smoking when he returned.

"Joe, you haven't s-smoked since Connie died."

"Once in a while. Jesus, Ned, I just smoked a cigarette, right in front of you! You're zoned out."

I took fast drags to get the tranquilizing effect. Why not smoke regularly, I thought. The worst has happened.

"Ned, this backfires, you got to keep me out of it. They'd arrest me. And it's got to be just between us, just you and me—no Tad Sullivan, no nobody."

"Joe, I know you won't r-r-rat on me. You think I'd r-rat on you?"

I laughed again. "That's funny the way you say it, like a gangster in the movies. You in that eyepatch."

"I see a lot of m-movies, Joe. Sometimes in my head I see f-fucking movies."

EIGHTEEN

❑   ❑   ❑

"HOW CAN YOU defend the guilty?"

My blunt attack unsettled Marvin Isaacson. He had been led to expect a debating-society atmosphere but he was getting the Inquisition—live and in color: gunmetal gray. Logan made him wait under hot lights while the director pretended to test camera angles. By showtime he was wilted and tense. I strolled onto the set in fresh makeup fifteen seconds before the cameras rolled.

"How can you defend the guilty, Counselor Isaacson? How can you defend murderers?" I fought against the icefire, glaring at the sleazoid who had defended the butcher of my children.

"Everyone has . . . I'm not the judge or the jury." Marvin's voice was high and unsure. His tie was already askew, the ponytail mussed where he twirled it with his finger. "The way the system works—"

"How can you defend a murderer!"

"Everyone is innocent until proved guilty. If the government cannot prove—"

"If a murderer *tells* you he's guilty like Franklin Delano Hollowell did, like Boogie Brown did—"

"I don't ask . . . that's privileged—"

"*Privileged.* Do the victims get any privileges, Counselor?"

"The way the system works—"

"Oh we know how the system works, Counselor—that's what bothers us. We don't think the system makes any sense when the question of guilt gets lost, when the question of truth gets lost—"

"A criminal trial is not fundamentally a search for truth, it is—"

"You admit it! You admit it! If a criminal trial isn't a search for truth, then what is it? A game? A game you try to win by lying, by forcing the police to play by all the absurd, formalistic rules that protect the guilty from society instead of protecting society from the guilty—" The icefire raged. I swallowed some air while Marvin huffed fiercely. His hand was trembling as he twirled the ponytail.

"Guilt is irrelevant," Isaacson said primly, arching his neck. "The only issue is, Can the state prove its case? If the government cannot prove—"

"You mean if you can trick the jury, or suppress evidence—"

"Someone has to stand up for the accused against the power of the government, make the government prove its case! The defense lawyer serves the system whether there's a conviction or acquittal! And there's a difference between innocent and not guilty!"

"There's a difference between innocent and not guilty? You lawyers are something." I fought to control my voice against the icefire. "Are you saying that one of your murderers can be both not guilty and not innocent? *At the same time?*"

"Yes! Yes! Not guilty does not mean *innocent*! The Scots say *not proved*. In our system the burden—"

"Would you defend your wife's murderer?"

"That is not . . . that is repulsive."

To make Isaacson look sinister we were shooting him ECU—extreme close-up—so his head was too large for the

frame and every eye movement and bead of sweat accentu-
ated. His makeup was lousy and the lighting brutal—Logan
was using all the tricks. The shot of me was wider and
therefore less sinister, my makeup was perfect, my chair a
little higher.

"I want to ask you about the Hollowell trial. One day in
court a friend of mine said, 'Watch this—when the jury gets
settled, Hollowell will take out a package of Life Savers and
offer one to Marvin, and a little later they'll be conferring and
Marvin will put his arm around him and hug him like a son.'
And that's exactly what happened! He predicted your little
slimeball tricks to make a rapist and murderer seem warm and
humane! And everybody knows that Frank Hollowell
wouldn't offer a Life Saver to anybody on this earth unless it
was poisoned! Is this what you mean by *serving the system*?
Making a murderer seem like a nice guy?"

Isaacson was trying to interrupt me but the words wouldn't
come, only gurgles and gestures. He was twirling the ponytail
demonically.

"I don't have to . . . obviously the ground rules—"

"Ground rules, there are no ground rules! Don't try your
slimy tricks in this court! Why do you oppose the death penalty?"

Logan and I knew that an irate Isaacson couldn't resist this
one.

"The state shouldn't be in the business of killing people!
Capital punishment is institutionalized revenge! It's—"

"What's wrong with revenge?"

"It's barbaric—"

"Don't you want to avenge the murder of your wife? Just
a little bit?"

He squeaked something unintelligible and turned deeply
red, his eyes narrowing to slits. He knew he'd made a terrible

mistake appearing on the show, and I loved his agony. We had expected him to walk out, so the tech had bungeed his chair down and snagged his microphone cord.

"Leaving early, Counselor? Good riddance! Your tricks won't work in this court, it's not a *game* here, we deal with truth in the court of public opinion, and you lose, Counselor! Court adjourned!"

He was tearing at the cord and shrieking so loudly his ravings were unintelligible. Finally he extricated himself and stormed out—with Casey, our best cameraman, in hot pursuit off-the-shoulder, capturing every antic swing of the ponytail. We had set up lights in the parking lot. As Marvin struggled to unlock his car, his hands trembling so violently he couldn't insert the key, he whirled and thrust an upraised middle finger at the camera—and simultaneously at the occupants of one-point-one million homes. Mad Dog Marvin. Cut and print.

The red lights glowed on my camera and I leaned into it. "Here on *Crime and Punishment* we think a trial ought to be a search for truth. You got a problem with that, go to law school, they'll love you. Back in two minutes."

After the commercial I adopted my David Brinkley intonation. "A final point. A disturbing point. We've gotten calls from people asking how to contact Avengers. We don't know how to contact Avengers. If we did, we'd tell the police—because these self-styled Avengers are serial killers who take the law into their own hands and murder innocent people. For God's sake, folks, let's keep all this in perspective—and remember what our mothers and fathers and priests and ministers and rabbis taught us. Court adjourned. Good night."

In Logan's office it was Bollinger's again. Four bottles. The switchboard was swamped; twenty to one pro-Colby. New York wanted *Would you defend your wife's murderer?* and Marvin flipping the bird in the parking lot. Janie was sitting on Logan's grand oval desk facing his chair, her knees under her chin and her beguiling legs not exactly locked in the modesty position. She winked at me several times and I decided to stay until they asked me to leave.

"Joe," Logan said, ostentatiously bending forward to slurp Janie's knee, "we're back on track, baby. Nothing like a good slaughter for the ratings. We've had calls for Avengers? Holy holy. Take a number. 'Remember what our mothers taught us'—that was beautiful, Joe. Crime and punishment . . . Janie, it is a crime to have legs as luscious as yours and a punishment—"

My cue. I took it.

NINETEEN

❑   ❑   ❑

WEARING RUBBER GLOVES, he types on the old Olympia.

To Joe Colby:

We are not "serial killers." We are AVENGERS
who punish defectives and their allies for cause. We
demand a private taping to state our case. Time and
place will be disclosed later. Observe strict secrecy.
Think of Ellie.

Avengers

*He removes the letter from the typewriter and rolls in an
envelope. Home or office address? Home, like the others. First
thought best thought. He types the address, extracts the envelope and inserts the letter and the photograph of Elly Briggs
taken from a distance with the long-lens Nikon.*

*He moves to the metal shelves and begins preparing for the
work ahead. A flash of irritation unsettles him.* Serial killers!
He could explain it on television.

*She arrives and soon they are ready. They leave the damp
chamber and make their way up the bank and along the hidden trail. She carries a small handbag and a pair of shoes. He
carries an automobile license plate. At a certain point they
make a turn and emerge from trees behind a large outbuilding*

which they enter through a door hidden by vines. They rear-
range certain items, affix the license plate and drive away in a
small car that no one looking into the building could have seen.
    "Wearing the new ones?" she asks.
    He nods. "Yes. They're tight."
    "But you like that."
    "Yes."
    "I want you to shave. Too much hair shows. Your balls too."
    "You shave me."
    She laughs and reaches for him. "I knew it."
    "Not now, check the wig."
    "The wig is fine. Don't worry, I'm doing all the work."
    "I don't worry."
    As usual, she gets out at the Visitors Entrance of the immense
stone structure and he drives to the parking lot. He parks and
pretends to read a book. A few of the other cars are occupied
too. He understands why some people don't go inside. In less
than an hour she returns and they drive away.
    "Any problems?"
    "So easy. Where do they find those guards?"
    "He understands everything?"
    "Oh yes. You should have seen his eyes. He said to save the
radio for Hollowell, that's the only way on Death Row until
you're above C-level. Asked about Boogie, who screwed up."
    He checks the mirror. "Did you notice a station wagon?"
Before she can answer he abruptly turns right, then right again.
    "Don't spook yourself. All these turns." She strokes his leg.
"When I showed him the photograph he almost jumped
through the glass. I said, 'Clay, we know your mother won't
try to hide again, will she?' Of course he denied everything.
Where are you going?"
    "Slight detour. We're in character, may as well take advan-
tage. Minimum John's house. First thought best thought."

"I thought we had some shaving to do. First thought best thought."

He drives slowly through an affluent neighborhood of wide streets and broad lawns behind hedges. They look into a nearly hidden driveway.

"His Jeep?"

"Security."

"Full-time?"

"Off and on. I know the schedule."

"How'd you find out?"

"Patiently. Like a good detective."

She reaches for him. "What's first thought best thought?"

"First thought is church. Best thought may be rifle."

TWENTY

❏   ❏   ❏

ELMO FINN REACHED inside his herringbone jacket and brought out a revolver. He snapped open the cylinder, shook the bullets into his hand and passed the gun, butt first, to me in the back seat. We were in Elly's Buick on the way to Burl Devine's Sentinel Gun Shoppe. Elly was driving.

I gingerly closed the cylinder. "Where's the safety?"

"You saw too many early Bond movies, Joe. Revolvers don't have safeties. Double-oh Seven didn't know either."

"Jesus, I don't like this," Elly said. "This could be a big mistake."

I twirled the gun like a desperado. "Should I get a revolver or an automatic? Or a rocket launcher?"

"Revolver has fewer problems but holds fewer rounds. Takes longer to reload. But if you need to reload you're in a shootout, and if you're in a shootout you better hope somebody mounts up and rides to the sound of the guns."

"You have many shootouts in Vietnam?"

"They called them firefights," Finn said without answering my question.

Burl Devine's Sentinel Gun Shoppe was an immense establishment in an aging suburban shopping center. The heavy bars on the windows made it look like a prison. Ahead of us several customers displayed their unloaded weapons, cylinders and chambers open, to the uniformed guard at the metal detector inside the door. Finn flashed some kind of ID and the guard waved us through.

Burl had a vast inventory. Rows of rifles and shotguns in freestanding floor racks. Handguns in glass cases cushioned with velvet like jewelers' trays. Holsters of every kind, shirts and fatigues in camouflage and hunters' orange, Kevlar vests, serious-looking longbows and knives, videos and books. The clerks wore their shirts outside their pants, but the bulges on their hips were obvious. We made our way to the rear where Burl Devine awaited us in a three-piece pinstripe, striking his curator's pose. I had told him we were researching a show on buying a gun. He didn't expect Elmo Finn.

I introduced Elly to Burl, who bowed from the waist and took her hand in both of his.

"The Countess," Burl purred.

Elly inclined her head and smiled.

"And this is my firearms advisor—"

"Colonel Finn," Burl said. They shook hands. *Colonel.*

"How you doin', Sergeant," Elmo Finn said.

They held the pose, looking squarely at each other. Colonel Shakespeare and Sergeant Nutbeam.

"Burl," Elmo Finn said, finally breaking the eyeclinch, "what's hot in home defense for these two good citizens? Something easy."

Burl bounced up and down on his toes and winked at Elly. "Colonel, I suggest the Mossberg pistol-grip twelve-gauge shotgun with double-aught birdshot, *recommended for black bear* as it says right on the shell box. Same as I carried in a black-and-normal. Don't plan on huntin' ducks or nothin', do you?" Another huge wink.

"We don't plan on huntin' nothin'," Elly said, mimicking Burl's inflection. "Joe thinks the ducks may hunt him."

"Watch out for Isaacson, Joe. That's one bleeding heart needs a transfusion. You made him look goofier'n me."

Suddenly Elmo Finn was all business. "You hear something, Sergeant?"

"I *seen* somethin', Colonel, right where we're standin'. Who but Marvin Isaacson his own self drops in the other day and purchases certain firearms. Wearin' bedroom slippers like a fruitcake. Had a wild look about him. Some people say I have a wild look."

"What'd he buy, Burl?"

"It's all on the forms, legal and proper. Remington pump twelve-gauge, Smith three-fifty-seven, six weeks of lessons, five hundred rounds."

"Mr. Gun Control," I said derisively.

"A liberal who's been mugged, Joe, very schizoidal species. Avengers mugged him first, then you mugged him in everybody's livin' room."

A heavyset clerk with three prim women in tow stopped to confer with Burl. Commander Nutbeam said something about Mace being good for "enraging, not disengaging," then turned back to us.

"Everybody's buyin' somethin'—you oughtta see upstairs! Sentinel Security is swamped, all the lawyers and judges have panicked. Woulda started Avengers myself, I'd know this!" He threw Elmo Finn a challenging smile, then went to a display case and got out the Mossberg. He racked it open with a flourish and passed it to me across the counter. I struck a few poses, squeezing the trigger, then swung the barrel toward Elly. Elmo Finn grabbed it hard.

"First rule, Joe. Never point a gun at someone unless you intend to shoot."

"It's empty."

"Especially if it's empty. They're the most lethal."

Burl said, "And Rule Two is, Never shoot 'em unless you intend to kill 'em."

Finn let go of the barrel and I offered the shotgun to Elly.

She raised her hands in protest and backed away a few steps.

"I'll wait, I'll wait," she said. "Take lessons first. I'm not so sure about this."

I bought the shotgun and signed us up for lessons. Burl handed me the state form and said, "All answers are No. Just check all the No boxes." When I hesitated, he said, "If anything's a Yes, can't sell you a gun." I scanned the questions—criminal convictions, mental illnesses, affiliations with subversive organizations—and rapidly checked off the No boxes. Gun control at work.

We said good-bye to Burl and went next door to the sandwich shop for coffee. We took a corner booth.

I said, "Could Burl his own self buy a gun? He's a Minuteman or whatever, they want to overthrow the government."

"What's a black-and-normal?" Elly said.

I told her how a black murder suspect once collapsed and nearly died in the carotid-artery chokehold of Sergeant Burl Devine. When Burl finally released him, the suspect pitched forward on his face, unconscious, and the EMTs were hard-pressed to revive him. Later, Burl explained to us reporters that the mishap had occurred because the veins and arteries in black people don't open up as fast *as in normal people*. Burl's racist theory was front-page for a month. The Bubba cops immediately dubbed their cruisers "black-and-normals."

"Was he disciplined?"

"Suspended, demoted, finally forced to retire. But there's plenty of Burls left."

"With four balls?" Elly said.

"Marching around in the woods with AK-forty-sevens they all *think* they got four," Elmo Finn said.

After the coffee came, I said, "Colonel Finn, holding that shotgun I felt funny, same as when I tried to break into jail. I could almost see Boogie Brown in front of me. I could see myself pointing the gun . . ."

Elly reached for my hand and held it.

"They say revenge is wrong," I said, "but I can barely stand it sometimes, knowing what that animal did to my children. I still want to kill him, I can't help it. Did you feel that way?"

Elmo Finn sipped the hot black coffee. He seemed to be composing an answer. "It's wrong by law," he said finally, "the law we write with our heads in marble chambers. But the laws of the heart . . . I know how you feel, Joe. My fiancée was murdered. Senselessly, savagely, like Buzz and Belle. I wanted revenge. People said I was wrong." He looked at me intently. " 'Everyone can master a grief but he that has it.' "

"Shakespeare?"

"I did what felt right to me. Here." He tapped his chest. "Not here," pointing to his head.

He suddenly straightened in his chair and his voice became brisk.

"Joe, will you be ready when they ask for equal time?"

"Sure—but they'll mail in a tape. How could they do a taping with me and not get caught?"

"We can be there fast."

"I know. And they know. That's why they'll mail it in."

"Joe, stay alert on all fronts. True believers like Marvin Isaacson can rationalize anything, and now he's armed to the teeth. Marvin Isaacson and Burl Devine are two sides of the same coin."

"Some coin," Elly said.

I said, "Well, we got the shotgun now, we're getting the dog. . . ."

"Doberman's better than the Mossberg. He'll warn you to get the gun."

Elly said, "I don't want to keep it loaded, Colonel. Do we have to?"

"Any kids around?" He went pale, stared helplessly, finally looked away. "Jesus, Joe, I'm sorry."

I nodded and waved it off, but the icefire flared inside.

"In your situation, keep it loaded. You can't say, 'Hold on just a minute,' while you chamber a round."

"We could just shoot 'em in the leg," Elly said. "What did Burl mean, never shoot except to kill?"

"He means you don't want your target healing up at tax-payers' expense—and paying a return visit."

TWENTY-ONE

❑ ❑ ❑

"VICTIMS, JOE, THAT'S our hook! We're on the side of *victims*!" Logan Murphy folded his manicured hands self-righteously on the edge of the oval desk. "Interview your Savages, Joe. Let your Savages tell their stories," he pontificated. "Unrehearsed. Unedited. Unvarnished."

I wanted to say, Shut up. I was scared.

Logan fixed his eyes on a corner of the ceiling. He had nothing to do this morning and wanted someone to do it with. "Must be careful about *exploiting*—"

"Logan, there's something—"

"No, let's do victims next—keep the emotional stuff going."

"I've—"

"Don't be afraid to argue with me, Joe. We need creative tension."

"Goddamnit, listen, Boss!"

I talked for ten minutes. For the last five Logan was pacing, softly muttering "holy holy." When I finished we high-fived.

"The mother of all interviews! Joe, don't tell the cops. These people are killers. Simple as that."

"It's Elly, Logan. I can't take any chances with her, so I have to take a chance with Elmo Finn and the cops. They could arrest me."

"Then they'll have to arrest me too."

"They're going to be pissed, Boss. It's like interviewing the enemy in wartime and not telling your own troops where they are. We can kiss our insider trading good-bye."

"Fuck 'em, people will understand. It's like paying a ransom to kidnappers—you're afraid not to."

"I'm going to keep a record of everything."

"Write it all down! Write down that I advised you—*directed* you—to tape the interview before telling the cops. The story comes first. No, Elly comes first. Then the story. Then the cops." He shrugged. "No choice. Holy holy."

"Wish me luck. If I don't show up before sunrise, call Elmo Finn."

"Let's hire a bodyguard for tonight!"

"No, Boss. If I'm going to do it, I'm going to follow their rules."

"You're right. Holy holy. Ask Janie to come in."

I waved Janie in and hurried through the basement to my car. I drove too fast to a suburban mall and pulled to the curb at a certain entrance. Ned got in.

"Sorry," I said.

"No problem. Is it w-what I hope?"

"Yep."

"God."

We got a six-pack of beer at a drive-through. I made Ned watch for suspicious cars while I circled the block a few times. Then I swung onto the circumferential and began driving around the city.

"Could someone really be f-following us?" Ned was breathless, which was curious for a man in an eyepatch who walked dark streets with a gun.

"Goddamn right."

He reached inside his coat and produced the Glock. "Fuck 'em, p-partner."

I laughed. Everybody wanted to fuck 'em today.

"Ned, what I'm going to tell you is a crime and you will be as guilty as I am. Or almost, something like that. Conspiracy. You understand?"

"Tell me. I been c-conspiring for years."

"Yesterday I got a letter from Avengers demanding a secret interview—they sent a photograph of Elly I've never seen! Then this morning I get a call. 'Go right now to the pay phone outside the Seven-Eleven where you buy beer. Remember Elly.' The line goes dead. I start shaking like a leaf. I go to the pay phone, I'm there maybe a minute and it rings. Same voice. 'We will tape the show at midnight tonight at your house. Bring a Sony Betacam and two umbrella lights. Be alone. Remember Elly.'"

"Tonight! They're c-coming tonight?"

"Ned, you have to keep totally quiet."

"Sure." We drove silently for a few moments. "Joe, why tell me?"

"Just in case. If something goes wrong. Logan's the only other person who knows and . . . I don't know, he might not admit it. I'm afraid to tell Elly, they threatened her. We just bought a shotgun, she's already hyper enough, thinks the house and everything else is bugged. Worst-case scenario, someone may have to talk to Elmo Finn." I finished my beer and cracked a fresh one. "There's another reason I'm telling you, Ned. I promised you something."

"Oh yes. Y-yes. I'm a customer, Tad S-Sullivan is too."

"Forget Sullivan!" Ned jumped at my outburst. "Goddamnit, Ned, nobody else! I shouldn't be doing this at all, but you're my friend. But no strangers."

Ned made a shaky palms-up gesture. "No p-problem, J-Joe."

"How much have you talked with Sullivan? We don't know anything about Tad Sullivan!"

"Joe, S-Sullivan asked *me* about contacting Avengers. We

105

d-dreamed up the classified ad, don't you remember?"

"Don't you remember I said *nobody else*? Goddamnit, are you and Sullivan some kind of package deal?"

"No. Of course not."

"Have you talked with anyone? Julia?"

"J-Julia? What do *you* think?"

"Ned, if I put you in touch with them I'm guilty of something. Just interviewing them makes me guilty of something."

"J-Joe, is my w-word g-good enough?"

I couldn't look at him. "Of course, Ned, of course it is. You know that."

"You have my w-word."

I held out my palm and he slapped it and held on tightly. Something shivered through me, like a warning.

"Ned, can Elly stay at your place tonight?"

"Sure."

"She thinks I'm pulling an all-nighter with Logan."

"Sure. I'll t-try to restrain myself. But J-Julia's a heavy sleeper, especially s-sedated."

I laughed. "Elly says you turn her on. Must be the eye-patch."

"We'll p-practice menage-ing tonight. Be all r-ready when you can make it a t-t-trois."

Another warning wrinkled through my head. I banished it.

"There was something I didn't tell you about the voice on the phone."

"You r-recognized it."

"It was a woman."

TWENTY-TWO

□   □   □

AT THREE-FIFTEEN THE next morning I telephoned Logan Murphy and Sergeant Steve McDade. At four-fifteen I was yawning on the sofa in Logan's office, afraid to close my eyes. Logan was perched on the windowsill behind his desk, sipping gin. At four-twenty Patterson and McDade burst in. Steve was carrying a thermos of coffee. I almost laughed.

Without a glance at Logan, Patterson said, "Joe, you know your rights, you may want a lawyer."

I waved indifferently from the sofa and tossed Steve a manila envelope containing my hour-by-hour record of events and the original note from Avengers trussed up in the usual plastic bag. I had not mentioned Ned.

Steve the speed-reader absorbed everything in a rush, handing each page to Patterson as he finished. He placed a tape recorder on the coffee table and turned it on.

"Where's Elly?" Steve said.

"She wasn't there. I'd rather not say."

"How many of them?"

"One."

"The woman?"

I shook my head. "Man."

"Who was it?" Steve growled.

"I don't know. He wore a mask like one of those political masks. I didn't recognize it. He had a voice-disguiser gadget, made him sound like a robot. Check the tape."

"Did you recognize anything at all about the person? Any glimmers? Hunches?"

"No. And I was trying to."

"Tell us everything. From the moment he got there."

"I had already set up the camera to shoot through a bed-sheet, get a silhouette effect as a disguise. I thought they'd want something like that. At midnight there was a knock on the door. I opened it and the mask scared me to death. He was a little shorter than me."

"Clothes."

"Suit and tie. Dark suit, seemed too big. Loose fit. Some kind of thin leather gloves like driving gloves. After a few minutes I realized I couldn't see one inch of his skin. He had black running shoes, Reeboks, I think."

"You're absolutely sure it was not a woman."

"Yes. No, not *absolutely*. Pretty sure."

"Weapon?"

"Revolver, I could see the bullets in the chambers. Small black revolver. He kept it pointed at me the whole time."

"Why'd you wait until after three to phone?"

I stood up and went to Logan's bar for a drink. My third. Or fourth.

"That won't help."

"Well arrest me then, goddamnit! My nerves—"

"You guys help yourselves." Amazingly, Logan had decided to play genial host.

"This ain't no fuckin' social call! Why'd you wait to phone?"

"I didn't wait to phone! This wasn't just a straight interview, no interruptions! We stopped after each question and answer. Usually he made me do several takes. I had to pee three times."

"Did he pee?"

"No."

"Did you use the bedsheet?"

"No. He tore it down, he just wanted the camera on a blank wall while I asked the question, then pan over for his answer. No zooms, no close-ups. Very sterile. If he had asked me, I could have jazzed it up some. But I didn't volunteer."

"Chair?"

"I had set up a folding chair. He didn't like it, he wanted a stool so I got one from the kitchen. You can't see it in the shot."

"How many questions?"

"I don't know. He handed me a stack of index cards with typed questions. The famous typewriter, looked like. You can watch the tape. I wasn't counting." I tried to stifle a yawn but couldn't.

"Bored with all this, Joe?" Patterson said, giving me the Look. Treblinka version.

"I'm tired, Captain. This has been a hard night. And day."

"Not as hard as it will get."

Logan slapped the oval desk with his big hand. I jumped, the cops didn't. "Don't threaten anybody here, you fuckin' storm troopers! Don't make any fuckin' threats to my people!"

Patterson shifted the Look to Logan, who glared back, red-faced but defiant. The defiance was one part spunk, nine parts gin.

"Did he come in a car?" Steve asked.

"I don't know. I didn't hear a car, before or after. He just materialized at midnight."

"What time did he leave?"

"Two fifty-five. I made a note."

"Tell us exactly what you did when he left."

"I listened at the door for a few seconds, heard absolutely nothing, then poured a very strong drink and waited ten minutes like he said. Fixed another drink. Then I went to the phone."

"Give me the key to your house. Is Elly there?"

"No." I gave Steve the key. They made me go over the story again, interrupting with sharp questions, jumping all around the chronology. At one point Steve had to load a new cassette. Finally I said, "Just look at the video, it's almost an hour of footage. See for yourself."

"Oh, we'll look at the video," Patterson said. "We'll be the only ones who'll look at the goddamn video."

Logan exploded again from behind the desk. "Fuck you, storm troopers! This interview is going on the air tonight! *Crime and Punishment*, seven o'clock, and we're going to promo it all the livelong day! Go read the First Amendment! Go—"

"Fuck the First Amendment," Captain Avery Patterson said acidly. "Joe Colby and Logan Murphy, you are under arrest for obstruction of justice, conspiracy to obstruct justice, aiding and abetting a felony, compounding a felony and tampering with evidence. Steve, read 'em their rights—slowly, these assholes are pretty stupid."

Logan made the mistake of getting on his high horse and refusing to be handcuffed, whereupon Patterson slammed him into the wall and wrenched the cuffs on. The stuff on Logan's credenza got knocked to the floor, including the gold badge in the Plexiglas case emblazoned *Friend of the Police*. Logan Murphy, the rugged superexecutive, squealed like a toddler. His nose and wrist were bleeding. I simply turned away from Steve, my hands proffered meekly behind my back. As I did so, Harry Covington charged through the door.

"Judge Burkett was *still up*, Cap. Reading poetry and drinking brandy! Piece of work, approved both search warrants."

"Harry, contact everybody on Elmo's list for alibis. Wake the fuckers up."

"Juanita was with me, Captain," Harry Covington said.

I tried a new tack. "Steve, I forgot something. Guy named Tad Sullivan, new member of our Victims Group. He's been asking around about contacting Avengers."

"What'd you tell him?"

"Nothing."

"What'd Ned Cromartie tell him?"

"I can't imagine. Nothing."

Covington and Kim Whitten and several uniforms were setting up shop as we were conducted outside. Logan recovered his chutzpah and demanded to make a phone call. Steve said there might be a phone at Headquarters. I had a flash of insight.

"Steve, Sullivan's a cop, isn't he?"

TWENTY-THREE

❑   ❑   ❑

WE WERE BOOKED, fingerprinted and photographed by
dawn's early light. And by noon's stern sun back on the
streets. My second arrest in eight weeks and still they couldn't
hold me. I told the typewriter cop I was a known desperado,
he already had my fingerprints, and without an upward glance
he muttered, "Shut up, asshole."

They finally let Logan make his allotted call, and he phoned
Channel Nine's corporate attorney, who had always despised
his mousy practice and jumped at the chance to raise unshirted
hell at Police Headquarters. Then they threw us in the tank
with the drunks and disorderlies. Logan and I had nodded off
on the cold cement floor when a bailiff xylophoned the bars
with his nightstick and marched us to the office of Prosecuting
Attorney Bucky Webb, where our corporate lawyer embraced
us like prisoners of war.

Bucky, the compulsive plea-bargainer, offered a deal: a vol-
untary ban on the interview until the police could review it
thoroughly. "Twenty-four hours!" Logan bellowed. The corporate lawyer bobbed his head and roared off a string of First
Amendment precedents that he must have memorized within
the hour. Patterson ignored the lawyer and gave a gruff nod.
Then they released Logan but escorted me in a stiff formation
to Patterson's office, where Elmo Finn and another dude were

waiting. I had never seen the new guy, but I knew who he was.

I poured a cup of coffee and slumped into a soft chair facing the big Sony. I stared at the new guy, who stared back. He was as tall as Finn but a little stockier. Not fat; solid. He wore pressed faded jeans, a black linen sport coat over a black T-shirt and western boots. And a sour, turned-down mouth that seemed impervious to a smile. Except George Graves didn't smile. He went to the corner of the big office where a video camera was mounted on a tripod.

"We're going to tape this for the record," Finn said.

"Who do I have to fuck to get off this movie?" Graves growled. I cackled despite my fatigue. Network had warned me about this crusty jacket-and-jeans videographer and side-kick to the bounty-hunting Elmo Finn. *He plays the clown—don't fall for it.* Like Finn, George Graves had been CIA. In Vietnam.

I said, "I get *your* first interview, right, El-mo? We have a deal?"

"Deal," Finn said pleasantly. "You can even have cancellation rights."

"You'll want those," Graves said, fiddling with the camera.

"Joe, this is George Graves."

"I know. Mr. Graves's bad reputation precedes him." We shook hands and Graves's mouth twitched slightly. I was to learn this was as close as he ever came to a smile.

Finn was ambling back and forth, lazily swinging the sawed-off six-iron. Captain Queeg massaging the steel balls. I giggled again. I was punchy.

"I guess they didn't mail it in, did they, Joe?"

"No they didn't, El-mo. But they did mail in a threat to Elly. I couldn't take any chances."

Elmo Finn shrugged. "You didn't hear anything until the

knock on the door?" Finn said. Suddenly the gray eyes were
fiery lasers.

"No."

"How many knocks?"

"Three or four. I don't know. Three."

"You open the door, the mask startles you, he motions you
to move back."

"Yes."

"With which hand?"

"Right. I think."

"Holding the revolver."

"Yes, I saw the gun. No, I guess the gun was in his left
hand."

"You sure it was a revolver?"

"I could see the bullets in the cylinder."

"About this size?" He held up a small black pistol.

"Yes, about. Like a detective special."

"He yanked the bedsheet down as soon as he saw it?"

"Yes. Not immediately—he studied it a few seconds."

"With which hand?"

"With . . . I'm not sure."

"Which hand adjusted the voice device under the mask?"

"Right. Gun in left, must have been the right."

George Graves, wearing headphones now, came out from
behind the camera and adjusted an audio recorder I hadn't
noticed. They were double-taping me for some reason.

"Where was the microphone?"

"Camera mount."

"Both of you sound off-mike."

"No wonder."

"When he looked through the viewfinder, which eye?"

"Left. I think."

"Did he make you sit on the stool when he looked?"

"Yes. How'd you know?"

"Did he change the framing?"

"Yes. He wanted a head-and-shoulders shot."

"Your first setup was too wide?"

"Too tight."

"Did he use his hands to demonstrate the framing he wanted?"

"Yep."

"And when he used his hands to demonstrate the framing you didn't see his wrist or arm—as his sleeves were pulled up? A piece of skin?" Finn dropped the six-iron and pantomimed the motion.

"No. He wore gloves. Nothing showed that I saw."

"Describe the shoes."

"Black Reeboks. There was a little color somewhere, like a logo."

"How do you know they were Reeboks?"

"I must have seen the name, I don't know, that's all I can tell you. I wasn't looking at the goddamn shoes! I was looking at the goddamn gun!"

We watched the tape. "Looks like the Iranian hostages," Graves said. He was right—drab set, stark lighting, my voice eerily off-camera and off-mike: "This is Joe Colby, offscreen, and the person you see is a spokesman for the group known as Avengers, who is being interviewed at his demand. The first question is: On this program I called Avengers 'serial killers.' Is that correct?"

"No. We are not serial killers. We are avengers who punish defectives and their allies. We make them feel the pain they cause others. To do this, we must also punish a few innocents—but innocents will die in any event. Fewer will die our way. The injustice system does not protect society from criminals, it protects criminals from society. The name of this program, *Crime and Punishment*, is ludicrous. It should be *Crime and Plea Bargaining, Crime and Parole, Crime and Com-*

munity Service. We are restoring justice to the injustice system."

"Those cadences," Finn said as George Graves paused the tape. "He could be reading from a cue card."

"It's the voice device," I said. "Makes him sound robotic."

"Could he have been a woman?"

"Steve asked that. I don't think so."

"Did he walk like a man?"

"Yes. I mostly walked ahead of him."

We went back to the tape and listened to the distorted voice droning behind the mask.

"The urge to avenge is as natural as thirst and hunger . . . What is unnatural is to deny it. . . .

"Justice should mean guilt or innocence, not winning or losing a case. . . .

"Average murderer serves only eight years. . . .

"Rehabilitation doesn't work . . . prisons should be cages. . . .

"We should exhume the bodies of Karl Menninger and Earl Warren and desecrate them on the courthouse steps. . . ."

"I almost asked him to explain that one," I said. "It sounded so . . ."

"So what?" Finn asked.

"Old Testament."

Graves restarted the VCR. My off-mike voice seemed to emanate from a cavern.

"How and why did you choose your targets—Mrs. John Lodge, Mrs. Marvin Isaacson, Nasturtium Brown, Duane Hickman?"

"The targets chose us."

"What can we do to persuade you to stop?"

"Change the injustice system to a justice system."

"But surely you've made your point—surely more killings cannot help your cause."

"Avengers is not a cause. It is a result."

Graves hit the rewind button. Not again, I thought.

"Joe," Finn said, "until his one-liners at the end, your questions take three minutes, his answers take eighteen. Why didn't you ask some follow-ups, probe a little? It's not your style to sit idly by."

"Like watching a fucking play," Graves growled. "You two didn't rehearse, did you?"

"Why didn't you ask about the little boy?" Finn said. "He's dead, too—whether they meant to shoot him or not."

I sank deeper into the chair. I was drained. "You guys ought to be fucking critics. I didn't push this guy because—Jesus, it was too unreal. Surreal. The lights are throwing this goofy shadow behind him, he looks like Edgar Allan Poe and sounds like Mr. Magoo and you can't see his lips move and he's killed four people and he's holding a gun on me—oh I don't know, El-mo, I guess I should have *pissed him off*!" I snapped my head toward Graves.

"What does *rehearse* mean, George? What the fuck does *rehearse* mean?"

Graves ignored me and lit a cigarette with an old Zippo. Network had told us he allotted himself six Marlboros a day. I resolved to drive him to seven.

Finn said, "Could the gloves have been women's gloves—going up the sleeve?" His mouth had turned down like the mournful faces in the Haitian ghetto on the wall.

I took some deep breaths. "Maybe. I don't know. They weren't like any men's gloves I ever saw. Thin leather, supple—he could easily hold the gun and work the mask. I'm not an expert on fucking gloves."

"When he handed you the three-by-fives, were they clipped together—with a paper clip or a rubber band or something?"

I laughed. "Sherlock Fucking Finn—I don't remember, I don't know, I didn't notice, what the everloving fucking hell difference would it make? The cocksucker's killed four people and he was pointing a gun at me!"

Steve appeared with a fresh pot of coffee. He filled my cup first. "God's restorative, gentlemen." He topped off the other cups, filled his mug labeled *Mug* and sat down next to Elmo Finn on the sofa.

"I agree with him about Earl Warren and Menninger," Steve said. "Founders of the be-nice-to-scumbags, it's-all-society's-fault school of criminology. If they get an exhumation order I'll take annual leave and go piss on both of 'em."

"I thought Menninger was a psychiatrist," I said.

"He said punishing criminals was a crime. So barbaric."

"Piss on him for me," I said. "I'll introduce him to Boogie Brown."

"Okay, now he's leaving," Finn said, lasering back to me. "Interview's over. What does he do, everything, step by step?"

I sipped the hot black coffee and decided to demonstrate as I talked. I rose slowly from the chair. "He stands up . . . adjusts the mask, right hand . . . waves me to go ahead of him. Like this. I go down the hall to the front door. I stand with my back to him, like this, he says, 'When the door closes go back to the studio'—I remember thinking, How odd to call it a studio, it's just a spare room—'and wait ten minutes before you call anyone. We expect the interview to be broadcast in toto.' That was another funny thing—in toto. Sort of quaint, my dad used to say that. Then the door opens and closes. I stand there trying to hear something. Nothing. I go back to the studio and fix a double. And call Logan and Steve."

Detective Kim Whitten came in. "Joe, your house will be a crime scene until further notice." Then to Elmo Finn: "No tire tracks but two partial footprints. Maybe Reeboks."

Even though I was exhausted, I felt the icefire. Tire

119

tracks! Footprints! The dull stodgy forensics parade—but all their science couldn't match Marvin Isaacson's lies and chicanery.

Finn narrowed the lasers. "We think the mask is George Orwell."

"George Orwell?" I laughed. "George Orwell?"

"*1984*," Kim said.

"Big Brother is watching you," I said, resting my head on the back of the soft chair. "Are Avengers Big Brother?"

"All the pigs are equal," Steve said.

"That's *Animal Farm*," Graves said.

"George Fucking Orwell," I said. "Are you sure? This is getting crazy."

Finn, swish-swishing again, said, "Joe, we're setting up community meetings so people can learn about home defense, let off some steam. Will you give us some promos?"

"Sure, fax me the details. We'll cover the actual events."

"No, live cameras would change the dynamic. Prepublicity will do fine."

I thought, You may be Sherlock Holmes, Mr. Elmo Finn, but you don't know shit about television. *Change the dynamic.* Hell, TV *was* the dynamic.

It was noon when they let me go. Finn asked again for an indefinite ban on broadcasting the interview. I shrugged. Out of my hands. We had a deal.

Outside it was hot and bright. I walked a few blocks and called Ned from a pay phone. A few minutes later he picked me up in the Explorer.

"You're hot, Joe. B-Big news."

He had the all-news station on, and Channel Nine's promo boomed out. "Joe Colby's exclusive secret interview with an Avenger . . . one of the serial killers wanted for four murders . . . special edition of *Crime and Punishment* Thursday night at seven . . . the interview the cops don't want you

120

to see . . . Joe Colby one-on-one with the notorious Avenger . . . Thursday night at seven on Nine . . . your crime and punishment channel!"

"Were you s-scared, Joe?" Ned's eyepatch was slightly askew.

"Hell yes, I was scared."

He fumbled with a cigarette and I gave him a light.

"Joe—"

"I told him, Ned. He asked me who wanted their services, who had called in. I told him about you and Thorp."

"You told him about Thorp?"

"I told him everything—the mugging, the eyepatch, the way you walk the streets with a gun like an Avenger yourself."

Ned tried to say something but couldn't.

"He kept asking, Ned, I kept talking. He made sure of the name. Darnell Thorp. Three-Finger Thorp."

"God. I can't b-believe it."

"Ned, you have to forget all this now. If the cops find out, I'm fucked. You're fucked. I shouldn't have done it."

I looked at Ned. He was crying. I thought I knew how he felt. He could see a door closing.

TWENTY-FOUR

❑   ❑   ❑

"*THE REACTION HASN'T been positive. We have to face it,*" she says as he pulls into the curbside lane and slows down.

He checks the mirrors, then abruptly turns right and speeds up.

"*No one's following us,*" she says. "*Easy.*"

"*Odd car.*" He continues working the mirrors as he makes several aimless turns. "*You can't tell yet—the responsive chord's always slow at first.*"

"*The reward has tripled! Three hundred thousand! There's your* responsive chord!"

"*What about the bumper stickers?* Me and Avengers Don't Dial 911! *Plenty of people understand. They just don't have typewriters or microphones.*"

"*You should have said something about the little boy, like an apology. Not an apology, but—*"

"*Oh, sure. That would've been great—the soft side of Avengers. Why didn't* you *do the interview?*"

He makes still another turn and follows a serpentine course for several minutes.

"*I warned you about the mask.*"

Silence.

"*No one thinks you're the great avenger, they think you're the great fanatic. George.*"

"*It was the* only *mask. You know that.*"

"You looked like a fanatic, you sounded like a fanatic. That voice gizmo, I told you. First thought worst thought."

He remains intent upon the mirrors.

"You don't have to drive like a cop."

Silence.

She says, "Of course you're still considering the Day of Vengeance. The big holy day."

"Of course."

"Of course. Of course."

"There'll be plenty of people. You don't have to worry about it."

"Of course I won't worry, George. You'll get plenty of people. Of course, George."

He pulls into a large church parking lot and drives slowly around the perimeter.

"Every Thursday night," he says. "Choir practice. Over at nine-thirty. Drives home alone."

"Better than shooting from the trees. If the roads are clear."

"If the roads aren't clear, move on, of course. Want to second-guess some more?"

"Yes I do. The interview was too ... mental."

"Mental."

"Not emotional enough. Now you know how it feels. That's emotional. You could do another one, leave George out."*

He snickers. "Ladies and gentlemen and morons you missed the point Stop analyzing the fanatical George Orwell and focus on punishing murders and rapists and lawyers and judges Goddamn you're stupid Now we have to do this all over again Mr. Colby don't just sit there, ask something. . . ."

She stifles a laugh.

"Let's go see our friend at Central," he says. "Keep him motivated."

"Ten thousand dollars ought to be enough motivation. He only asked for five."

"We added Three-Finger Thorp to the list."

"Another bad idea. Why not let his mother tell him?"

"We should tell him. We're already in character. First thought best thought."

"Whatever you say, George."

"Speaking of second-guessing, how about the Reeboks in the Dumpster?"

"A Dumpster full of garbage."

"Not perfect. The tires and clothes were perfect."

He exits the church parking lot, circles the block twice, then turns onto the circumferential highway and heads toward Central Prison.

He says, "How about sending this when Thorp's over? 'Done. Destroy this note. Avengers.'"

"I don't know. Maybe."

They pass through the checkpoint with no difficulty. She says, "No, I don't like it. No note."

"Maybe you're right."

"First second-guess best second-guess."

He drops her at the Visitors Entrance and continues to the parking lot, where he pretends to read. As usual, some of the other cars are occupied. He closes his eyes.

"To Ned Cromartie. Done. Destroy this note. Observe strict silence. Avengers."

Yes.

TWENTY-FIVE

❏   ❏   ❏

CRIME AND PUNISHMENT was now a certified smash. Three of our first four shows had gone national—Captain Avery (We Work for God) Patterson, Marvin (A Trial Is Not a Search for Truth) Isaacson and George Orwell, the masked Avenger. Only Commander Nutbeam had bombed.

"Got to stroke the buzz, Joe," Logan decreed. "Got to get Elmo Finn on soon. He's running the circus."

We decided to attack on home ground and invited Elmo Finn and George Graves to lunch. At high noon we strolled into the Press Club, where the free spirits hailed us and the bluenoses ignored us, as usual. George Graves in jacket and jeans was already sipping grapefruit juice at Logan's corner table. Logan and I ordered manhattans.

"While we're waiting for Colonel Finn," Logan said unctuously, "tell us his *real* story."

"Sure. Nothing to it. Elmo Finn's your garden-variety genius who devoutly celebrates Shakespeare's birthday and devoutly believes that the reason God made day and night is daytime's for golf and nighttime's for sex. Balance of nature."

"When is Shakespeare's birthday?" I asked.

"April twenty-third. Finn always insists on a group reading, a very *spirited* reading. We do the swordfights."

"Holy holy." Logan was overdoing it. I wanted to elbow him.

"Mo's even got a parrot who spouts off a little Shakespeare. Falstaff—disgusting bird."

Logan cackled, drawing a few stares.

"April's his big month, got to be careful in April," Graves said. "Shakespeare and the holy days."

"Passover or Easter?" Logan fawned.

"Masters. Augusta."

We laughed dutifully and Graves took a tiny sip of juice. He drank like a reformed tippler.

"What about that day in September?" I asked.

Graves's face clouded over. "You've done your homework, Colby. He won't talk about that."

"When his fiancée died?"

He turned stone-faced. The manhattans arrived just in time.

"Elmo told me a little about it," I said. "He followed his heart and got revenge, which is exactly what I was trying to do when I got arrested."

Graves took another sip, then glanced around the room.

"You were there too, George, I know that. I've seen some clips. What I can't figure out is why the cops didn't prosecute."

George Graves's tiny twitch-smile appeared briefly. Still he said nothing.

Logan said, "So you're Elmo Finn's videographer and faithful Indian companion."

"We're fairies without the sex."

Logan laughed too eagerly and Graves's mouth screwed into the twitch-smile again. "I met Elmo Finn in Vietnam. He had just graduated from VMI and turned down a Rhodes."

"You were both in the Phoenix Program?" Logan asked too quickly.

"Phoenix was already over."

"What the hell *was* Phoenix?" I asked, knowing the answer.

Again Graves seemed uncomfortable, and our chances to get Elmo Finn on *C&P* were disappearing as fast as VC cadres during the Phoenix Program.

"Interrogation program."

"We heard it was more assassination than interrogation."

"Ah, the critics—the critics come down from the mountaintop after the battle and shoot the wounded. It was a war. People got killed."

The noise level had ratcheted up as the elite of the Fourth Estate hoisted second and third rounds. I scanned the room to snub the snubbers.

"Finn turned down a Rhodes?" Logan said admiringly. "I'd have given my left one for a Rhodes."

"He wanted to go to Vietnam. Seems quaint today, doesn't it? We did two tours each, then he disappeared. Just vanished. A few years later I'm reading about a kidnapping, victim rescued from a buried coffin by commandos, and there's Elmo Finn in the photograph. Looking away from the camera but I could tell. Took weeks to track him down. I said, 'What the hell have you been doing?' and he said if the statute of limitations ever expired he'd tell me."

"Did he ever tell you?" Logan and I asked as one.

George Graves twitch-smiled and seemed to shrug. Could have meant anything.

"Finn graduated from VMI?" Logan babbled. "Stonewall Jackson. 'Let us cross over the river and rest in the shade of the trees.'"

"Let us cross over the river and play thirty-six," Elmo Finn said, sliding into the empty chair.

"Ah, Colonel Finn," Logan chirped, "we've been hearing your résumé."

"Pay no attention, it changes every month."

Finn's drink was designer water, no ice, so we went ahead

and ordered lunch—steak sandwiches for Logan and me, lasagna for Graves, two salads for Finn, dressing on the side. He made an entry in his notebook.

"My Duke training. Have to follow the system."

"Follow the bouncing anal retentive," Graves muttered.

"You're not fat," Logan said.

"And as part of my lifetime reward I'm having dinner tonight with Detective Second Grade Kimberly Whitten."

"You're probably not too fat to fuck," Graves said.

"I was never too fat to fuck."

"Yes you were."

"Too fat for you."

"Did I complain?"

"Fairies with*out* the sex," Logan wheezed. "That's what we heard."

"That's last month's résumé."

People were looking at us now. I said, "She wears three guns, Elmo, be careful."

"Holy holy," Logan boomed, "you think you're about to get lucky and *bang*!"

"That's the idea. You journalists, so pithy."

"Will you tell us where the third gun is?"

"I'll show you the video," Graves said.

More howls, but our laughter was fleeting, like fireworks fading into a black sky. The specter of Avengers was always at hand. As if to prove it, Finn opened his notebook to a page covered with tidy handwriting.

"Update. Last twenty-four hours. Dr. Snavely, the psychiatrist who testified about *helpless rage* in that murder case—poor murderer couldn't help himself. Shot dead in his office, note from Avengers.

"Last twenty-four hours. Stalker terrorizing a schoolteacher who wouldn't go out with him, she gets a restraining order which he ignores, finally as the cops drag him away he yells, 'You'll never get rid of me!' Wrong. Shotgunned last night parking his car. Handwritten note from Avengers."

"Handwritten?" I said. "The others were typed."

"Can't tell Avengers without a scorecard. Last twenty-four hours. Child molester, just released from Central, supposed to go live with his sister, middle-class neighborhood. House torched, sister in shock, pedophile unaccounted for. Note taped to a Community Watch sign—'No Perverts Allowed. Avergers.'"

"Holy holy! We got to get crews out!" Logan was half out of his chair.

"You're covered, Logan—McDade's already briefed your people. Last twenty-four hours, still at Central, two convicts found dead side by side in the laundry. One mutilated—castrated and knifed in the eyes, lowlife named Darnell Thorp. Three-Finger Thorp. The other victim was a druggie, wrong place, wrong time. Lifer named Clay Crabtree did it. They think."

"Doesn't sound like Avengers," I said.

"Except for the odd coincidence that Three-Finger Thorp mugged your pal Ned Cromartie, and Ned Cromartie's credit card was found in Duane Hickman's shoebox, and Duane Hickman was a victim of Avengers."

"Holy holy."

"Last twenty-four hours. Sheriff Monahan's turning the county jail into a cage like Avengers demanded. No movies, no TV, no smoking, no porn. No hot lunches—sandwiches and fruit. No coffee—you want a cup of coffee, don't get sent to my jail. And the High Sheriff wants to deputize a posse with jeeps and cell phones. Burl Devine's boys are knocking each other down to sign up. ACLU's in shock."

Logan was standing now. As the waiter arrived with the

orders, Logan grabbed the check and signed it. "Joe, we got work—enjoy your lunch, gentlemen—Elmo, how about coming on *Crime and Punishment*—can we buy you with two salads?"

"Sure, been bought with less. Thought you'd never ask."

TWENTY-SIX

❑   ❑   ❑

HARRY COVINGTON DRAPED one arm around Juanita Daley in her standard flowering dress, the other around Kim Whitten in her standard blazer and khakis.

"My two partners!" he crooned as the photographer snapped away.

"Chocolate and vanilla," I whispered to Elly. "That's my kind of affirmative action."

The Thunderbolt, the preferred watering hole of the police and their hangers-on, was closed to the public for the evening. Private party honoring the newly engaged Harry Covington and Juanita Daley—Detective Smooth and Mother Savage. The tables had been rearranged to create a tiny dance floor, and a rock group named Bomb Sniffing Dogs thundered from a makeshift bandstand. The affair was off the record—no official partying with mad-dog killers on the loose.

Elly and I stood alone in a corner nursing vodka and tonics. I still felt ill at ease among my old Homicide buddies. I wondered if anyone would come over.

"There's Ned and Julia," Elly said. "Saved."

Most of the Victims Group—all the Savages and even a few Other-Cheekers—had turned out. Deirdre, the hand-wringing facilitator who bawled when Juanita hissed Marvin Isaacson out of Group, had posted herself near the bandstand, a purple miniskirt baring her thunder thighs.

Ned and Julia Cromartie, clutching tall brown drinks in sweaty glasses, made their way to our corner. Even at a cop party their drab clothes stood out; missionary chic. Ned was jumpy, gulping the bourbon and shooting me dark looks with his uncovered eye. Julia, thin and mousy, had wrapped her glass in napkins and held it with both hands.

"At least Ned knows somebody here. There's nobody I know." Julia had already worked up to full whine. She had been Connie's best friend, and had never accepted Elly, my illicit love. Even after Connie died.

"Permit us to introduce ourselves," Elly said in a good Count Dracula. "Elly Briggs and Joe Colby. We're nobody."

Julia colored slightly. "So pleased to meet you, nobody. I thought it was you."

Ned rolled his eyes. Soon he and I went outside, leaving the girls to catfight. The night air was pleasant. We walked half-way down the block.

"They s-snuffed him," Ned whispered, his hand trembling as he lit a cigarette. I lit up too. I wondered if he'd been this jumpy trolling for muggers.

"Just what you ordered, Ned. Sounds odd—*snuffed.*"

"What the fuck would you c-call it! You're the expert, you know the individuals."

I stared at him. "What do you mean, *I know the individuals*? What the fuck's wrong with you? What's wrong with Julia—"

"Leave J-Julia out of this."

"Did you tell her, Ned? Goddamnit, don't lie to me! Are you drunk?"

"Not yet."

I had to relight my cigarette. I was up to a pack a day.

"Why'd they have to k-kill the innocent guy? He was only in for p-possession, he didn't hurt p-people."

134

"I don't know, Ned, and there's no way to ask. Leave well enough alone."

"Well enough is not . . . w-well enough!"

"Are you drunk?"

"They killed an innocent p-person, Joe! I didn't want them to k-kill an innocent person. Just Darnell Thorp! Just Darnell Fucking Three-Finger Fucking Thorp! Why'd they have to k-kill an innocent person?"

"I don't know, maybe he saw something. You can't order a fucking murder and expect some kind of Letitia Baldridge conduct. You kill somebody, shit happens."

"They broke the agreement."

"What does that mean, Ned? There was no *agreement*, I just did what you begged me to do—tell the Avengers about your situation. Which seems to have been a big mistake since you can't live with the consequences. Did you tell Julia?"

"I didn't *beg* you to d-do anything—and I certainly d-didn't intend for an innocent person to be killed. This c-c-came out all wrong."

"Good, Ned, you've come to the right place. The whole Homicide Division is right inside, I'll introduce you to Commander Avery Patterson and you can confess that you commissioned a murder but you're dissatisfied with the results and would like to throw yourself on his mercy. I'll warn you though, his mercy cannot even be *seen* with the naked eye. You will be arrested and prosecuted and go to prison and I will tell them that I didn't set up a goddamn thing, I just gave Avengers your name and you must have set it up on your own. And fuck you."

"They sent me a note."

"Does it mention me?"

"No. It just said, 'D-Done. D-Destroy this note. Observe strict silence.' "

I lit another cigarette and looked around. Other people were filing out to escape the smoke and Bomb Sniffing Dogs. We moved farther down the block.

"Ned, let's calm down, both of us. I did you a favor. You don't like the result. But you have to live with it."

"What if I'm w-wearing a wire?"

I was stunned and probably showed it. "You're trying to implicate *me*? Are you crazy, you're the hit man here, Nedski! I'm just the messenger!"

"I'm not w-wearing a wire, I don't even know w-what I'm saying."

I stared at him coldly. "*Observe strict silence* is very good advice, Nedski."

I left him standing there and went back inside. I squeezed through to the bar and ordered a double vodka. John Ewell, tall and alone, was standing nearby and came over. He was dressed all in black and looked even thinner than usual.

"Joe, can I tell you something?"

"Sure, John, what is it?" We drifted away from the bar. I was still seething.

"It's great isn't it, Juanita and Harry?"

"It sure is. They're good people."

"The best. Just the best. I love Mother Savage."

"So do I, John." We took big swallows. John cracked an ice cube with his teeth.

"I got a video, Joe, in the mail. A video of Duane Hickman . . . the urn actually . . ."

"Did you tell the cops?"

"No."

I studied his face. He seemed in full control.

"I watch it a lot."

"Maybe you should tell the police, John."

He looked somber. "It came a while ago. They'll want to know why I waited."

"Tell 'em you didn't know what to do. Tell 'em the truth—you're glad the son of a bitch is dead."

"I love seeing that urn smash in, over and over. I ought to feel different, I guess. But I don't."

"Don't let anyone tell you how to feel, John."

I fished out a cigarette and John gave me a light, holding his glass in his teeth. I thought it might shatter.

"I'm not going to tell them, Joe."

"Fine. It's your call, John." I wondered why everyone was telling me things the cops didn't know. I got two fresh vodkas and made my way back to Elly.

"You were right about Ned," I told her.

"I think Burl Devine should give up a couple of balls. He's got four and Ned's got none."

We drifted back into our corner. I couldn't see Ned or Julia anywhere. Elly leaned into me, insinuating her C-cups with just the right jiggle. I shivered. Across the room Logan Murphy was power schmoozing with Elmo Finn and George Graves. Elly and I went over holding hands.

"Gentlemen and Logan," I said. Elmo Finn and the Boss were dressed Fraternity Row—navy blazers, khakis, cordovan loafers. Graves was Skid Row—old seersucker jacket and pale jeans. He bowed slowly from the waist.

"Countess. I am charmed." Graves's face was bright.

"Let me introduce her first, George," I said. "Countess Elly Briggs, George Graves. A commoner."

"Get your watchdog yet, Countess?" Elmo Finn said, the gray lasers gleaming at Elly.

Logan leaned over and gave Elly a wet kiss. They're all drunk, I thought.

Elly said, "We're holding out for a Doberman, Sherlock, already trained and vicious. With an arrest record."

George Graves threw out his chest like a pitchman. "You looking for a *dog*, Countess, you looking for a *watchdog*?

How would you like to have a very watchful Limey *bulldog*? Looks like Churchill, acts like Stalin. Elmo—Sherlock— wants to dump him. I'm *quite* sure."

Elly pretended to ponder the question. "Does the dog have any defects?"

"Just one. Gas. Never lie to a countess. Actually, now that I think of it, Dr. Watson ain't worth a farthing as a watchdog, he can't concentrate with the gas. But have you ever considered a watch*bird*, very chic, I got a perfect specimen who's also on the block. Falstaff—Sherlock's imperial cockamamie. He'd scare off anybody including the Doberman."

Elmo Finn was chuckling with the rest of us. He seemed to regard Graves as his jester.

"A watchbird—I like that."

"Forget it, Falstaff's too fat. Couldn't fly without a motor. But what about a watch*cat*, Countess, talk about chic. No, forget that too, Macduff's so cross-eyed he bumps into the wall, he's the worst of the bunch. Countess, you can't believe what I have to put up with." Graves turned to Finn and squared his shoulders. "Colonel Finn, sir, Colonel Sherlock- on-Avon, I'm goin' on work stoppage till that goddamn me- nagerie has been relocated in good homes. Strike *good homes*."

"Can the bird talk?" Elly squealed. She and Graves were having a high time. Neither could have walked a straight line.

"Can the bird talk?" Graves said, lolling his head and squinting up like a pirate. "Countess! Falstaff can do solilo- quies! 'Lay on, Macduff!' 'How now!' 'Kill the lawyers!' Elmo reads him all this fuckin' Shakespeare."

Elly spewed her vodka everywhere. Logan was listing to and fro like a buoy in a gale, laughing his basso executive laugh. Everyone was rollicking.

Suddenly, Juanita Daley, as drunk as everyone else, popped up before us and escorted Elly and me away from the others.

"Joe, Joe, Elly, you are so dear to come. Finally I have a

man like you, Elly. I mean like you *have*, Elly, a dear man like Joe." She giggled and I hugged her. Major maracas. "Joe, Joe, I have an idea for your program. The punishment side of *Crime and Punishment*. Show what it's like on Death Row, what kind of *domicile* it is for the poor murderers, compared to the graveyards where the victims are. That animal Hollowell's got fifty-eight square feet and a color TV, and my Debbie's in a pine box, Joe, six feet down."

I nodded and hugged her again. This was part of her litany.

"Did you know I was raped once," Juanita said loudly. "I told my Debbie about it just to scare her. Make her think. Maybe she was remembering . . ."

"Juanita," I said, "they're going to execute Franklin Delano Hollowell. He can't appeal forever."

"Oh yes, yes, they're going to, I know they're going to. If they don't, *somebody* will."

TWENTY-SEVEN

❏　　❏　　❏

ELLY AND I left the Thunderbolt to the heavy throb of Bomb Sniffing Dogs. Elmo Finn was a half-block ahead of us.

"Going our way?" I yelled.

Finn was walking back to Headquarters, Elly and I to her realty office, and our paths coincided most of the way. The sidewalks were empty and we strolled three abreast with Elly in the middle. The talk was desultory—we agreed that the party would roar on for hours; that everyone was drunk, but Harry and Juanita were drunker; that convicts should have to listen to Bomb Sniffing Dogs around the clock. Elly called Finn "Sherlock" and teased him about George Graves and the menagerie.

After several blocks I craved a cigarette. Elly and Finn waited outside while I went into a nondescript saloon. As soon as I entered the bleak, smoky barroom, I knew I'd made a mistake. A dozen faces turned toward me, black, hard, suspicious. Everyone stopped talking. The only sound was the rap video pumping from the dinky TV behind the bar.

"You got cigarettes?" I asked the bartender in what I hoped was a confident voice. He was as black as asphalt, a giant in a sleeveless T-shirt, his head shaved and glistening. He stared at me, then turned and moved to the far end of the bar. I shifted my weight nervously, my hairline prickling. My pulse pounded in time with the rap beat. The customer nearest me slid off his stool and sidled between me and the door. He cocked his head menacingly. This is a movie, I thought, this isn't real.

"I got something for you."

"I just want to buy a pack of smokes. That's all."

"Just want to buy a pack of smokes that's all. I got somethin' else."

I turned back to the bartender, who crossed his arms and lounged against a cooler. The words "Boogie Brown" came from somewhere. My eyes had adjusted to the dark and I could see every snarl. Another man, thin as a blade, got off his stool and came toward me wielding a beer bottle with most of its label peeled off. Instinctively I stepped backward and raised my hands, trying to keep both assailants in view. They edged closer, matching me step for step. The thin man broke into an ugly gap-toothed grin. He shifted his grip on the bottle.

To my left I sensed movement and pivoted. Swiftly, without a sound, Elmo Finn took the first man from behind in a twisting headlock, then spun him around and into the thin man with the bottle. Both went down but the thin man scrambled up. Finn glared and shook his head at the giant bartender who was frozen in a half-crouch, reaching under the counter. The thin man lunged with the bottle but Finn grabbed the man's free arm and wrenched it violently behind his back and up. I could hear bone snapping and a scream and the bottle breaking on the floor. The bartender rose out of his crouch with a sawed-off shotgun but now Finn had a gun and fired twice into the long mirror, shattering glass and bottles. I hit the floor and rolled to the wall. Finn's voice cut through the echo.

"Drop it! Next one's in your mouth!"

My heart thundered in my head. In a mirror I could see the bartender trapped, the shotgun pointing down. He would have to swing it up to fire. Finn fired again. The bartender screamed and the shotgun hit the floor.

The first man lay unconscious. The thin man was moaning on the floor, probing his broken arm. Finn pointed at the bartender. "Come here now."

He shuffled toward us slowly, holding his ear, his eyes white. I struggled to my feet but my legs were airy and dead. I could barely stand. Voices muttered "Colby" and "Boogie Brown."

The bartender lifted the hinged flap and came out cautiously. "Get their wallets," Finn told him. When he didn't move, Finn slammed the gun into his ear. "Now!"

Blood streaming from his ear, the bartender fished out the two wallets and handed them to Finn, who tossed them to me. "Take out the driver's licenses." He turned back to the bartender. "Give me yours."

The giant shook his head.

Finn made a sudden spinning leg-whip move and crunched down hard on the bartender's instep. He howled and stumbled, and Finn caught him flush in the throat with a savage blow. He went down heavily. Finn handed the gun to me and motioned to the stunned barflies. "Shoot anybody that moves." I squeezed the small automatic with both hands and swept the line of faces, stool by stool. The smell of cordite was strong.

Finn leaned over the giant. "Give me your wallet." No response. Finn slammed his fist into the man's ear. Another wail. Finn spun again and delivered a kick to the face. "One more and you're dead."

Blood and tears streamed from the giant's face. He whimpered pitifully, then managed to produce his wallet. Finn extracted the driver's license and flung the wallet against the wall.

The first man was still unconscious, the other two in severe pain. Finn took the gun from me and faced the room at large.

"These driver's licenses will be available tomorrow at Police Headquarters. Sergeant McDade. I will trace the background of these dirtbags and alert my friend Roy. If they ever bother us again, Roy will punish them. Believe me, they do not want to meet Roy. *You* do not want to meet Roy. Where's the cigarette machine?"

A hesitant arm pointed to an alcove.

"You have change?" Finn asked me.

I couldn't utter "No" so I shook my head.

He went behind the bar and opened the register. I handed him three singles which he dropped into the drawer, removing twelve quarters. While I was getting the cigarettes I heard Finn on the phone. My hands shook so badly I had to tear open the pack with my teeth. After three tries I got one lighted, inhaled deeply and rejoined Finn, who was holding the room at gunpoint.

Within minutes we heard the sirens. There was restlessness on the stools, but Finn waved his gunhand and everyone froze. Steve McDade and two uniforms swept in, followed by paramedics with stretchers. Finn talked briefly with Steve, then took me outside. Elly sprang from the front seat of a cruiser and embraced me. I had to push her away to get my breath.

We walked a few steps in silence. Then I said, "How badly hurt was the big guy? You—"

"He'll recover."

"Did you shoot him?"

"No."

"Was that karate?"

"Some of it."

Again I stocked up on air. "Elmo, I don't know what to

say, except thanks. For riding to the rescue. I really screwed up going in there, I should have known."

" 'Out of this nettle, danger, we pluck this flower, safety.' "

"Well, thanks for plucking me. Let me ask you, is there really a Roy?"

Finn smiled distantly. "Oh yes. Roy thrives."

"CIA?"

He paused. "Roy ain't exactly an organization man."

An unmarked police sedan pulled up beside us.

"Here's our ride," Finn said. We got in and Elly held hands with both of us.

I said, "I can't believe what just happened. What *did* just happen?"

"I think somebody's telling you to quit smoking," Elmo Finn said.

TWENTY-EIGHT

❏   ❏   ❏

AFTER THE RESCUE Elly and I resolved to treat Elmo Finn differently. No more kibitzing, no more sniping. He might not be Sherlock Holmes but now everyone knew he was James Bond. My James Bond.

A few days later, I was in my office working up puffball questions for Finn's *C & P* appearance. Three sharp buzzes sounded on the intercom: Logan's distress signal. I trotted down the corridor and sailed past Janie into the big office. The Boss stood white-faced behind the oval desk.

"Guess who," he said softly.

"Who!"

"Avengers."

My heart thundered and skipped some beats. "They've arrested somebody!"

He frowned. "The latest victim, Joe. Guess who."

"I don't know. Who?"

"The mother of all Kodaks."

"Who!"

Logan sat down abruptly and braced his fists against the big desk. "Mother of all Kodaks, Joe. Judge John Lodge."

"Judge Lodge! How? He had a bodyguard."

"Last night, driving home from choir practice. Bodyguard was off duty for some reason. One of Burl's boys. Lodge had a gun but didn't fire it. Elmo Finn thinks it was a bump-and-shoot—bump you from behind like an accident, you stop, get out, bang bang."

"Are they sure it's Avengers?"

"Apparently. I want you to cover the press conference, Joe, and stick around afterwards. The cops will talk to you now— they need us again."

At City Hall I wormed into the rear of the same cramped pressroom where I had apologized to mankind for trying to break into jail. At the cheesy lectern, the mayor was issuing a rambling "Return to your homes" message. He was perspiring heavily under the lights. Fidgeting behind him were the Governor, the U.S. Attorney, Prosecutor Bucky Webb, the FBI Special Agent In Charge, the Chief of Police and Captain Avery Patterson. Each took a turn at the podium to counsel vigilance, calm and courage. I could almost hear a gathering stampede in the streets. Patterson displayed his strong-jawed, We-Work-for-God persona, but his words were disjointed: "Everything's under control but just in case we're bringing in consultants from other police departments, volunteer canvassers to locate witnesses, forensic experts, even a psychic from Key West who has had visions of the urn falling on Duane Hickman. And Elmo Finn, the famous detective, is also on the case."

As the reporters outshouted each other, I slipped upstairs to Homicide. Logan was right—the cold faces had thawed. Patterson's office was the same except some of the watercolors had changed places. In the cozy lamplight I shook hands with the usual suspects. I was glad to be back.

Steve took me aside. "That fucking interview may not be a total minus," he said. "Stirred up the Hotline."

"Good. Good."

We stood tensely for a moment. I took a chance. "Steve, I know you think I should have called you first but I sincerely didn't—"

"You sincerely didn't think we could protect Elly."

"That's right. Maybe I was wrong but I was sincerely wrong." Steve picked up the coffeepot and poured me a cup. His way of burying the hatchet.

Patterson returned from the press conference and sank into the big judge's chair. He was red-faced; one of my fellow inquisitors must have stung him. "Five different people called the courthouse switchboard about Judge Lodge. Said, 'Good riddance.' Unbelievable."

"Goddamn!" said Harry Covington. "That's as bad—"

"You got to be a victim to understand, Harry," I blurted out. "Minimum John always gave the minimum sentence, lot of bad guys walking—"

"I'm a victim, I understand!" Kim said, glaring at me, then looking around the room. "I'm a rape victim if you must know. Every year on that day I'm crazy, it all floods back. Of course, I'm still alive, Joe. . . ."

Harry said, "Kim, partner, I understand being a victim, I'm a *black man* if you haven't noticed. And I understand revenge against a rapist. But a *judge*? A judge's *wife*? A *three-year-old boy who was born with bulletholes in his back*?"

Patterson whistled sharply to restore order, and Elmo Finn, swishing the sawed-off golf club, ambled to the window and launched a review of the case. The detectives thumbed their notebooks. A civilian aide delivered fresh coffee and Steve poured refills. No one asked me to leave.

Steve: "Surprise, surprise. All prints on Judge Lodge's car accounted for."

Harry: "The witness was drunk, went outside to pee. Said he and the dogs shared the front-yard bathroom. Crash. Voices. Peeks around the hedge and sees a van pull away. Didn't get the tag because Minimum John was lying in the street."

Patterson: "FBI's megaballistic—federal judge shot, and his

wife had already been shot. We continue to cooperate but not subordinate. Elmo will stroke them if necessary. He loves the little G-men."

Graves: "In the true Hooverian sense."

General guffawing and ribaldry that startled me every time. Avengers on the loose, ha ha.

Harry: "Alibis on the Avenger interview are holding up, which means nobody's lying that we know of. Yet."

Kim: "Clay Crabtree got three visits from one Carol Crabtree. Guess what, Central can't find the sign-in sheets, why am I not surprised? Clay Crabtree says Carol Crabtree is his ex-wife but there's no record of any marriage. He's the hardest of the hard cases, borderline retard, dyslexic—but he sits up straight when she visits. Of course he says he knows nothing about Three-Finger Thorp and the other dude. But his mother Beulah just bought a TV, a VCR and two air conditioners. Paid cash."

Graves: "Cemetery manager ninety miles away had an urn stolen. Didn't realize it till they inventoried. Says flowers are swiped all the time. We're showing him the urn in question."

Finn: "Joe, what were Ned Cromartie's injuries when he was mugged?

Me: "He was beat up and stabbed. Hospitalized for a year."

Finn: "Stabbed in the eye?"

Me: "Uh-huh. He wears an eyepatch."

Finn: "And stabbed in the groin?"

Me: "Right. I don't know the specifics."

Finn: "So Three-Finger Thorp gets a shank in the eye and the groin—the same thing he did to Ned six years ago. Is this coincidence? Is this *Avengers*? If it is, why didn't they take credit like they always have?"

The only sound was Graves's tapping on his laptop. Then Elmo Finn said, "Joe, the FBI techs say your voice in the famous interview is kind of flat. The Valium Voice, they call it. Didn't sound scared."

"Jesus, I was plenty scared! And I did take a Valium. What's the accepted voice pattern for interviewing a murderer in a George Orwell mask who's holding a gun on you?"

"Point taken."

When the meeting broke up I walked with Steve to the coffee machine. "You should have seen Finn in action, Steve. Man. James Bond."

The rumpled detective laughed. "Bar full of rummies versus Elmo Finn. Unfair odds, they needed help."

"He's something."

"He's something else."

"All I wanted was a fucking pack of cigarettes."

"Bad habit, Joe."

I poured a half-cup from a carafe that was stained nearly opaque. "Finn's going out with Kim, did you hear? Is the captain jealous?"

"Hell no. Anyway, she asked him. Their first date was getting AIDS tests."

"How very modern. Dinner, dancing, finger pricking."

Back at the station I learned that my fellow reporters at the press conference had ignored all the big shots and zeroed in on the psychic from Key West. She loved the attention, strode to the podium wearing a floor-length sweatshirt and admitted she had requested items of underwear worn by Maggie Lodge, Ruth Isaacson, Nasty Brown and Duane Hickman. Something about vibrations or sentic cycles or whatever the hell. As it turned out, the portly psychic could have stayed in Key West and the other experts could have stayed home. Except one.

TWENTY-NINE

□   □   □

ELMO FINN SHOWED up in perfect TV dress: dark jacket, blue shirt, simple tie that wouldn't bloom on screen. I didn't tell him what we'd cover on the air, and he didn't ask.

I gave him an unctuous introduction—two tours in Vietnam, consultant to the FBI, how he chummed around with a serial killer to demolish his insanity defense, golf with two presidents. I didn't mention Finn's experience in the avenger department.

Then I said, "There's a story about you, Mr. Finn. You were assisting the police in a major city, just as you're doing here. The story goes, you loaded a Xerox machine with three sheets of paper. The first two said, 'Truth,' the last one said, 'Lie.' Then you convinced a reluctant witness to take a *lie detector test*—by pressing his hand against your Xerox Lie Detector Machine. Your first question was something like, What is your name? He touched the machine and gave his name, you press the button and out comes 'Truth.' Second question: Where do you live? He answers, the machine says, 'Truth.' Third question: Did you see somebody shoot Cockamamie Jones? He says no, out comes 'Lie.' He breaks down and spills the beans. Is this a true story, Mr. Finn?"

"Do you have a lie detector?"

I laughed, violating the tone Logan wanted. No joking around with Avengers at large.

"Mr. Finn, when you interrogate a suspect, is it fair to lie?"

"They lie to me."

"So . . . *everything goes.* What *wouldn't* you do to trap a perpetrator?"

"I wouldn't go on TV and say what I wouldn't do."

"Fair enough, fair enough." I was rattled. Impulsively I scrapped Logan's questions about the CIA's Phoenix Program. "Let's get to Avengers. This city is in turmoil, the country and the world are watching. Copycats are springing up. What can you tell us about the investigation—is there progress?"

"Yes. There is progress and plenty of it. Obviously I can't reveal details. I can say two things. First, anyone with information should call the Hotline. If you're not sure whether to call, call. Second, the police will be holding community meetings to discuss Avengers, home security, buying a gun—everything. These meetings will not be televised. Please attend if you have questions—or simply to listen and learn. We're all in this together."

Pretty lame, I thought. Is this the best Sherlock can do?

"Mr. Finn, is the psychic from Key West still . . . seeing things?" I almost laughed again, then added quickly, "still forecasting?"

"Yes. We don't understand extra-sensory perception but we cannot deny it exists. Sometimes it helps."

"Is it true that the psychic asked for the bodies to be exhumed?"

"I don't know," Finn lied. "We agreed no details, Joe."

After this mild rebuke I tossed up some puffies that allowed Finn to say whatever he wanted, which was basically Calm Down, Heads Up, Call Us. Then I opened the phones. The console lit up but the questions were the usual woolly, misinformed, delusional mix. Normal people don't call in. The show didn't fizzle but it was no home run.

Unhooking the mike, Finn said, "You went easy on me."

"I'm still atoning. Good job tonight—people will be reassured."

"I think I prefer anonymity."

"You sure weren't anonymous when your fiancée . . . Network sent us the clips. Terrible tragedy."

His jaw tightened. "Joe, we've both been to places no one should ever have to go."

"Sometimes I get this feeling inside . . ."

" 'Everyone can master a grief but he that has it.' "

"He knew it all, didn't he?"

"He knew me. Emily Dickinson said, 'If you have this book, why do you need another?' "

The technicians were gone now and the studio was empty. Elmo Finn seemed in no hurry to leave.

He said, "I was reading your high-school yearbook the other day."

I was stunned and probably showed it.

"Actually I was reading Patterson's yearbook. Didn't realize so many of you grew up together—Patterson, McDade, Ned and Julia, Harry Covington. You and Julia played the leads in the senior play."

"That's right—*Our Town*. We had to kiss on stage. It was my most embarrassing moment. Avery played the Stage Manager."

He leaned back a little. I was nervous and not sure why.

"I was thinking, Joe—this whole Avengers case is like *Our Town* . . . a little Grovers Corners inside the big city. Theoretically, Avengers could be anybody, but I don't think so. I think somehow this case is very contained. Sort of all in the family."

"The family?" I said.

He made a vague gesture and pushed back his chair.

"Elmo, are you getting close?"

"Yes."

I walked him to the door. "Any chance we could be in on the arrest? Cover it live? I think we've earned it."

He thought about it. "Maybe. From a safe distance. They have some firepower."

"I hope you get 'em, Elmo, that's what my head says. But down here I hope they get Boogie Brown first. If anybody on earth understands that, it's you."

The gray eyes darkened. "Joe, the system will get Boogie Brown, not a pack of wolves."

"That's what my head tells me. But my heart . . . isn't that what your special day in September is all about? I understand, Elmo—mine is June first. Every victim has a day."

We were standing close together, very still. Had I been too emotional? As he turned to leave, I said, "Tell me one thing, Elmo. Is Tad Sullivan a cop?"

He looked back. "Sure he's a cop. And a victim too."

THIRTY

❏   ❏   ❏

"YOU CAME SO fast," Elly whispered as I awoke from a sexnap and rolled against her. She giggled in my ear. "Like high school, slam bam thank you ma'am. I majored in P.E."

"I know—premature ejaculation."

"I carried Prolong in my purse."

"Did that stuff work?"

"Most of them would come while I was rubbing it on. I was a thorough rubber."

"Oh no doubt."

We fell together hungrily. Sex was our sanctuary. When Connie lay dying, sex. When Elly's sister committed suicide, sex. Even during the hours of unspeakable evil, Elly and I were screwing in her apartment, hiding from the world. If I had gone home instead. My litany of remonstration. I never finished the litany—the icefire consumed me and I centered on the vast malignity of Boogie Brown. I hated him as I hated myself.

When the phone rang we jumped like criminals. It was Ned.

"Joe, could be a problem with your federal return, depreciation and some stuff. May have to file amended."

"Sure, Ned, whatever. Will it cost me?"

"I don't think so. But I need the documents and worksheets back."

"Sure. Mail everything to you?"

"No, no, just bring them when you can."

"Sure, Ned. Save my ass from Leavenworth, partner."

"Sure. All right. Soon as you can."

We hung up. Elly looked baffled.

I whispered, "Ned's using our old code. He wants me—"
She clamped her hand over my mouth and pointed to the ceiling. We slipped into the bathroom, closed the door and turned on both faucets.

"Ned wants me to meet him right now at the Canebrake. He used our old code for sneaking off."

"He's talked to the cops."

"I think so."

"Well, if you get arrested again . . . third time's the charm."

"They'll crucify me this time. 'Why yes, Elmo, I did give Ned's name to Avengers. All he wanted was to kill some skell in prison. He was my friend, I had no choice.' Ned was the one who said, 'You won't turn me in, Joe! You won't turn me in, Joe!' And he's turning *me* in. Goddamnit!"

"Maybe not. Maybe he'll come to his senses."

"I think Elmo Finn will believe me. I tried to bond with him."

"You better *re*bond with Ned."

I drove Elly's Buick to the Canebrake and parked around back like the old days. I went in through the kitchen and slipped into the last booth in the darkest corner of the bar. Ned was already there. His glass was empty.

"C-Cops came. Harry and a w-white woman. Kim Something."

A pudgy waitress ambled over, too young to remember the old days. I said, "Double vodka and tonic, lime. And refill his." She sauntered away indolently.

"Jesus, was it always this dark?" I couldn't see Ned's eyes.

"He wants me to t-take a lie d-detector test."

"Why?"

"Why shit! Why do they w-want anything? *'Your credit card Mr. Cromartie had Darnell Thorp's f-fingerprint on it and now Darnell Thorp has been killed in p-prison the same way he assaulted you We don't b-believe in coincidences Mr. Cromartie We w-wondered if you could tell us anything more M-Mr. Cromartie.'* Shit!"

I willed myself calm. "What did you tell him?"

"Nothing! *'Yes my c-credit card was stolen in the mugging Yes I know John Ewell No I don't know how Darnell Thorp was killed.'*"

"Is that all, Ned?"

"I told him it didn't b-bother me all that much about Darnell Thorp. He said it didn't seem to b-bother anybody all that much b-but they had to investigate all homicides."

"Is that all, Ned?"

"I asked about the other person."

"The druggie. What about him?"

"I w-wanted to know more."

"Suck it up, Ned! *Suck it up!* You have to live with the consequences and you have to do it without involving me."

"I know what I have to do, Joe."

"You better know, Ned. Not just to protect me, although that *ought* to figure in somewhere. To protect yourself. Solicitation of murder. And Avengers warned you."

"Why would they c-care now? It's all over, just another scalp."

"They haven't claimed this scalp. They probably don't want their Central Prison associates identified. Pull one thread—"

"*Associates.* You make them sound—"

"Ned—"

"Don't worry, I d-didn't say anything!"

"What about Julia? What about Tad Sullivan? He's a cop."

"I don't think he's a cop."

"I *know* he's a fucking cop, Ned! Elmo Finn told me."

The bored waitress finally arrived with the drinks. We were silent until she left.

"So S-Sullivan was entrapping me."

"Congratulations, Plato."

"What should I do about the l-lie detector?"

"Refuse it. Tell 'em it's voodoo, high-strung people can't pass it. Tell 'em you don't want to. Fuck 'em. They're bluffing."

"They b-bluff good."

"Sure they bluff good. That's most of being a cop."

We had several more rounds before depositing two twenties under the ashtray and slipping quietly out the back. We sat in Ned's car and talked until we were okay to drive. I was sure he had told Julia something, perhaps everything. I didn't care if he totaled a tree.

When I got home Elly was asleep, the Mossberg on the floor beside the bed. A round was chambered; pop the safety and fire. Elmo Finn had told us to leave the chamber empty—it was easy enough to pump the first round in, and the unmistakable click-chink of a 12-gauge was a deterrent in itself. "Every criminal knows that sound," Finn had said. "And nothing scares them like a shotgun." But to me there was something scarier than a shotgun: the longing to use it.

THIRTY-ONE

❏   ❏   ❏

LOGAN WAS IN full strut behind the vast oval desk, back and forth, gesturing theatrically, his shirt open to reveal curly chest hair which I assumed he assumed made Janie squirm. Soon Janie in miniskirt and thong would find a reason to bend or twist or splay, which I assumed she assumed made us squirm. Not very subtle—but hell this was television.

"*Blood*, Joe, *blood*! That's our lifeline!" Logan beamed at Janie who beamed back and crossed her legs. I told myself not to look but disobeyed.

"Avengers. *Blood*. Isaacson. *Blood*. Captain We Work for God. *Blood*. And you yourself, Joe—blood to the infinite power, the embodiment of blood!" Logan stopped abruptly, as if he had gone too far. "You're the greatest avenger of all, Joe, delivering *Crime and Punishment*. The greatest avenger of all, wielding the terrible swift sword of truth, thirty frames a second." He gave me a long look and seemed satisfied. Then he found himself at the recessed bar and as if surprised by this good fortune decided to mix one. "Joe? Janie? Churchill said he took more from brandy than brandy took from him. Righto!" I shook my head. Janie said, "Sure." Her regular drink was anything and Coke.

"*Emotion* of course is what I mean. Emotion over intellect, blood over brains, heart over head. The blood shows, Joe, have gone national. The brain shows have gone toilet. And I'm afraid Elmo Finn was a brain show after the first ten minutes."

"We took a chance, Boss, that a world-class detective would arouse something."

"Aroused the head cases. Isaacson made people's blood boil, and Patterson, and George Orwell the Avenger and Elmo Finn could have made their blood *boil over* but he stepped on his dick because you didn't ask about Phoenix or his own career as an avenger. . . ."

Janie was giggling furiously behind her hands, no doubt envisioning the famous detective stepping on his member. Janie was our literalist, and God knows we needed one.

"I didn't think I should antagonize Elmo Finn! People *support* Finn and the cops—hell, so do we. Why go after him?"

Logan turned his mouth down and made the little dismissive wave that infuriated me. I wanted to bust him one.

He stopped in mid-pace and flung his arms beatifically. Another irritant. "I want to change the subject. I've been saving the pièce de résistance." He smiled his favorite sinister smile. "The bloodiest pièce of all."

"Pièce me."

"The court of appeals has overturned Hollowell's stay. The execution's back on, Bucky wants to fry him fast. This'll all come out today."

Logan grinned inanely. He loved it when his sources beat mine.

"Joe, don't get up. You want a drink, I'll fix you a drink, you need to be seated to receive the next pièce, weak V and T, I know, a weak little double vodka. Janie, we may need some Bolly, I got a feeling, I got a fe-el-in'." He was half singing and half dancing. If he swallowed one more canary I *would* bust him one.

Throwing back his shoulders, he began to intone in his anchor-man voice, a mélange of Dan Rather hype and Jim Lehrer cool. "This is Joe Colby, Channel Nine, live on Death

Row, the countdown has begun, the last minutes on Planet Earth for rapist and murderer Franklin Delano Hollowell . . . this is Old Sparky, the state's seventy-five-year-old electric chair . . . frantic legal maneuvering by Marvin Isaacson continues . . . Joe, *I want to televise the goddamn execution!*"

Janie began making zapping noises with her tongue and jerking and twitching in her chair. Tasteless and unfunny but I got a peek at today's thong, which was the idea. Baby blue.

"Death, live," I said. "Has it ever been done?"

"Hell no, it's never been done! There have been *unscheduled* deaths on television, some anchor in Florida put a bullet in his mouth on the six o'clock, but there's never been one we could *promo*!"

I thought Logan was crazy. "I love it, Boss."

"The libs like Isaacson always complain that executions are scheduled at midnight so people won't really notice, if we really want to kill people we should do it in the open, hang 'em in the public square. They think if people had to confront it, they'd turn against capital punishment. Let's find out! I think people will love it! Blood!"

"Logan—"

"Blood, my man, blood . . . if we are smart enough to go with the flow."

I was on full metaphor alert. The canary population was fading fast. Logan stretched and puffed behind the oval desk, milking his poses for Janie's benefit.

"Who says yes or no?" I asked.

"That's my man, that's my man, I roam off into the clouds and Joe Colby asks, 'Who says yes or no?' Commissioner of Corrections comes first, and he will say no because he's a bureaucrat and that's what bureaucrats say. AG will overrule him. I think. Anyway, the buck stops with the governor who supports capital punishment and needs conservative votes next year."

"Does he support capital punishment *in the living room*?"

"He'll support whatever his pollster says. Our job is to beat the drums."

Janie began boom-booming and flailing a mean air tom-tom. She usually wasn't quite this insipid. She and Logan must have been toasting blood all morning.

I said, "Logan, the liberals are right—people *will* be repulsed if it looks like a poor downtrodden hardluck wretch is being murdered by a callous government. So we have to show not just the execution but what *led* to the execution. *Crime* and punishment, not just punishment. Show Hollowell's crimes, his tattoos, we've got some gory footage, interview Juanita—make people *salivate* for Old Sparky."

"Yes, Joe, yes, show the *first* blood, then the *second* blood! Death Live! Network, here we come!"

It took twenty-four hours to get the attorney general's approval. I was impressed—Logan had as much bite as bark. The pundits went crazy—some pro, some con, all crazy. Logan was called a "ghoul" and a "pioneer." The national press converged and he held court like an emperor. I put in a call for Commander Nutbeam.

THIRTY-TWO

❑   ❑   ❑

HE TILTS BACK in the straight chair and swings his feet atop the battered desk. The room is mustier than usual; he tells himself to check the ventilation. He wishes she were here.

He recalls an ancient warning: Be careful what you pray for. You might get it. *He prayed for justice and got copycats. Imitation, the sincerest form of jackassery. Purity has been lost.*

He picks up a handwritten list and studies it again:

Cromartie
Ewell
Daley
Colby
Sullivan

He removes one name and adds another: Crabtree. First thought best thought.

He lowers his legs and gets to his feet. He reaches into the long shelves for the soft rubber mask, toys with it, presses it to his face. He recalls the evening clearly though it was years ago. He had refused to go until she cried. He sees himself buying the mask and adding the name tag above his heart: Eric Blair. *An inspired move. And the pretentious swellheads staring at the name tag, coughing falsely, obviously baffled. One person understood but didn't give it away. Finally he had turned to* the Big Brothers and Winston Smiths and Julias and crowed, "Eric Blair was his real name. I'm George Orwell."

Someone had lectured him stiffly—Big Brother stood for Stalin and the book was a critique of Soviet totalitarianism. So he gigged them again: "Okay, why'd he call it 1984?" More coughing and fidgeting. "Because he wrote it in 1948. He just reversed the last two digits." The lilt in his voice became a sneer.

Other images of that evening begin to intrude. She was right, he should not have worn the mask. That mask.

He returns it to the shelves and carefully lifts the portable radio in its special case. He is concerned that when the explosive is added the radio will seem too heavy.

THIRTY-THREE

❏   ❏   ❏

I DIALED NED'S private number, returning his call.

"This is Ned Cromartie."

"What's up?"

"J-Joe. I was just leaving. I'll call you mañana. It'll k-keep."

"Fine, okay. Mañana." I hung up and waited five minutes until he could get to the isolated pay phone two blocks from his office. *Mañana* was the signal. He answered on the first ring.

"Joe, I got two photographs from Avengers—D-Darnell Thorp and Julia! It's a threat!"

"They sent me Boogie Brown's picture and a note."

"I got a note, too—'C-Case closed. Observe strict s-silence.' "

"Mine said, 'Now he knows how it feels. Observe strict silence.' "

"What's g-going on, Joe? They're threatening me!"

"I don't know. They're reminding us to keep quiet. I agree—it's a threat."

"Reminding, threatening—Thorp's b-balls were in his mouth, Joe. How'd they t-take a picture?"

"I don't know. Sit tight till I see Elmo Finn."

"G-Goddamnit, Joe."

I hurried to Patterson's office, which these days looked

like a squad room. At a portable worktable Elmo Finn was tapping on a laptop computer. There were piles of books on the floor behind him. I recognized my high-school year-book beneath a hardbound copy of George Orwell's *1984*. George Graves was on the sofa balancing his own laptop on his knees. High-tech Hardy boys. At least Finn could roust barflies. Steve McDade was pacing and talking on a cordless phone. Patterson stood behind the cherry desk reading something.

Finn stopped tapping and looked up. "So we have an out-break of mail from Avengers. Juanita Daley gets a photograph of Marvin Isaacson—'Now he knows how it feels. Observe strict silence.' John Ewell gets one of Hickman under the urn—'Now he knows how it feels. Observe strict silence.' Joe get a picture of Boogie Brown—'Now he knows how it feels. Observe strict silence.' But Ned Cromartie says he got nothing. Joe, did Ned get mail from Avengers?"

"I don't know," I shot back, my pulse spurting. I wondered if I could defeat a polygraph.

"Ned Cromartie says Avengers didn't contact him and *he didn't contact them*. Direct quote—'I didn't contact them.' Why would he say that? How *could* he contact them, Joe? You're the only person who's seen one of them—the only living person. And George Orwell didn't give you his phone number."

"No. And I didn't ask for it."

"Ned says he has no idea why Darnell Thorp would be attacked the same way Ned himself was attacked. Did Ned somehow solicit Avengers to do it? Did he solicit Clay Crab-tree to do it? Is Crabtree an Avenger? Did the phony ex-wife, Carol, set it up? Did Avengers or Crabtree solicit *Ned*? If so, how'd they know to do it?" Finn turned abruptly to Avery

Patterson. "Let's get a search warrant, Captain. Lean on Ned Cromartie."

My pulse rocketed off again. Had Ned burned everything? If Elmo Finn got there first, Ned would crack.

I said, "What about the other guy? Didn't Crabtree kill two people?"

Steve McDade said, "The other guy just happened along. Wrong place, wrong time. Shouldn't have been at Central in the first place—wrong prison, wrong crime. Ought to be different cages for Dwight Weems and Clay Crabtree."

"Has Crabtree confessed? Off the record."

"No."

Elmo Finn went to the window and found enough space to swish the sawed-off six-iron. "Remember 1984? Think back. Reagan versus Mondale. Anybody attend a *1984* party? As in the novel *1984* by our chief suspect, George Orwell. *Big Brother is watching you. The Thought Police.* Et cetera. I admit this is a long shot."

"We all did," Patterson said. "It was my party, I was a detective then. 'It was a bright cold day in April, and the clocks were striking thirteen,' first line of the book, I always remembered that line. The party was in April. It was a costume party—I was sort of a showoff back then."

"Thank God you recovered," Steve said.

We burst out heartily. Designer furniture and Haitian art and Waterman pens and English tailors—thank God you stopped showing off, Commander.

Finn stopped swishing. "Did anyone wear an Orwell mask?"

"I'm sure they did, someone must have," Patterson said. "I remember a lot of Big Brothers. But at some point I was taken suddenly drunk. You remember, Steve? Joe?"

"I wasn't there," I said. "But I heard about it."

"Long shot," Finn mused. But his fire-flecked gray eyes were bright. "Churchill said that truth is so important in wartime it must be protected by a bodyguard of lies. That's what we have to penetrate. Avengers have been protected by a bodyguard of lies."

THIRTY-FOUR

❑   ❑   ❑

I HURRIED BACK to the station where Ned was pacing in the corridor. We went outside to the parking lot.

"Ned, you've got to burn that stuff! They're getting a search warrant!"

His eyes darted furtively. "I'm gonna sh-show it to them."

"No, Ned—"

"L-Listen, Joe! I'm not turning you in! I'll just s-say this stuff arrived after the . . . incident. Like yours did."

"And when they ask why Avengers would send you *any* message, how Avengers *knew* about you and Three-Finger Thorp, what will you say? You've already lied, Ned, you told them—"

"I know what I t-told them, Joe!" He moved away a little. "If Avengers are really c-cops they'd know about Thorp and me." The eye without the patch danced crazily. I tried to compose myself as Elly had taught me, find the center. My hands went into my pockets.

"Ned, if you crack the door open, they'll knock you down with it. You'll fuck yourself and me too. Not to mention what Avengers might do."

"But you talked to the p-police, Joe! You didn't *observe strict silence!*"

"I didn't talk, Ned, I listened. You talked enough to convince Elmo Finn you're lying."

"I am lying."

"Goddamnit, Ned!"

"What do they r-really know?"

"Nothing!" I lit a cigarette and struggled for calm. "But they do suspect certain things. They suspect that a lifer named Clay Crabtree killed Darnell Thorp, and they suspect it was somehow because of you, but they can't prove anything and never will if you keep your mouth shut and burn that goddamn stuff."

He flung his arms haplessly. We were standing between two lines of cars in the middle of the lot. Janie came out on the loading dock and motioned for me. I pretended not to see her.

"What about W-Weems?"

"Ned, Dwight Weems was no innocent dope smoker. He was a *dealer*, sold crack to kids, *junior high* kids, he may have rubbed out one or two competitors. He could have been helping Thorp in the fight."

Ned gave me a suspicious look. "Where do you get this?"

"I just came from Homicide, Ned. They tell me a lot of things off the record. For God's sake don't repeat any of this."

He walked away and came back. "Dwight Weems was a c-crack dealer?"

I nodded several times.

"Then w-why was he only convicted of p-possession?"

"Some kind of plea bargain, I don't know. Ask Bucky Webb. Let me tell you, Ned, *nobody* feels sorry about Weems *or* Three-Finger Thorp. *Nobody.*"

Ned whirled suddenly as if he'd heard something, then spun back around to face me. His hands went to the eyepatch. With a show of resolve, he promised to burn everything and stick to his story. I offered him a cigarette but he insisted on leaving. He walked away at a fast pace and didn't look back.

Our guest on *C&P* was Burl Devine, not in his poorly received role as Commander Nutbeam, but as Mr. Capital Punishment. Burl never missed an execution at Central Prison. He and his Cat-hat followers gloried in shouting down the love-thy-murderer chants of the "white robes"—the candle-bearing opponents of the death penalty who trooped in a slow circle outside the prison on execution nights. Burl loved the idea of televised death.

"I agree with Marvin Isaacson—miracle of miracles—we shouldn't do it in the dark." On my monitor Burl looked remarkably sane. Logan had loosened the framing to dim the nutbeam. "Used to hang 'em in the town square and leave 'em a while, damn good object lesson, today it's a few cycles of eighteen hundred volts at midnight while everybody's asleep. Let's do it in prime time!"

"Sergeant, some people say electrocution is cruel and unusual punishment. Capital torture, not capital punishment."

"Do they now? I say, look at what these animals did to get where they are. Talk about cruel and unusual—talk about torture! Look at Franklin Delano Hollowell, death's too good for that monster!" He took in some air and struck a professorial pose. "But there's other ways besides electrocution, you have your firing squad, five sharpshooters, strap him in a chair with a little yellow target over his heart and no one knows who fired the blank . . . or you have your lethal injection where you shoot in sodium thiopental for sleep and pancuronium bromide to stop breathing and potassium chloride to stop the heart and you have several people injecting but only one with the real stuff—"

"Burl, some say the death penalty isn't a deterrent."

"It'll deter *him*! It'll deter *him*! But the point is, we've never tried it. Only five out of a hundred who are *condemned* to death are actually *put* to death. The other ninety-five get around it with these crazy appeals. Death Row's the safest place to live in America—three hots and a cot—they're dying of old age. There's three thousand depraved defectives on Death Row, let's fry 'em all tomorrow morning and see what happens. See if that deters anybody! Smoke comin' out of their ears!''

THIRTY-FIVE

❑ ❑ ❑

BURL'S PERFORMANCE INSPIRED comic lyrics—"When Smoke Gets in Your Ears"—but the calls ran five to one pro-Burl and ten to one pro-death-on-TV. The next morning I visited the cemetery, something I was doing often. I parked on the narrow service road near the obelisk that dominated an acre of death, ascending like a phallus from its marble base with the chiselled letters: COLBY. Behind the phallus were the graves of my father and a few mismatched relatives. A space had been left for Mother. Then came the area Connie had called the "North Forty," with the fresh graves: Constance Kell Colby. Joseph Kell (Buzz) Colby. Annabelle Constance Colby. And the narrow slice of good earth reserved for me. One black midnight I prostrated myself there with the idea of never getting up. Pull the trigger, they'd find me atop my final resting place, just dig the hole and drop me in. But they'd have had to haul me somewhere for the chemicals.

I sat down against the sheltering maple and talked with Connie and the children. This had become a frequent ritual that comforted me. I spoke aloud, sensing their responses; hearing them. I talked about everything except Elly. I could see boys playing baseball in a distant field and remembered Buzz's last Little League game, when I arrived late and Connie chided me for stopping in a saloon. I huffed out of the bleachers and lounged behind the backstop, kibitzing loudly, embarrassing everyone. 'Swing hard in case you hit it!' I bellowed to Buzz in the batter's box, and laughed uproariously. Buzz in tears struck out weakly, fled to the dugout and refused to take left field. A replacement had to be sent in. Before I could apologize to him adequately, he was dead. My torrents of atonement in the soft shade of the maple had never eased my guilt. I had many penances to perform.

That night at Group, Juanita was waiting for me, hollow-eyed and trembling in her long dress. "Joe, Joe, I have to talk to you. Something terrible's happened. Harry got suspended." She steered me into a corner away from everyone. "Suspended, Joe. *Internal investigation.* They think he knows something about Avengers or maybe *is* an Avenger, maybe working with *Ned*—and *I'm* part of it!"

"With Ned—"

"It's that Elmo Finn!"

"Juanita—I can't believe this." I hugged her, stunned.

Deirdre, brandishing the usual sheaf of multicolored papers, called, "Seats, please," ready to plunge us into her frenzy of therapy. *Relaxation! Meditation! Inner child! Mantras! Closure!* Juanita and I escaped outdoors and sat on the stone steps in the balmy night. Nervously, I lit cigarettes for us.

"Joe, Captain Patterson told him nothing. Nothing! A gold shield for fourteen years and nothing." Tears welled in her saucer eyes. "How can we get married now?"

"Harry working with Ned? This—"

"And me—I'm part of it too. Put this on TV, Joe, make fools out of 'em. That Elmo Finn!"

The big doors opened and John Ewell came out. Group nights were his only respites from the bedside vigil at Presbyterian Hospital, where Gwen still lay comatose.

"What's wrong?" John whispered, standing awkwardly on the top two steps. He wouldn't join us until invited.

Juanita told him about Harry's suspension.

John said, "They searched my house, searched my office, they even talked to Gwen's nurses. They kept asking about Ned."

I looked toward the parking lot. "Where's Ned tonight?"

Juanita shook her head. "He wasn't doing Crossing Guard. He's never missed."

"Maybe they arrested him," John said. "If they'll bring in some two-ton psychic from the Keys and a CIA assassin and then suspend the best detective on the force, they're out of control. Completely." He smiled oddly. "And Avengers are *in* control."

THIRTY-SIX

❏   ❏   ❏

HOMICIDE WAS ASTIR with the indignation cops reserve for skells, defense lawyers and the ACLU. Steve, shirttail flying, took the pot, I grabbed styrofoam cups and we hustled into Patterson's office. Everyone was there except Harry, whose absence made him seem very present.

In the surreal lamplight Patterson was working on a chart that appeared to be a timeline. On the corner of the cherry desk was a two-foot stack of 101s—Interview Reports. There must have been fifty or more.

"You heard, Joe?" Patterson said.

I took the hard chair and sipped the scalding coffee. I was jittery. "Is this about Harry?"

"What about him?"

"I don't know. Juanita said he's been suspended."

"That's off the record." Patterson edged toward the Look, then away. "There's something else. Isaacson has a new angle to get Hollowell another stay of execution—*incompetent counsel.*"

I stared dumbly, not getting it.

"Isaacson's arguing that *he* was incompetent. He made intentional mistakes along the way, very diabolical. Now he says that because counsel—*himself*—was incompetent, Hollowell deserves a new trial."

"He'll probably get one," I said. "Justice is blind, deaf, dumb, paralyzed and brain-dead." The icefire roared inside me.

"There goes your televised execution, Joe."

"So we'll do the next one. Governor's signed off—somebody's going to fry on the air."

A uniform opened the door and motioned abruptly to Steve. He and Elmo Finn hurried out and returned a few minutes later, with drawn faces.

"Joe," Steve said. "Brace yourself, Joe."

I froze, the cup halfway to my lips. I could see every line in Steve's face. "Joe, Ned Cromartie is dead. He's been killed."

I half stood, then fell back. "Ned. Not Ned. Not Ned. Ned *Cromartie*, are they sure?" I looked from Steve to Patterson to Elmo Finn. I stood up, took a step and sat down again. The coffee cup fell to the floor. "Where—oh my God—Julia." I stood up again.

"A men's room in an old building near Ned's office."

"A men's room? Oh my God—how?"

"Stabbed."

"Ned? Stabbed?" I let out a crazy laugh. "Ned was stabbed years ago, that's how he lost his eye." I looked around wildly. "Has anyone told Julia? Oh God."

"She's been told. Or being told."

"I should be with her. They were our best friends." I looked bleakly at Elmo Finn. My eyes were wet.

"I'll go with you," Finn said. I didn't protest even though I should have gone alone. I went down the back stairs holding the rail with both hands. We took an unmarked police sedan.

"A men's room? Was it robbery—that's how Ned almost got killed before. God, this isn't happening."

"Could be robbery, wallet's missing. Kim's at the scene."

"If his wallet's missing . . . how did they identify him? Maybe it's not—"

"Something in his pockets."

"Men's room—there's no other suspicions, are there? Julia will die—"

"Don't know." Finn was driving slowly, obeying all traffic laws. I wanted him to gun it. "Steve said it's that kind of men's room, Joe. Vice stakes it out."

"Oh, Jesus. Ned was *not* gay. I knew him for twenty years. If Julia—she couldn't bear to read in the paper that her husband was killed in some homosexual rendezvous—Elmo, can you keep that part quiet? As a favor, I'll owe you."

He called Steve on his cell phone and passed on my request. He listened for a moment, then said, "Let's check all calls from that phone, last three months. Six months."

Ned's secret pay phone—the mañana phone. My number would show up. I'd tell the cops that Ned couldn't talk privately in his office, which was true.

"I appreciate it, Elmo."

"You okay?"

"I'm numb but my heart's pounding. I need a drink, I don't think I can face Julia. God, this isn't happening."

Julia met us at the door with dry eyes though her face was streaked. Two of her neighbors were there and scurried into the kitchen when they saw us. Julia had obviously taken something. We embraced and I held her for a long time. Elmo Finn went to the living room and waited.

I sat beside Julia on the slipcovered sofa where I'd spent too many nights after too many drinks. As if remembering, she got up and poured me a full glass of vodka, her hand steady. It hadn't hit her. In a soft voice Finn asked if anyone had a grudge against Ned.

"No, no, Mr. Finn. Joe, could anyone—" My heart fluttered as her eyes filled. I hoped Finn wouldn't ask too many questions. "Ned was . . . you know, Joe, since the mugging . . . but I don't know anyone . . ." She looked at me fearfully. "He was gone a lot, some nights he didn't get home until after midnight. He said it was work. Was it work, Joe? I would call his office and get voice mail. Was it a woman, Joe? Please tell me the truth."

I squeezed her hands and assured her there was no woman.

"You would know, Joe," she said bleakly. "You would know. What was he doing all those nights, Joe?"

I shook my head.

"May I see his desk, dresser, any papers he kept here?" Elmo Finn said.

"I found this," Julia said, producing two items from the patch pocket of her denim skirt. She handed them over without looking at them.

Elmo Finn spread them side by side on the coffee table. " 'To Ned Chromartie.' Misspelled—there's no *h*. 'Done. Observe strict silence. Destroy this note. Avengers.' "

Julia straightened herself primly. "The photograph is very hideous."

Finn turned it face up. "This is a police photograph."

"What in God's name . . . is that Darnell Thorp?"

"Yes," Finn said. "Your husband identified this man as one of his assailants. I know this is difficult, Mrs. Cromartie, but we've found that talking through the details can help a little. We know nothing can help very much."

"My picture was there, too." She looked at us desolately, uncomprehendingly, tears streaming now. She fumbled in the patch pocket for the second photograph. I looked away.

"What was my picture doing with those things?" she sobbed as it dropped to the floor. "I've never even seen that picture before. Joe, what in God's name was he doing all those nights? Joe, please . . ."

I hugged her again. Fiery tears flowed from my eyes. "Julia, Julia . . ." I didn't know what to say.

"Tell me, Joe! My husband has been murdered and I find this note from the Avengers and that horrible photograph and my own photograph . . . I never knew him at all. Joe, what was he doing all those nights?"

"Julia, I promised Ned."

"Promised him!" She pulled away from me. "He's dead, Joe! Murdered! Promised him! Promised him what?"

I took her hand but she wrenched it away. The two neighbors came through the archway with a tea service. They looked at us and turned back.

"Julia, after the mugging Ned was very angry. Maybe he snapped a little. He bought a gun and walked the streets at night, hoping to find them."

"Bought a gun? No, not Ned, not my Ned. Oh my God, walking the streets . . . why didn't someone tell me?"

I couldn't look at her. "Julia, remember how we'd all be going somewhere and Ned would point to the houses with bars on the windows? 'Look at those windows, look at those windows. The wrong people are behind bars.' He couldn't live behind bars."

"When did he contact Avengers?" Elmo Finn asked.

"Contact Avengers!" Julia cried. I thought she might faint. Everything she believed in had collapsed in an afternoon.

"Do you know, Joe?" Finn's voice was unrelenting.

"Elmo, when they identified Darnell Thorp, Ned went kind of wild. He asked me how to contact Avengers. I told him to forget it, it was crazy, but I know he talked to Tad Sullivan about it. Maybe others. Then Thorp was killed and . . . he didn't say and I didn't ask."

Julia fumbled in the patch pocket for a bottle of pills, her hand trembling so violently she couldn't remove the cap. When I tried to help, she rose stiffly and headed for the kitchen without a word. Her friends burst out to receive her. Finn and I left quietly.

In the car he said, "Tell me everything."

I went over Ned's demented "trolling," how I thought he'd

183

given it up, how I wasn't positive he'd *ever* done it. I said I was disdainful when he wanted to contact Avengers.

"Could he have been part of it, Joe?"

"No no no. I don't see how. Maybe Three-Finger Thorp's old pals blame Ned for Thorp's murder, maybe this is just good old homeboy payback."

Finn was driving more slowly than before. A few horns complained but he didn't seem to hear them.

I said, "Whatever Ned did, I want to help catch the son of a bitch who did this."

"You believe she's been in the dark like she says?"

"Julia? Yes, I believe her."

We were crawling along now.

"Why would the homeboys blame Ned?" he asked.

"You guys didn't have any trouble," I said.

THIRTY-SEVEN

❏ ❏ ❏

*H*E PUSHES THE *Olympia to the back of the wooden desk
and arranges three newspaper clippings side by side:*

"HOLLOWELL SEEKS FOURTH STAY OF EXECUTION. Isaacson Alleges His Own 'Incompetence.' "

"VETERAN HOMICIDE DETECTIVE SUSPENDED. Decorated
Black Officer Subject of Internal Investigation."

"ACCOUNTANT FOUND STABBED IN GAY RENDEZVOUS.
Secluded Men's Room Often Vice-Squad Target."

*He sweeps the clippings into a desk drawer, repositions the
Olympia and begins typing.*

To Elmo Finn:

   Ned Chromartie was our friend. We will avenge
his murder.

Avengers

*He seals the note in a prepared envelope, removes the rubber
gloves and rises. He crosses to the quilted mattress where she
lies naked, sleeping, her soft exhalations punctuating the damp
silence. She is breathing too rapidly. Perhaps a dream.*

*He removes his shirt and panties and kneels at the foot of
the mattress. He leans forward, swirling her toes softly on his
tongue. She stirs and reaches for his hair, as she always does.*

An hour later they rise and dress. They leave one at a time, obeying the daylight rules. Before long they are on the road in the hatchback with a new license plate.

They drive past the trailer park twice from both directions, then turn in through the ramshackle wooden gate and take the perimeter road, which is unpaved like all the roads. They see only a few people. No one pays attention. They park in a pre-selected area and walk through the dust to Number 71, a drab single-wide trailer with closed curtains and a cinder-block stoop. Beulah Crabtree immediately opens the door.

They sit around a stained linoleum-topped dinette table. Beulah Crabtree, hatchet-faced, watery-eyed, offers iced tea or gin; they decline. From his handbag he produces a wallet and displays it on the table. Beulah looks inside.

"He talked, Beulah. No one talks. He was once our friend, like you . . ." She nods anxiously, her frail upper body weaving from side to side. From an envelope he counts out fifty one-hundred-dollar bills as Beulah Crabtree intently counts along, her lips moving silently. He pushes the stack of bills toward her.

"Is Clay sure about the guard?"

"No problem, Clay knows him good."

"Clay must be totally confident."

"He is totally confident, no problem." Beulah Crabtree pushes back the sleeves of her sweatshirt, sweeps the money into a frayed tote bag and zips it closed. She bobs and laughs, displaying gaps in her teeth.

"Beulah," he says, "it may be possible to reduce Clay's sentence. You cannot tell him yet. Chances are good. Did you hear about Hollowell getting another stay?"

Beulah Crabtree nods frenetically. "Won't do him no good when he tunes in!" With a witch's grin she points stabbingly at the rectangular box labeled Panasonic *that the visitors brought with them. "A real boombox!" she cackles.*

"Beulah. Nothing is funny about this. Recite the plan, step by step."

Chastened, she speaks nervously with erratic hand gestures. He interrupts several times to correct her. She becomes more agitated, both hands flying antically. He makes her demonstrate a certain maneuver with the radio. Finally he lifts his hand to quiet her.

"Are you scared, Beulah?"

"No! What's to be scared? This is a good plan, no reason—"

"Beulah." He leans across the tiny table, his tight sweater bunching oddly.

"Falsies," Beulah Crabtree says. "Wore 'em myself for years, give you a profile and no blubber to haul around! You take hormones?"

"Beulah."

"You got some hair on you."

"Beulah, if you ever hide from us again—"

"Never, never. I just got spooked till Clay explained. We're on the same side. The same side. Why you wearin' gloves, this heat?"

Soon they leave the trailer and walk toward the car along the dusty road. In the heels he has trouble on the uneven surface. As they cut through an overgrown picnic area, a wiry man leaps out from some bushes and blocks their path. He is wearing camouflage fatigues, a leather vest and an Australian-style military hat with an upswept brim. A badge of some kind is pinned to the vest. Jammed into the pocket of his fatigues is a cellular phone.

"Posse! Posse! Citizen Patrol!" He pushes both hands toward them. "Routine, ladies. Questioning."

The taller Avenger reaches for the shoulder bag.

"Whoa there, ma'am—"

"May I show you something, Officer."

"Show me . . . well I ain't . . . Whoa! Look at that! Well, you *understand, I seen you goin' into Crabtree's which her son's a murderer and she's killed people herself. Call her Bonnie Parker."*

The sheriff's posseman rattles on as the three amble deeper into the trees. The shorter Avenger scans in every direction and signals with her eyes, as they have practiced. From the shoulder bag he brings forth the big automatic with the silencer and shoots the man in the face. He falls quietly. The Avenger fires again, and again.

In the car she says, "They'll match the gun."

"Maybe not."

"Maybe not."

They stare fixedly ahead as he turns onto the circumferential. She leans toward him and drops her hand to his leg. "Let's not fight. Only four more."

He squeezes her hand. "Four more."

"And no Day of Vengeance." She waits for his response but there is none. He drives carefully below the speed limit.

"Death Row," he says finally, "may not be the safest place in America."

THIRTY-EIGHT

❏   ❏   ❏

"WHAT DO THESE people have in common? Joe Colby . . .
Elly Briggs . . . Logan Murphy . . . Janie Thomas . . . Harry
Covington . . . Juanita Daley . . . Tad Sullivan . . . John Ewell
. . . Deirdre Olson . . . Burl Devine . . . and the Homicide Division of the police department?"

"Cast of Avengers," I said. "Like *Murder on the Orient
Express*, everybody did it."

Elmo Finn didn't smile. "Ned's pay-phone calls. He made
more calls from that phone than anywhere else."

"He was paranoid about the office. I thought he was afraid
of his boss."

We were alone in Patterson's office. Ned's funeral had
ended only two hours earlier and Julia was already on a plane
with her sister. She was still in semi-shock when I said goodbye. I wondered if she would ever return.

I said, "Okay, Elly and me make sense, Juanita and John
were in Group, Deirdre ran Group, Harry was investigating
him. And Sullivan was entrapping him."

Finn didn't bite. "How about the others?"

"Burl Devine? I have no idea. Who else?"

"Logan Murphy."

"Ned was Logan's accountant. I got him the job."

"Janie."

"Home or office number?"

"Both."

"I don't know."

Finn was hunched over Patterson's cherry desk, a phone-company printout spread before him. "One of Sheriff Monahan's citizen posse bought it yesterday in a trailer park. Amateurs playing cop."

"I didn't see it in the paper."

"They didn't find him till this morning. The High Sheriff may get some defections now."

"You see what Fletcher wrote in the *Herald* about televised executions? 'Logan Murphy and Joe Colby give journalism a bad name, and that's hard to do.' The viper."

"Your fellow journalist."

"Fuck journalism. It's all rock and roll to me."

I got back to the studio as Harry Covington, tonight's guest on *C & P*, strolled in. He was dapper, as usual, and unruffled for a suspended detective under internal investigation. "Ask me anything, Joe, except about my suspension." That was okay—Logan and I had worked up a little surprise.

"Detective Covington," I began somberly as the cameras rolled, "you're black and I'm white. When I see young black males coming toward me on the sidewalk, I feel apprehensive. Is that wrong?"

"Yes it is, Joe. It's wrong."

"Okay, then answer this. Blacks make up only twelve percent of the population—but they commit *fifty-five percent of the violent crimes.* Now, if you factor out women, children and older people, who commit very few crimes, you end up with young black males—a tiny percentage of the population—committing about *half the violent crimes.* Young black males are the most dangerous predator on earth. If people weren't apprehensive they'd be crazy."

Harry surprised me. He answered calmly, more in sorrow than anger.

"Joe, you're condemning everyone for the crimes of a few. Most young black males are not lawbreakers. The great majority."

"Okay, what's the percentage? Isn't it like prostitutes and AIDS? Not all prostitutes have AIDS, but the percentage is so high you avoid all of them."

My goading didn't work. Harry folded his hands on the gunmetal gray desktop, exuding long-suffering patience with us honkies. "Joe, you've had a terrible personal experience with a young black male. I understand that. But most victims of black crime are also black."

I nodded. "Good point, Detective. I've met a lot of black victims in my support group."

"The real criminal is crack cocaine, Joe. That's what's killing us."

"That's a subject for another show. Let's get to Avengers. When is this going to be over, Detective—or whatever your current status is."

He ignored the jab. "Avengers are terrorists and will be caught sooner or later. But I'm not surprised that vigilantes have appeared. The justice system isn't producing justice, it's simply accommodating the people *in* the system—judges, lawyers, criminals. A trial isn't about justice, it's about trivial procedural things that only lawyers and judges care about. So there's no public confidence that the guilty will be punished. So we have Avengers."

Harry had managed to defend both the blacks and the rednecks. He was as smooth as Patterson or Elmo Finn. What the hell had he done to get suspended—and why wasn't he bitter?

After Harry's segment, I leaned into the camera, extreme close-up, head cocked to the exact angle Logan wanted. The teleprompter began scrolling but I didn't need it.

"Once I tried to break into jail so I could get at the murderer

191

of my children. I was caught, I apologized, I was given another chance. Now I am withdrawing part of my apology. I am sorry for what I did, but I am no longer sorry for *wanting* revenge. We are told to turn the other cheek, that vengeance is wrong. But why does it feel so right? My precious children were savagely and senselessly killed by an animal who was not convicted although eleven jurors said there was no reasonable doubt. My heart cries, 'Get even.' My heart cries, 'Settle the score.' I believe this feeling is basic, natural and *human*. It is inherent in our species. It comes with the territory. I have decided to trust the agonized impulses of my heart and to ignore the lofty contrivances of my head. Especially the lofty contrivances of other people's heads who have not walked in my shoes. Shakespeare said, 'Everyone can master a grief but he that has it.' If you want to turn the other cheek, fine, but don't preach at me. We are what we are, I am what I am. I still ache for revenge and I will until the books are closed. I do not apologize. *As they do unto you.*"

I stared grimly into the camera while we faded slowly to black. Before I could unhook the clip-on mike, the phones were flowering and in Logan's office the Bolly flowed and flowed. When I got home Elly was asleep but I managed to get her awake. And keep her awake.

THIRTY-NINE

❑   ❑   ❑

MY SERMONETTE ROILED the waters. Network ran a thirty-second excerpt and booked me on the tabloid show. Newspapers published anguished editorials—"Eye for an Eye," "Fire with Fire," and, of course, "As They Do Unto You." I was the Prince of Darkness and loving it.

Two mornings after the broadcast, as Logan and I continued to gloat, Elmo Finn and George Graves showed up unannounced at Channel Nine. "Don Quixote and Sancho Panza," Logan boomed, "wandering in the wilderness—Janie, bring 'em on back."

Janie was all twitch and wiggle in front of the celebrated detective, holding his chair, touching his arm, serving coffee and pastries, delivering folded notes to Logan. I saw today's thong twice. Finally the Boss dismissed her with an executive gesture.

Finn said, "Didn't know you had one of those gold badges Patterson gives out. *Friend of the Police.*" Logan reached for the Plexiglas case and raised it above his head like a boxer with a trophy.

"I've got one too," I said, "because of one story we ran and two we didn't." I remembered the night when Logan's Friend of the Police crashed to the floor as Patterson slammed him into the credenza to force the cuffs on.

Logan, grinning his monkey-wrench grin, balled up one of

Janie's notes and tossed it to me. "A guy's gonna call you about a bumper sticker. 'As They Do Unto You.'"

"A bumper sticker? Jesus, Boss, I don't know—"

"Oh, he's gonna print 'em up, doesn't need permission—just wants you to have a little piece of the action. Elmo, you see the *Herald* today? Whaddya think, did Joe desecrate Shakespeare?"

"Shakespeare will survive even Joe Colby."

"What about the posse member who didn't survive? Was it Avengers? We hear yes."

"Probably," Finn said. "Odd that it happened at the trailer park where Clay Crabtree's mother lives."

"Coincidence?"

"That would be even odder."

Logan had to take a call from Network, so Finn, Graves and I moved to my tiny office. Finn settled into the canvas director's chair, and I rolled in an extra chair for Graves.

"Can we dig around some, Joe?" Finn said. "We thought a fresh . . ." His voice trailed off. These guys were stuck, tilting at windmills.

"Sure. Stream of consciousness?"

He nodded ambiguously. "You were with an Avenger for three hours. During all that time, for whatever reason, an impulse, a caprice, did someone's name cross your mind? However much you discounted it? Or repressed it?"

"No, not really. I was pretty jittery. I was having strong second thoughts about what I was doing."

"Have you ever been hypnotized?"

"No." I realized that Graves was operating a tape recorder. A little cheeky, I thought; he should have asked. "You want to hypnotize me?"

He shrugged and shifted lower in the director's chair. He seemed in no hurry. I wanted to speed this up.

194

"Joe, did the voice device require him to touch it with his hand?"

"Yep—to activate it or whatever. I told you, position it. He had to reach under the mask."

"You never see that on the tape."

"He did it before each scene. That's what they were, scenes."

"Did the gloves give him any trouble with the gun? He was holding it in the wrong hand. He was right-handed."

"How do you know?"

"Several indications."

"No, he seemed to hold the gun okay."

"Joe, think about the voice on the phone, setting up the interview. Could it have been a man impersonating a woman?"

"No. I'm almost positive."

"And the Avenger you interviewed couldn't have been a woman impersonating a man?"

"You guys have asked this over and over. It was a man, ninety-ten."

"Ten percent is a lot."

"Okay, ninety-five to five. Ninety-nine to one!"

"How long did it take you to get to the pay phone?"

"At the Seven-Eleven? Not long. Five minutes."

"The call came from another pay phone around the corner."

I stared open-mouthed. "You mean she was right there all the time?"

"Nearby."

"Why?"

Finn shook his head. "I'm still on the hows, Joe. After you got the two phone calls in the morning, you had thirteen hours before the interview took place. Think about where you went, who you saw. They might have followed you—making sure you weren't working with the cops."

"We've been over all this before, Elmo. There's nobody I remember being out of place. You'd think I'd have been supersensitive to everything but now it's just a blur. They had threatened Elly, I was mostly scared all day—of Avengers one minute and you guys the next."

"You knew Ned for a long time."

"Twenty years. My best friend, I guess."

"He asked you how to contact Avengers."

"Yep."

Finn's gray eyes angled up at me now, sharp, intent.

"Why didn't you do it for him? You had three hours."

"Do it for him? You mean set up the hit on Three-Finger Thorp? It's a crime, for one thing. I've had enough brushes with the law."

"Was it hard not to?"

"Hell no. I sympathized with Ned but not that much."

"Ned told Tad Sullivan that you'd help."

"Who knows what the hell Ned told anybody? I always knew Sullivan was a cop."

"How do you think Ned *did* make contact?"

"I don't know. Are you sure he did?"

"Yes."

"Well, he was calling all over creation from that pay phone. I guess he must have found them, or they found him."

What irony—Ned was in the ground and I was still lying about him. I realized I had two cigarettes burning and casually stubbed out one of them.

"At your house, Joe, how much did he know about the camera and the setup?"

"He knew what he wanted. Shoot the blank wall during questions, pan over for answers. Very static."

"That seems strange to me—his best chance to state his case and he downplays the production values. Static, as you say.

But in the snuff videos he pans, zooms in and out, fades to black. Understands technique."

"Maybe he was nervous. Maybe he has a videographer, like you." I winked at George Graves, who twitched back.

"Any chance you've forgotten something, Joe?"

"No, I don't think so. Like what?"

"Like asking the Avenger to snuff Boogie Brown."

I snickered and shifted in my chair. "I think I'd remember that, Elmo."

He stood and stretched. "Seems odd, Joe, the man who tried to break into jail to get Boogie Brown . . . who got an offer from Avengers to do the job for him . . . who admits he still wants revenge, *as they do unto you* . . . seems odd that when this man is alone with an Avenger for three hours, he doesn't close the deal." Finn's gray lasers slammed in.

I shrugged, palms up. "Well, I didn't. Obviously I didn't—Boogie Brown's still alive." Inside the icefire surged. My face and neck were burning.

Finn gripped an imaginary golf club and took some swings. "The police photo of Darnell Thorp chewing on his privates—somebody made extras. There's one behind the bar at the Thunderbolt, one above the urinals at the Blue Steel. Burl Devine's got a giant blowup in his office. Somebody even sent it to the KGB with a note: 'Carrying on the tradition.' Patterson's ballistic."

A vital clue comprised. I could hear Avery Patterson's roar.

The door opened and Logan lunged in, as we had planned. "Okay, boys, Press Club, my treat. Get the little gray cells stimulated, Quixote." With a theatrical gesture, he brandished a red-white-and-blue bumper sticker: As They Do Unto You. "Get 'em while they're hot! Burl Devine just ordered twenty-five thousand."

FORTY

❑ ❑ ❑

FOR HOURS HE *has been typing on the old Olympia. Finally
he stands and takes a few steps to relax his legs. He goes to the
cooler for beer, drinks half the bottle and flops onto the quilted
mattress. He falls asleep quickly.*

*Soon there is a coded knock at the entryway but he does not
hear it. The knock is repeated, slightly louder. Then a key turns
in the lock and the door begins to swing inward. He awakens
with a shiver. As she closes the door and straightens up he is
aiming the big automatic at her chest.*

"God!" he whispers fiercely.

"You didn't answer."

"I was asleep. How did you get in?"

*"Put that down. You want me to stand out there till you
wake up?"*

"Did you have another key made?"

"Yes."

"Why?"

She shrugs.

"You carry it with you?"

"Today I did."

*He extends his hand. She gives him the key and picks up the
beer and drinks. "There's a strange car near Beulah's. Could
be cops."*

"Her phone's tapped."

"So send her a note."

"Maybe. That might be dangerous too."

"A mail screen?"

"It's possible."

He picks up a batch of newspaper clippings from the desk. "Look at these. Send some notes—Court Adjourned."

She studies them and shakes her head. "I don't like it. Why?"

"There is no why."

"Oh. Just first thought best thought."

"It works."

"The theory of absolute randomness. The theory of absolute bullshit."

"Contrived randomness. It works. It's working."

"Okay. I promised." She goes to the shelves and selects the items she needs. "Let's do it."

Two hours later they are outside following the secret trail, abiding by all their rules of movement. They encounter an unexpected noise that freezes them for five minutes and requires certain backtracking. With a flash of displeasure he remembers the farmer on the green tractor. But their schedule allows for contingencies; they have plenty of time. Before long they are proceeding circuitously in the white van, which has been changed in appearance and now has a roof rack holding two bicycles.

He drives by the trailer park but the strange car is gone. "Could have been cops, could have been Clay's pals waiting to ambush us," he says. "Or nothing."

She does not answer.

"Almost caught up on our memoirs," he says.

"Oh wonderful. You tell me not to write anything down, and you're writing everything down."

"Not everything. Maybe we'll mail it to Joe Colby."

She laughs and they ride in silence for a while. Several times *he repositions the shoulder bag on the console between them.*

"Nervous?" he asks.

"No. Yes."

When they reach the target area, he slows down.

"Where is he? We're right on time."

"I don't know. He'll be here. Pinochle game's at nine, always. Just drive the Cruise route."

He turns right and proceeds at a moderate pace, circling the block.

"See him?"

"No. Don't slow down too much."

Again he circles the block. She says, "There he is, just going in. He's late. Go back to Jump. It takes him five minutes in the store. There's never much traffic."

"I know."

This time he traverses three sides of the block and pulls over at a certain point, leaving the engine running. They have clear lines of sight even though it is dusk.

She says, "There he is, coming out. Okay. Okay. When he passes the pole."

He swings the van back into the street, drives to the intersection and turns right. There is no traffic. As they pull alongside the pedestrian, she lowers the tinted window.

"Mr. Pitts, Mr. Pitts! You little darlin' you, gonna be late your pinochle game you don't ride with me. I give you a nice ride and you give me somethin' out of that nice paper bag Mr. Pitts don't you recognize me! I tell your brother Sam you can't hardly see nothin' you little darlin' I tell Sam maybe brother Paul gettin' old ha ha."

Mr. Pitts has stopped walking. He stares at her with an uncertain smile. She opens the sliding door of the van and gestures suggestively.

"One ride for one beer. And maybe one kiss. And maybe two, my sister's drivin'."

Mr. Pitts looks into the van, places the paper bag on the seat and climbs in. She closes the sliding door and raises her window as the van pulls away fast.

"Hey now! What—I lives—"

Without looking back the driver says, "Paul Pitts, how much did Isaacson pay you to vote not guilty?"

"Who—"

"Shut up! How much money did you take to save Boogie Brown?"

Paul Pitts dives for the door but cannot open it. In the front seat she leans over to hold the wheel for the driver who swings around and raises the big automatic with the silencer and shoots Paul Pitts three times in the chest. When the body comes to rest he fires two more rounds.

"He fell the wrong way!" she says. "Go on to Drop! Go on to Drop!"

He grips the wheel tightly and forces himself to slow down. She is halfway into the back seat struggling with the body.

"Hold on! Almost there."

He turns into a dark street and proceeds to a remote area of vacant lots and abandoned houses. At a preselected point he pulls over, gets out of the van and comes around unhurriedly to the passenger side. The sliding door is open. Together they lever the body up and roll it out of the van onto the grass. Breathing heavily, he returns to the wheel and they drive away. Soon they are on the circumferential highway around the city.

"Dead weight," she says. They laugh sputteringly.

"Five rounds."

"Yes." She examines the brasscatcher and counts five casings. "Still hot. Five, check."

"The note?"

"Oh no, the note! Getting him out—"

"It's okay. It's okay. Don't worry." He reaches for her hand. "It's okay."

"It's a mistake. We practiced enough. I should—"

"It's okay."

"There's a lot of blood. A lot."

"That's why I used three seat covers. Three carpets and three seat covers."

They exit the circumferential and follow a serpentine route, finally stopping in a wooded area. They pile the seatcovers, carpets and gloves onto a plastic tarpaulin, then roll up the tarp and fasten it with bungee cords. They drag the misshapen bundle to the edge of a drop-off and push it over. It rolls and slides down the slope into a vast collection of refuse. A half hour later the van is in its hiding place. In the comfortable darkness they make their way along the path through the trees to the embankment. They drop softly to the tiny clearing below. Within seconds they are inside.

They remove all their clothes and stuff them into an opaque six-ply plastic bag. Carefully they take off each other's wigs and return them to the shelf. Then they collapse on the mattress.

"Wish we had a shower down here," she says. "I should make you lick me."

"Make me."

Later he says, "Think about this. Send a copycat note."

"Perfect!" She laughs and laughs. "We were good tonight. Rolled with the punches."

"We were prepared."

She pulls him close to her. "Will you give up on the Day of Vengeance? You've fooled them all. Let's disappear. First plan best plan."

"Maybe you're right."

"I am right! You know I'm right! Who could you trust?"

"Victims. They have pure motives. Gangbangers. Maybe some Phoenix alumni."

"Phoenix? Assassins?"

"Assassins. Bring 'em in out of the cold."

FORTY-ONE

❏   ❏   ❏

JANIE STRUGGLED INTO my office with a two-foot stack of overloaded manila envelopes.

"It just keeps coming, Joe. We stayed till midnight last night just to sort all this stuff. You and Logan and your big ideas."

"Death live, Janie—everybody's got an opinion."

"I wish they'd keep it to themselves."

She tossed each envelope onto its proper stack on the floor in front of my desk. "There. Now all the little goofballs are in your court." She sashayed out like Marilyn.

My private line rang. It was Commander Nutbeam his own self, who was calling twice a day to report new evidence of his fifteen minutes, which was stretching into a career. I had created a star.

"Burl, what's up?"

"Congratulations, Joe—nobody but Boogie left now."

"What—"

"Hot scoop. The famous holdout, juror number nine. The nigger Isaacson bribed. Dead on arrival absolutely fuckin' dead."

"Paul Pitts? Burl, we haven't heard anything."

"You're Avengers' poster boy, Joe. Boogie's the only one left."

"Are you sure about this?"

"Ask your buddy Elmo Finn. Speak of the devil, I got something for your profile."

"Burl, how do you know we're doing a profile?"

"I got spies everywhere." His laugh was full of phlegm and malevolence. "Elmo Finn was definitely Phoenix. One of the Company's assassins."

"Phoenix was over when he got to Vietnam. We checked."

"Bullshit. Maybe they tore up the letterhead but the shop stayed open. And Elmo Finn was behind the counter. You know what they did when they wasted some gook? Left an ace of spades in their mouth. The Phoenix calling card."

"Okay, Burl, what is this? You should *like* Phoenix, you should *love* Phoenix, hell if you'd been over there you'd have been *running* Phoenix!"

He laughed again, like taking a bow. "Phoenix was all right. But Finn took an . . . unwise turn. He killed seventeen people, not all gooks, either."

"Who says? Who could back this up?"

"Assassinations, Joe."

"I can't use this without a second source—that's the Logan Murphy Rule. Call Channel Two—they'll run something off the bathroom wall, but we won't."

"I admire men of principle, damned if I don't." He hung up with another satisfied laugh.

As soon as I was off the phone, Logan breezed in and began pacing. In my cramped office he could take only three strides in each direction, so he was whirling like a dervish. He had a yellow pad in his hand, always a bad sign.

"Finn, Finn, Finn, you Lazarushian-leather Elmo Finn, though I've belted you and flayed you, by the living Gawd that made you, you're a better man than I am, Elmo Finn!" He beamed down at me. "Kipling!"

"Bar's open, I see."

He laughed and consulted the yellow pad. "Unimpeachable

sources. Elmo Finn inherited mucho dinero. That's how he can get away with charging no fee. Lives on Longboat Key, in Sarasota, has a place in Manhattan. Finn's fiancée was carjacked, raped, left for dead and died. The story is that Finn and Graves hunted down the killer and executed him in an utterly Peter the Great fashion. Everybody's got a different set of gory details. If any of them are true, do not—repeat do not—piss these people off. Talk about avengers."

Finally Logan exhaled and I jumped in. "He killed seventeen in Vietnam. Not all gooks."

"I was just about to tell *you* that. My sources say seven and they were all legitimate. Phoenix was over."

"They *said* it was over. What's an illegitimate kill in war?"

"Good question."

"Logan! What the fuck am I doing? Jesus! Burl Devine just told me that Paul Pitts was killed yesterday. The holdout juror in Boogie Brown's trial, could be Avengers. We ought to do a newsbreak."

"Holy holy! Why didn't you say so?" he thundered.

"I'm going crazy."

"Write it fast." He buzzed the control room and got them stirring.

Janie came in with more mail. She had isolated one envelope. "This looks suspicious," she said.

"Don't handle it!" I shouted. I took it by the edge between thumb and forefinger, slit the envelope carefully and fished out the note. The three of us read it as it lay face up on my desk.

Joe Colby,

When Paul Pitts voted Not Guilty he himself became Guilty. Court adjourned.

The Avengers

FORTY-TWO

❏   ❏   ❏

"I'M RUNNING OUT of plastic bags," I told Steve McDade as I deposited the Pitts note on his desk in the squad room. He looked up blankly, as if I had interrupted something deep. He dispatched a young detective to hand-carry the note to the lab, then stared glumly at the coffee machine which was wheezing toward a full pot. He scrambled up and grabbed the carafe, allowing the unfinished stream to sizzle on the burner, and headed for Patterson's office. "Bring some cups."

Patterson was on the phone. Elmo Finn sat behind his worktable under We Work for God, pecking at his laptop. Still chasing Avengers in cyberspace like a latter-day Quixote; a good hook for our profile.

Patterson hung up. "The homeless dude stabbed under the bridge Saturday night—one skell killing another, we *thought*. Hell, a goddamn wino *confessed*. Now Avengers say *they* did it because the dude had AIDS and was trying to bite people. Which was true. The note is *genuine* Avengers."

"What note?" I asked. "Who got it?"

"Elmo—he also got one promising to avenge Ned's killing."

Elmo Finn said, "There's also a tavern killing, sleaze named Garren, just released from Central after four years for manslaughter, his old girlfriend picks him up, they stop at the first bar for a drink and Garren doesn't return from the john because he has a near-death experience with a ball-peen hammer and a total-death experience with an eight-inch serrated blade. That was weeks ago, suddenly Avengers are claiming it. Note was typed on the famous Olympia portable."

"Who got that note?" I asked.

Finn tapped his chest.

"Well, goddamnit."

"We didn't think you'd be jealous, Joe," Steve jibed.

Finn went to the coffeepot, which was resting crookedly atop several police magazines on one of Patterson's antique tables. He poured himself a cup and a refill for Steve. I waved him off. Steve, shirttail three-quarters out, his paunch more prominent, had been pacing since we came in. Patterson stood behind the judge's chair, leaning on the high back, his head on his arms. I was the only one sitting down.

Elmo Finn said, "So. We have two *genuine* Avenger notes claiming killings they probably didn't commit. And now comes Paul Pitts, the infamous Boogie Brown juror." Finn threw me a sympathetic glance when he said *Boogie Brown*. I tried to look deadpan but I expected the icefire, and there it was, right on time.

"There was no note on Paul Pitts," Finn went on, "but Pitts was shot with the Avengers' gun. Note could have blown away."

A beep sounded. Finn picked up a cell phone, listened for a moment and hung up.

"The plot thickens. The note that Joe just brought over is *not* genuine—or at least it wasn't typed on the Olympia. There's another thing—it starts *Joe Colby comma*; that's different. And it's signed *The* Avengers; they never used *The* before. But the gun matched. So, *apparently*, we have two copycat murders that Avengers are claiming—and one Avengers murder a copycat is claiming."

"Curiouser and curiouser," Steve said.

"Maybe not," Elmo Finn said.

"You understand it?"

"I don't think we have to. 'Fair is foul, and foul is fair.' These are pink herrings."

"What's a pink herring?" I said. "A pale imitation of a red herring?"

"Exactly," Finn laughed. "Meaningless diversions. The answer is that there *is* no answer. Except the bodyguard of lies."

"That's why we love him, folks," Steve said.

"I don't get it," I said. "Are they getting smarter or dumber?"

Elmo Finn pondered for a moment. "They're getting scared. Joe, try to empty your mind for a moment. Make it blank. Listen only to your feelings."

I nodded, almost rolling my eyes.

"You talked to a female Avenger on the phone. You spent three hours with a disguised male Avenger. Now forget everything you've said before and just go with your feelings, your instinct. Could either of them have been black?"

I hesitated. Finn said, "Don't think. Feel."

"No . . . maybe. I can't rule it out. The woman's voice was white, I'm almost positive. But the man—the man I think *was* a man and *probably* white. But he could have been black. Maybe that's why he never showed an inch of skin."

The door opened and Harry Covington came in. He began a discussion with Patterson and Steve that I couldn't hear.

I whispered to Elmo Finn, "Is Harry back on the team?"

He winked. Curiouser and curiouser hardly covers it, I thought.

"Elmo, we're doing a profile of you for *Crime and Punishment.* Can we mention your current . . . friend, the actress or whatever. Sandra, I think. Just to personalize the story."

"Dancer. Sure. Sandra and I have a good relationship—we fight like we're married and fuck like we're not."

211

Steve, who was listening, said, "Oh, the joys of being single. My wife and I kvetch like we're married and screw like we're embalmed."

"Exactly the word she used," Harry said. "Embalmed."

Patterson hung up from a twenty-second call. He was getting a lot of them. "Okay, there was a witness to Paul Pitts. Pitts got into a two-toned van with a bicycle on top. Black girl in the passenger seat, don't know about the driver."

"Can we report it?" I asked.

"Sure. Report hell out of it, maybe somebody else saw it. Run the Hotline number."

"We run it all day long, Captain, everybody's memorized it. You getting any calls?"

"Plenty, we had to put extra volunteers on."

The door opened and George Graves made a signal to Elmo Finn, who abruptly went out. Patterson and Steve went tête-à-tête behind the desk.

I leaned toward Harry and whispered, "What was your suspension all about? Juanita was very upset."

He made a face and shrugged. "History. But listen to this, Joe. Some farmer called the Hotline. Real cracker. Said one time he got lost on his tractor trying to take a shortcut through the middle of nowhere and some guy just materialized out of the trees and showed him where to go. But maybe he dreamed it."

"Got lost?" I said. "How do you get lost on a tractor?"

"Well, you start by drinkin' a quart of first-run moonshine. Straight. Then you puke. Then you grab a travelin' quart and fire up your old John Deere and head out on back roads and old creek beds and across fields and you see roads that aren't there and after about two hours you're so fuckin' lost you can't find the sky and some dude just looms up out of the mist and never says a word just motions with his arm and you chug off and get lost again about two dozen times and finally hit a paved road and turn over in a ditch and survive because you were too goddamn drunk to die. And many months later you remember the ghost in the woods and think maybe that was an Avenger and you call the police but you can't pinpoint your location within a hundred square miles. And Sherlock Holmes thinks it's a clue."

"I assume I can't report this," I said to Harry's amusement.

He said, "Sherlock thinks Avengers have a base of operations off the beaten track. They got to hide vehicles, disguises, cartops, flowers—they can't just whiz in and out of a suburban driveway. Maybe this farmer stumbled onto it."

"How long ago was this?" I asked.

"Six months."

"Six months!"

"Avengers have been in business at least that long. Sherlock says."

Harry's story spurred me. I decided to be a reporter again. "Is there anything solid we can report, give the public a little hope? Or let me interview this farmer?"

Patterson broke in. "Farmer's off-limits for now. Maybe after hypnosis."

Again the phone rang. Steve hustled out for coffee. Harry leaned toward me and said, "This Elmo Finn—I was suspicious. But no more."

"I know he's good in a saloon fight."

Harry whispered, "You should listen to him interrogate. He's got tricks—if the Supremes could see him . . ."

I wanted to ask whose constitutional rights Sherlock had violated. But didn't.

"He does some goofy stuff, Joe, like readin' old high-school yearbooks. But then he went out to interview the cemetery manager about the urn and the stolen flowers and came back with aliases for Avengers, post office boxes, unbelievable. He found this farmer in a stack of two thousand Hotline cards, he and Graves just sat there all night reading card after card. He gave a lecture to the Hotline volunteers on how to listen and take notes and they applauded. Applauded! He keeps sayin', 'Howdunnit, then whodunnit.' "

Patterson was scribbling notes from his phone conversation. I said nothing, hoping Harry would continue.

"You want to know what Finn's been asking?" Harry opened his notebook. "Who attended Boogie Brown's trial regularly? Who attended Hollowell's? He wanted all of Lodge's rulings in death-penalty cases—the full written opinions! Who Duane Hickman's friends were. A list of goldsmiths within a fifty-mile radius. A list of survivalist camps, weekend warrior playgrounds. Stuff from the Probate Office. A meeting with all the librarians in the country! Librarians! All the heads of Civil Defense for the last forty years!" Steve returned with a fresh pot. "Jesus, there was more, I haven't kept up with everything. When we ask, 'What for?' he just smiles. 'A little idea, a little idea.' We tell him where to find it and off he goes. And that goddamn Graves. Jesus."

Patterson hung up. "Mail intercept at Central Prison. Clay Crabtree got an envelope with nothing in it except one thing— a photograph of his mother."

FORTY-THREE

❑   ❑   ❑

THE NEXT MORNING, Janie slouched into my office holding the envelope with tweezers.

"Joe, I opened it, I'm so stupid."

I cleared a space on my desk where she laid the envelope as if it were explosive. She stepped back and expelled a lot of air. I took the tweezers and extracted the note.

> To Joe Colby:
>
> We demand another interview on "Crime and Punishment" to correct misimpressions. Be prepared for our call. Observe strict silence.
>
> Avengers

I squeezed open the envelope and looked inside. "Was there a photograph?"

"No. Just the note."

I dialed Steve McDade and read him the message.

"Elly's picture?" he asked.

"No, not this time."

"Hurry, Joe." He hung up.

I knew what to expect at Homicide. As I walked into Patterson's office, I said, "Why do I think I'm about to become a guinea pig?"

215

"We'll have people close at all times," Patterson said. "Whenever they call, wherever they tell you to go, we'll be there. And we can bring in the cavalry like that." He snapped his fingers like a gunshot. I flinched.

"One small detail, Captain. These people are killers and your people aren't."

"We'll protect you, Joe."

"You got a killer, Captain?"

The Look. "If necessary."

"Who decides *if necessary*? I want a gun."

"Fine."

"How about Elmo Finn? I want Elmo Finn."

Steve said, "Joe, I been a police a long time. Never lost nobody yet."

"You never had Avengers before."

I retrieved a styrofoam cup from the wastebasket and got coffee from the pot on the magazine. My hand shook as I poured. "This stuff is strong but not strong enough." I looked around the room. Everyone's eyes were on me. I went back to the hard chair.

"So I play along with these killers and follow them anywhere and wear a wire and somehow at the last minute James Bond will burst in and save me."

"If bursting in is required. Avengers *need* you, Joe, don't forget that."

"If they come to my house the cavalry could already be there."

"Elmo says they probably won't. Avengers have their own video equipment, they'll shoot the interview at their location with their camera."

"I don't want to wear a wire—"

"No wire, Joe. Transmitter. Undetectable."

"*Undetectable.*" I set the styrofoam cup on Patterson's desk and rubbed my eyes. "Can I have my old bodyguard again?"

"No."

"Why?"

"Too cumbersome. Guinea pigs don't have bodyguards."

"Bullshit!" I slapped Patterson's desk but he didn't react and the coffee didn't spill. "What's *cumbersome* for you might be just *perfect* for me! You want me to be the bait and I want somebody who'll shoot the cocksuckers! Whether it's George Orwell or George Washington or George Raft!"

"Who's George Raft?" Kim said.

"Before your time," Steve said. "Gangster actor."

"George Raft didn't need three guns," I said, glancing at Kim. I must have sounded deranged.

Elmo Finn and George Graves came in, relieving the tension a little.

"How'd it go?" Patterson asked.

Finn took in our expressions, got out the six-iron and began swishing lazily at the window. "Clay Crabtree wants his mother in Witness Protection. So I say, 'She's not a *witness* to anything, is she, Clay?' and he says, 'Sure she's a witness, she knows plenty of stuff,' and I say, 'What does she know?' and he says, 'I don't know *exactly* what she knows,' and I say, 'Will she tell us what she knows?' and he gets this glum look and says, 'Probably not.'"

Everyone laughed louder than necessary, including me.

"I ask, 'Who sent your mother's photograph?' and he says, 'No idea,' and I say, 'You're lying and screw you *and* your mother unless you tell us everything. We know your phony wife Carol Crabtree is an Avenger and what have they got on you, Clay, that's worse than what *we've* got on you which is life without parole,' and he says, 'Can my sentence be adjusted?' and I say, 'Yes, it can be adjusted from life to death.' This seemed to spook him."

Hearty laughter this time, not as forced.

"Bottom line, he's scared to make a deal and scared not to."

The Big Three were eyetalking like hell. Suddenly McDade jumped up and began spaziering, slicing a path from the door to the window and back.

"Mo, we got a time problem here. When did this Carol Crabtree visit Clay the first time?"

"The perfect question," Finn said. "The answer is, *too soon.* Obviously she went to demand something from Crabtree. But not to kill Three-Finger Thorp—nobody knew about Thorp. Not to kill Dwight Weems the druggie—he was an innocent bystander."

"Which brings us back to Franklin Delano Hollowell," Steve said.

The phone rang as if punctuating his words. The call lasted only a few seconds. "Authentic," Patterson said as he hung up. "The real real Avengers wrote the note about the second interview. Not the real fake Avengers or the fake real Avengers."

Harry chimed in. "We got real Avengers who kill people and write real notes. We got copycats who kill people and write fake notes. We got copycats who send *real* Avenger notes. With Paul Pitts we got an Avenger kill but a copycat note. Or something."

"More or less," Kim gibed.

Steve said, "What we got is Avengers taking credit for some things they did, not taking credit for others, and sometimes taking credit for what they didn't do. Why?"

Elmo Finn smiled. "To make us ask why."

Finn's answer seemed to satisfy everyone and the meeting soon fragmented. I was surprised they hadn't pressured me harder to be the guinea pig. Then Elmo Finn said, "Let's get a drink," and he walked me down the private steps and out the private door and three short blocks to the Blue Steel Bar and Grill, where a lot of off-duty cops were noisily getting plowed. And where a certain photograph of Three-Finger Thorp graced the urinal wall.

We took a corner booth. I got several waves from cops I didn't recognize. *Crime and Punishment* was a big hit among the thin blue line. The saloon was fragrant with tobacco, and I lit a cigarette without asking Finn's permission. I was close to two packs a day now.

"You ever smoke?"

"Quit years ago and I've missed it every day since. I love it when other people do."

I took an ostentatious drag and exhaled a cloud.

He said, "Joe, we need you, we can protect you. And catch these psychopaths once and for all."

"Will you be involved?"

He nodded.

"This ain't Vietnam, Elmo. Can't leave the ace of spades in their mouth."

He was dead still but the gray eyes weren't. A touch of red colored the Apache cheekbones.

"What do you want me to do?"

"Whatever they say. And carry a small concealed device."

"How small? The ones on TV—"

"I'm borrowing one."

"From Langley, Virginia."

"State of the art."

"Elmo, what's that agency hangout near Langley? Beer joint, chili dogs, football on TV? Very campy place, all the spooks loved it."

"You're testing me?"

I nodded to the gray eyes.

"The Vienna Inn. Before David Wise's book exposed it."

"Okay. Okay. Maybe the stories about you *are* true."

"Résumé changes each month."

I forced a slight smile.

"Joe, are you afraid? That's logical. Or are you dragging your feet hoping that Avengers will somehow get to Boogie Brown before we get to them?"

I lit another cigarette and the icefire swept through me in a rush, then coiled in my gut like a predator. Malignant. Permanent. I took several strong puffs and coaxed a tiny bloom of serenity from the nicotine. I blew out a long stream of smoke.

"Yes, I hope they kill Boogie Brown. Of course I do." I looked squarely into Finn's hard face. "You know what I mean."

Again a shimmering in the eyes. I couldn't read it but I could feel it.

At length he said, "My fiancée was murdered like your children were murdered. Savagely, senselessly. Then the killer was terminated and I felt good about it, and still do. So I know how you feel, Joe."

Terminated. Company patois. Spookspeak.

"You killed him?"

Elmo Finn exhaled a long breath. "I found him. He tried to get away. But failed."

"So you did kill him. You got your revenge."

"He would have killed me, Joe. He tried to. It was almost a . . . duel."

"How did you find him before the cops?"

"The cops were there. They saw it."

"Were you prosecuted?"

"No."

"I heard that you and Graves . . . *medieval* was the word. Medieval." I lit a fresh cigarette from the butt and my hand was steady. "I saw you in action, I can believe it."

"Joe, some of the stories about me . . . I don't correct them very often. Mythology's good for business."

He had explained everything and nothing.

"Joe, the system will retry Boogie Brown—prosecute him, convict him, execute him. Bucky Webb's panting for another shot. The first jury was eleven to one *for* a first-degree conviction. Isaacson's arguments *failed*. Only Pitts held out, and we know why."

"You're something, Finn. *Do as I say, not as I do.*"

"In my case the cops wouldn't investigate."

"So you—"

"So I was glad when he was terminated. I thought justice was done."

"That's what your day in September means."

He looked at me from far away.

"Will you ever get over it?" I asked.

"No."

"Neither will I. I have this feeling inside, like burning and freezing at the same time . . . sometimes I go out to the cemetery and just lie on the grass, right next to Connie and the kids, in the exact place I'll be buried someday, and talk to the gravestones. Talk to *them*, really. We're all together except I'm on top of the ground and they're underneath. One really bad day I left a note on my desk and went out there to blow my head off—they would have found me right there on my own gravesite, my final resting place, just dig the hole and drop me in. Crazy."

"We all do crazy things, Joe. 'Everyone can master a grief but he that has it.' "

I put the cigarettes and lighter in my pocket. "How will you set it up? Bug my phones, bug my car, stick this magic CIA transmitter up my ass?"

"Won't be that bad. We won't—"

"No transmitter on my body, anywhere! They'll find it."

"It won't be detected. You have a handgun?"

"No. I should have bought a Bull*dog* instead of that Bull*pup* shotgun."

"The Ruger?"

"Charter Arms," I said.

Elmo Finn seemed confused. "I never could keep them all straight. How about a five-shot revolver, compact?"

"What if they search me?"

"You can explain it. He brought a gun to your house."

"What about the transmitter?"

"They won't find it."

"*They won't find it.*" I lit another cigarette. "When do you want to install the bugs?"

"You may consider them installed."

"*Installed—you've already bugged me?*"

"Thought Avengers might call you."

"Avengers *did* call me! The woman!"

"We missed it. You took the call at Janie's phone."

"Did you bug my house? You bugged my house! So when Elly and I are messing around, all you voyeurs at Homicide are getting off!"

"Just a phone tap, Joe. Not the house. Otherwise we'd have heard the famous interview."

" 'We're all on the same side!' No wonder cops have a bad name!"

" 'To do a great right, do a little wrong.' Lots of bugging, Joe. Not just you."

I threw the cigarette on the floor and stomped it violently. "Who? Ned and Julia? Juanita Daley? John Ewell talking to poor brain-dead Gwen? Burl Devine talking to the black helicopters? Duane Hickman ordering pepperoni and sausage? Who the hell else? Good company, is that what you're saying, I'm in good—"

"Joe." Finn got to his feet. "You don't let us follow you, we'll follow you anyway. In or out?"

"Of course!" I shouted. "In!"

A commotion came from the bar as a news bulletin flashed on TV. Finn and I strained to listen.

"... explosion at Central Prison ... criminal defense attorney Marvin Isaacson and Death Row inmate Franklin Delano Hollowell ... lawyer-client conference ..."

I looked around but Elmo Finn was gone.

FORTY-FOUR

❏   ❏   ❏

I SCRAMBLED TO a pay phone and called Elly. She had just returned to her office after showing houses to a dizzy boomer couple.

"Are you sitting down?"

"I'm almost lying down. The buyers from hell."

"You were right. Our phone's been bugged from the beginning."

"We're all on the same side, we're all on the same side—"

"I know. You were right."

"Always chasing the wrong people. Did they hear . . . you know."

My pulse was throbbing in my temple. "They probably have circle jerks playing the tapes. I'm sure we're bugged right now. Hello, Elmo, hello, Steve, fuck you. Turn on the TV—there's been some kind of explosion at Central Prison—Hollowell and Isaacson were involved."

"Both of them?"

"Apparently. We'll talk later."

"Into the fucking microphones."

I walked around aimlessly, took a cab for a few blocks, got out, doubled back, took another cab. If an undercover cop was following me, he was damn good. I saw nothing, and I was looking.

I went into an unfamiliar bar that was almost deserted and

ordered a double vodka. I asked the bartender to switch the TV from *Gilligan's Island* to Channel Nine's *Special Report*. We watched for a while. Another double vodka.

He said, "How they do it? Get Isaacson and Hollowell in the same room and blow 'em up? Always got everybody lookin' the wrong way."

I said something noncommittal, sure that he had recognized me.

"That Boogie Brown must be sweatin' turds. Bet he's next."

I tossed him a good tip and headed back to my car. It was Group night. I wanted to take Ned's place as Crossing Guard, but when I drove up, John Ewell was already in position. He had just come from the hospital.

"The doctors say pull the plug, Joe, but I feel something when I hold her hand. Today when I told her about Isaacson getting blown up, I felt something. She knows, Joe. She understands."

"Fuck the doctors, John. They're just like cops, all they want to do is close the file. Fuck 'em."

"Fuck 'em! Fuck 'em! Joe, I'm glad about Isaacson. You should see him in court—it's just a game."

"Oh I know, I know. And Juanita knows."

"Of course, Joe, I'm sorry. You know better than anybody. And Juanita knows. I'm sorry, Joe."

"Not better. The same. We all know the same, John."

He embraced me awkwardly. Then people began arriving and we were busy escorting them in. When Juanita drove up John and I ran to her. She was wearing the same white gown she had worn to the aborted execution.

She embraced both of us at once. She said, "I was snappin' beans this afternoon when I heard about Hollowell, the bulletin came on, and oh, how somethin' lifted off my heart. Somethin' I've been carryin' for twelve years. I didn't know it was so heavy, I can just float now."

The three of us stood together for a long time, occasionally whispering something. Finally we went in. We were crying.

I said to Juanita, "I'm glad Harry's back on the reservation. What was that all about?"

"Something's still not right, Joe. Doesn't make sense, suspended, unsuspended. They didn't explain nothin'. I don't trust that Elmo Finn."

Deirdre lost control earlier than usual. Everyone wanted to reminisce about Ned, and we told stories about the eyepatch, the nighttime trolling down mean streets, the Crossing-Guard service so no one would become a victim *going* to Victims. Almost everyone was crying now. Someone brought up the explosion at Central Prison, and Juanita took over and joyously told them she could float now. She wondered if she would still wake up at four-fifteen every morning.

Deirdre tried to spin us back into the pop-psych cocoon. *Outlets, feelings, closure.* One of the mousy women who never spoke whirled on her. "Have you ever been raped? Have you ever had a loved one slaughtered? Have you? *Have you?*" Deirdre turned crimson. "Then shut up! This is closure for Juanita, you pisswilly! The animal who killed her daughter is dead!"

We Savages were stunned for a moment, then roared and applauded. Deirdre ran out, the Other-Cheekers soon followed and we knew the Victims Support Group had just closed, never to reopen. So the Savages danced out of the dank chlorine-smelling Y and pushed a lot of tables together in the bar across the street, and hugged and cried and railed against pisswillies, and drank innumerable toasts to closure—as encountered this very day by attorney Marvin Isaacson and Franklin Delano Hollowell.

FORTY-FIVE

❑   ❑   ❑

HE CHANGES THE *license plate on the hatchback and drives to the trailer park, making two evasive detours. He knows this is the biggest risk yet. He parks the car and walks unhurriedly along the dusty road toward Number 71. A white man in his fifties is spray-painting cinder-block halves which he is using to line the perimeter of his trailer plot. Tiny boundaries of a tiny life; the Avenger stifles a twinge.*

"How you doin', buddy," the painter says cheerfully.

The Avenger nods stiffly. "Can't complain."

"Who'd listen!"

The Avenger smiles as he walks past. Before he can knock at Number 71, the door opens.

"Oops! Who you?" She peers at his face. "Who you? Who you?"

"I have something for you," he says quietly. "Let me in."

"Who you . . . where—"

He wedges past her and goes to the stained dinette table where he takes a seat in one of the mismatched chairs. He snaps on the radio and turns the volume up high. For a moment she stands motionless at the door, the combativeness of her creased face betrayed by anxious eyes. Then she slowly crosses to the table and sits down. They lean toward each other to whisper under the noise.

"You're older than the women," Beulah Crabtree mutters

raspily, staring intently at his face. "It's the gray hair. Don't see your kind around here."

"Shut up. Have the police been here?"

"What? Louder."

"Have the police been here?"

"The police?"

"Have they?"

"They might of dropped by. I know some police."

"What did you tell them?"

"Nothin'. I don't tell police nothin'. Now you answer me somethin'. Where's my money? Where's Clay's deal?"

He reaches inside his coat and produces a bulky envelope. He counts out fifty hundred-dollar bills and pushes them across the table. "You did a good job. How did the guard get hurt?"

She cackles. "Two with one blow, two with one blow. Ought to be worth more." With a plastic toothpick she stabs a half-smoked cigarette out of a plastic ashtray and lights it. "The guard's okay."

"Did you pay him?"

"He sat right where you're sittin' now."

"We've decided to pay you a bonus."

"How much?"

"Double."

"Double double, toil and trouble." She raps her bony knuckles against the linoleum tabletop. "We've earned it."

"How many times have the cops been here?"

"Who's countin'?" She cackles so piercingly that he winces despite the radio. "Three or four. They sit out there, unmarked car, think they're invisible."

"Tell Clay to stay cool. Don't take any deals they might offer."

"Don't you worry about Clay, he ain't takin' no deals from no cops. When do I get the bonus?"

"Don't you take any deals either, Beulah."

They talk for a few more minutes. Then he leaves and re-traces his steps to the hatchback. The spray-painter is sprawled on a folding lounge chair drinking beer. A younger man, sitting on the ground with his back against the trailer, is drinking with him. The Avenger nods and makes a small wave.

"Miller time!" the painter says.

"Always," the Avenger responds. He is not far from the hatchback. He gets in and yanks off the gray wig. He starts the engine and checks the rearview mirror. Both men are staring at him.

Later as they lie naked she makes him retell the story.

"Are you sure he saw you when you first walked by?"

"Yes, goddamnit. He was painting cinder blocks. He said something, looked right at me."

"And when you left there were two of them?"

"I just walked past them."

"And you took off the wig inside the car or as you were getting in?"

"Inside, goddamnit."

"And they were looking at you?"

"Yes, I think so. Yes."

"Are you sure they could see you?"

"Yes, goddamnit, I think they could see me."

She rolls away from him so they are no longer touching.

"Details," she says mockingly. "Details always mattered before."

"Talk about details, you can't even find the fucking farmer."

"I'll find him."

"You'll find him."

"But if someone hadn't decided to direct traffic in the woods one stupid night, I wouldn't have to find him. How's that for a detail?"

"Hypnosis won't work—he's an alcoholic. His memory is totally fried."

"Maybe they'll get him drunk again."

He rolls against her. "Did you look at the ventilation ducts?"

"I could barely find them. They look the same. Nothing's wrong."

"They're not working the same, the camouflage looks different. Couldn't you see that?"

"No. You're the one who's seeing things." Again she eases away from him. "But I'm the one hearing things. Like helicopters."

"The foliage and stuff look disturbed."

"An animal. The wind. You ought to worry about something real—like helicopters. Black helicopters."

He presses against her again and this time she turns into him.

"You seem to want to fuck me," she says, raking his penis with her nails.

"Yes," he groans.

"You have to earn it. Detail work."

FORTY-SIX

❏　❏　❏

ELMO FINN AND George Graves were seen everywhere: at the county courthouse where Graves camped for days; at the National Guard Armory where Finn conferred with the adjutant general; at Burl Devine's gun shop and Ned Cromartie's old accounting firm and Juanita Daley's beauty parlor; at tony restaurants where Finn jotted down calories with Detective Second Grade Kimberly Whitten, who couldn't have hidden one gun, let alone three, in her micro-minis; at Presbyterian Hospital where John Ewell still felt an "awareness" in the cold hand of his brain-dead fiancée while the physicians rolled their eyes; at the *Herald* where Fletcher bowed and scraped and brought forth a column gushing over Elmo Finn, and even made something of George Graves.

I called Fletcher. "Nice column, Wes. The great Finn obviously impressed you."

"Fuck you," Fletcher barked. Like most cupcake columnists, he loved imitating the old-time hardass newshounds.

"Okay, fuck me, I still liked your column."

"He was prowling through the morgue, Joe. Governor called, we had to give him the run of the place."

"What was he looking for?"

"Who the hell knows—some of it wasn't even on microfilm."

"You think he's onto something?"

233

"Hell no. Chasing his tail."

"Did you know Finn and Graves were part of the Phoenix Program? Assassins."

"Killers hunting killers—I should have used it."

"That's *our* angle, Wes. But I'd like permission to quote from your column on the show. Maybe have you on soon."

"Sure, Joe, sure. Quote your ass off. I ain't all that telegenic."

"Telegenic is out. *Real* is in."

"I ain't nothin' if not real," the print journalist cooed like a sycophant. Television was a plug-in drug on both sides of the screen.

While I was parrying with Fletcher, Homicide was in turmoil. None of the cops ever told me, but George Graves gave me the story later, when it was all over. The murder police were in Patterson's office, pondering the note Juanita Daley had received.

To Juanita Daley:

Case closed. Observe strict silence. Live in peace.

Avengers

Why *Live in peace*, the cops wondered? A different tone. Were Avengers closing up shop?

As their discussion continued, a uniform came in with the mail. Patterson rifled through it, then handed an envelope to Steve, who glanced at it and continued theorizing. Finally, almost absentmindedly, Steve opened it. Suddenly he went pale and sank heavily into a chair, something slipping from his fingers. Elmo Finn got to him first. Face up on the floor lay a photograph of Steve's daughter Cassie. It bore a stick-on label: *next*.

"They've threatened Steve's daughter," Finn said, handing the photograph to Patterson.

Steve scrambled up and grabbed a phone. "Get two uniforms to Madison High School, pick up Cassie McDade whatever class she's in, bring her here. And pick up my wife at home, bring her here. Now!" He clicked off and dialed another number. "Rachel, they've threatened Cassie. Listen to me, don't talk! We're picking her up. And you. Watch for the officer." He hung up breathlessly.

Elmo Finn asked, "Is this the way Cassie labels things? *Mug, badge*? Same kind of label?"

"Yes." It came out in a whisper.

A pall descended on the lamplit office of Homicide Commander Avery Patterson. Later, when George Graves and I compared notes, we realized that at the same time Steve was dispatching squad cars to safeguard his family, a black taxi driver was entering Channel Nine's reception area and flashing a plain envelope: '*Joe Colby—Immediate Attention.*' He seemed agitated and insisted on waiting for an answer. The alarmed receptionist rushed straight into my office and nervously thrust the envelope into my hand. I ripped it open. Inside was a typed note: '*Now. Your taxi is waiting.*'

Without a word I rose, yanked my blazer off the back of the chair and half-trotted to the front. The taxi driver was already outside behind the wheel. I wondered if the transmitter was working, if the undercover team that I had never sensed nor seen was really in place, if choppers and commandos and Elmo Finn would vault into action.

I got into the back seat and the cabbie wheeled out of the semicircular drive, headed for the expressway. I looked around but could see no car, no van, no human being reacting to what was happening. "You'll never know we're there," Elmo Finn had said.

The taxi shot up the ramp onto the expressway. The driver turned to look at me; an inscrutable black face I had never seen. He was perspiring.

"I'm dropping you at Copper Creek Mall, main entrance. You're supposed to go straight to the food court, turn right and go to the men's room. Change into these clothes." He tossed a bulging grocery bag into the back seat. "You're supposed to take off everything you're wearing, everything out of your pockets, your belt, everything, and put it in the trash can. You have eight minutes. Come back to where I dropped you, I'll pick you up. You can recognize this cab—two forty-nine. Number's on the door. Two forty-nine. Get in fast. You got it? You look older than you do on television."

"I am older than I am on television."

"I don't like this but I have to do it. No hard feelings."

"No. No hard feelings. What's your name?"

He hesitated. "James." He was as nervous as I was.

I kept looking for an undercover vehicle—a drab sedan keeping its distance, a phone company truck, a chopper in the sky. Nothing.

We reached the mall quickly. In the empty men's room I went into a handicapped stall, stripped naked, then put on the underwear, sweatsuit, socks and running shoes from the bag. Everything was too large. The transmitter was a brass button on the sleeve of my blazer. Finn's instructions had covered this contingency. I was to rip off the button and carry it in my hand or shoe, then discard it when I reached the final location. The cavalry would have me pinpointed. I ripped it off and wedged it into my shoe, then stuffed my clothes into the trash can. I slipped the revolver into my shorts and secured it with the drawstring of the sweatpants. The weight pulled the sweats down and I had to retie them. Amazingly, no one came in. The last item was a slouch hat. I jammed it on my head and strolled briskly back to the entrance, holding the revolver against my leg.

Number 249 rolled up immediately and I jumped in. As we sped away I looked for pursuers. Nothing.

"Where to now, James?"

He said nothing.

"You want to be on TV? Take me back to Channel Nine right now and we'll do an interview. Right now. You'll be famous, the police will protect you."

Still no response.

"You can say I had a gun, I forced you. I do have a gun."

Hesitantly, James said, "Mr. Colby, they showed me a picture of my son."

"You're missing the point here, James, big time. Police are going to be looking for me. Hundreds of police. Which means they're looking for you, too."

James drove on as if I hadn't said a word.

"Hundreds of police, James."

"Mr. Colby. With all due respect, shut the fuck up. I'm playin' the hand I was dealt."

He drove onto the circumferential, took an immediate exit and got back on in the opposite direction, drove for five minutes, reversed again, then veered onto the Interstate and finally exited at a truck stop just off the highway.

As we came to a stop, James said, "Stand at the big wall map inside. Someone will come for you."

He zoomed away and I was stranded. My eyes flicked everywhere. No cavalry. Nothing.

I adjusted the gun and pushed through the double glass doors and went across to the huge glass-enclosed road map on the wall between Men and Women. From the *You Are Here* arrow there were red and blue lines radiating everywhere. Lines of escape.

For nearly an hour I loitered, pretending to study the map. Motorists and truckers came and went. Children found the *You Are Here* arrow and squealed to their parents. When the cafeteria line thinned I hurried in to buy a cup of coffee. After another half hour I sat down on a narrow ledge not too far from the map. Before long a truck driver going to the cafeteria stumbled and jostled me slightly. Apologizing quickly, he patted my shoulder and moved on. I recognized the signal; it was Graves, though I didn't recognize *him*. After a few minutes I went into the men's room where he was waiting. He still looked like a stranger. Even his eyes were a different color.

"We think it's a dud," he said. "But call Elly and have her pick you up, just in case someone's watching."

"Elly had buyers today, she's unreachable."

"Call Janie."

"Okay. Where were you guys?"

"Later." Then he was gone.

Janie unhesitatingly agreed to pick me up. I had the feeling she was expecting me to call. Twenty minutes later I climbed into her convertible.

"Logan's on location," she said.

"Where? What's happening?" My heart raced.

"Some farmer got shot. Or shot at. I didn't quite get it."

"A farmer? I should be on this story."

"Mr. Finn called from an airplane. He said you were busy."

FORTY-SEVEN

❏   ❏   ❏

ELMO FINN WORKED the cab driver hard but his story held up. The day before, a woman—it sounded like a woman—had called his dispatcher and scheduled James to drive her to the airport the next day. She gave her name as Diana Rigg. He picked her up at a downtown hotel and thought it curious that she had no luggage. But every passenger was curious these days.

Diana Rigg said, "I asked for you specifically, James. You were so courteous the last time."

He didn't remember the last time but the compliment pleased him.

A few minutes into the trip she tossed something onto the front seat. He picked it up and found himself staring at a photograph of his ten-year-old son. He was puzzled, then with a start realized he had never seen the picture before. He twisted to look at his passenger, who was pointing a small black pistol at his face.

"Drive," she said. She explained what he must do to protect his son—deliver an envelope to Joe Colby at Channel Nine, drive him to Copper Creek Mall, wait while he changed clothes, drive evasively to a truck stop off the Interstate, deposit Colby, disappear. She made him recite the details three times as he drove randomly. Then, at a traffic light, she bolted from the cab and vanished among the pedestrians. Immediately he drove to Channel Nine and followed orders.

Elmo Finn bristled at the woman's alias. Diana Rigg was the actress who had played sultry Emma Peel in *The Avengers*, a sixties' British TV series. According to Graves, Finn said, "It's the endgame," and of course it was, but Graves always made Finn sound prescient. James described this Diana Rigg as black, forty or so, with a sharp nasal voice.

The cops questioned me briefly and complimented me on keeping the transmitter functioning.

"Where's your wallet, Joe?" Steve asked.

"Jesus! In the fucking trash can."

"We got it. And your watch and keys."

"Jesus. I was spacier than I thought. Did you guys scare them off? They must have seen you."

"They didn't see us," Elmo Finn said. "Maybe it was a test."

"A test? All that trouble for a test?"

"They take pains, Joe. Which is why they're still at large."

"So now what? Same plan? The invisible cavalry tracks me night and day and I get the button sewn back on?"

"We can put it under a skin graft."

"Great. Why not in a tooth?"

"Can do."

"Jesus. I'll stick with the button. Elly can sew it back on."

Finn said, "They suspected a transmitting device. That's why they made you change clothes."

"No shit. Elmo, did you give Wes Fletcher an exclusive interview?"

"No."

"His column *sounded* like it."

"No."

"Did you—"

"No."

"Fine. Maybe we'll do a show on how you guys fucked up today while I'm risking—"

"Get out of here, Joe," Steve McDade whispered coldly. His words snapped like a whip. I pulled the high-tech button from my shoe, set it spinning on Patterson's cherry desk and strode out. No one said a word.

I stopped by the station but Logan and Janie weren't there. I went to buy vodka and ice and cigarettes and then to meet Elly. She jumped up when I came in.

"Logan called," she said hoarsely.

"Fuck Logan."

"Did you ever see them?"

"Not until I saw Graves at the truck stop. But I blew up and stormed out of headquarters."

"First thought best thought."

I poured vodka. "Drink this. Toast your spectacular failure."

"I got as close as I could."

"I had half the goddamn police force running up and down the Interstate and you can't get to a fucking hayseed."

"Nobody saw me."

"You hope."

"Of course if you hadn't let the son of a bitch see *you*—"

"Shut up."

"Fuck you." She finished her vodka and poured more. We drank silently until she said, "Joe, let's stop this, let's find the center. We've got to get back on the same side. What's done is done. The question is, what do Avengers do now? To get Boogie Brown?"

"I don't know! I don't know! We've hit four people inside Central Prison and can't figure out how to do one little nigger in the city jail."

"Maybe Clay Crabtree knows a prisoner. Or Beulah. You want to talk to Beulah?"

"Maybe. But we can't visit the trailer again."

"No. Absolutely not."

"Not enough wigs in the world."

She nestled against me. "Two wigs was brilliant. The great Finn must be in a spin. You like my poetry? What's his latest theory anyway?"

"He's running in circles. They all are. Steve's frantic about his daughter."

Elly packed our glasses with crushed ice and filled them with vodka. "Let's stay here tonight and get drunk and fuck."

"First thought best thought."

She rolled against me on the quilted mattress. "The best part is, only Boogie is left. Only Boogie."

"Are you going to keep visiting that apartment on your anniversary? Can you let it go now?"

"I won't know until the day comes. I think so."

I pulled her closer. "I never asked you something."

"What? Ask me. He's dead now."

"He put on a condom before he raped you. Did you give it to him?"

"Did I give it to him? Did I give him the condom? No. But he made me put it on."

"I thought you talked him into it because of AIDS."

"AIDS had nothing to do with it. DNA. The rapists wear condoms so the cops can't trace them."

"Dickprints."

"Rubber gloves for fingerprints and rubbers for dickprints."

"So you put it on him."

"Yes. Don't you want to know if it turned me on?"

"Yes."

"I hated it but my body . . . responded. Partially. Afterwards I hated my body. I couldn't have sex for two years."

"He's dead now, Elly. You can let go."

"I wish I could've cut off his dick and made him eat it."

We kept drinking. She said, "Did you hear a noise?"

"Yes. Generator."

She nodded uncertainly. "Smell something?"

"Nothing unusual."

"So, you finally asked your big question. Did I enjoy it? So typically male. Fuck you."

"You can ask me a big question. So typically female, misunderstanding everything."

She turned on her side and propped herself up. "I do have a question. Did you mean to shoot the little boy?"

"Of course. Boogie Brown's son. As they do unto you."

"Why'd you pretend it was an accident?"

"I thought it might bother you."

"You *thought*. First thought worst thought." She reached for the bottle and filled her glass.

She said, "After Boogie, no more, no Day of Vengeance. Just Costa Rica."

"Just Costa Rica."

"They'll go crazy when it all stops."

"They'll search around the world."

"And never find us."

She sat up and sniffed the air. "I do smell something, Joe."

"The ventilation. I *knew* something had happened to it."

"Maybe it's clogged. Go check."

"It's too dark."

"You said you could come and go blindfolded."

"Blindfold me and I'll come."

"Go fix the pipes and come back naked."

I unbolted the door, opened it silently and stepped outside. I listened to the darkness; nothing. As I turned to close the door, Elmo Finn took me from behind with a vicious twisting headlock. I tried to yell but couldn't. I tumbled into unconsciousness as McDade and Patterson flashed by low and fast with guns in their hands. If Elly screamed, I didn't hear it.

EPILOGUE

❑   ❑   ❑

by George Graves

BY THE TIME it was finally over, and the murderous Avengers, Joe Colby and Elly Briggs, had been captured and locked
away, the reward fund had grown to three hundred fifty thousand dollars. Everyone agreed that it should go to Elmo Finn.
He had charged no fee for his services, working for the reward
only, and he had solved the perplexing case. Everyone agreed,
that is, except Elmo Finn, a purist and a perfectionist who
takes his ethics seriously, with a good deal of starch. Thus,
while the others sat dumbfounded, I was merely exasperated
as my stubborn friend looked across the table at the governor
and said, "Sir, they killed nine people after I got here, and if
Elly Briggs were a better shot, it would've been ten."

I was exasperated because Elmo was being too hard on himself, and because we had made plans for some of the money.
We were going to buy new Zings and Great Big Berthas, treat
ourselves to first-class seats on the Concorde and, at long last,
take the grand tour of the holy lands of St. Andrews and Car-
noustie and Troon. We owed it to ourselves, I insinuated re-
lentlessly, but I knew it was a lost cause. Elmo Finn would
not be satisfied until he had dissected every move we made
and every move we didn't make, cursed every failure, chased
after every loose end. "If we learn by our mistakes," he

groused, "I ought to be a goddamn genius by now." He refused to accept the reward.

That was Elmo Finn, the purist. Elmo Finn, the perfectionist, refused to accept the fact that no one could find the goldsmith. He came up with three or four schemes to track him down, but Captain Patterson vetoed them all. The homicide commander's budget was already in shreds, and he pointed out, gently but firmly, that we *had* found the gunsmith who made the suppressor and the brasscatcher; we *had* found the backwoods militiaman and would-be terrorist who taught Colby how to build a bomb; we *had* found the guard at Central Prison who slipped the radio-bomb through Inspection; we *had* found the soulless Beulah Crabtree, cowering in a bus station in Spokane. Elmo, the insistent perfectionist, argued that no matter what we *had* found, it was painful (to him) that we had *not* found the goldsmith who made the fake detective shields that lulled two people to their deaths, and therefore the case was incomplete. But Captain Patterson stood firm. He had everything the prosecutors needed—the fake shields themselves, and the George Orwell mask, and the license plates and typewriters and wigs and knives and guns and other instruments of vengeance seized from the bomb shelter that Joe Colby's father had built in the fifties, when President Eisenhower told Americans to build them.

What bothered Elmo more than anything, although it shouldn't have, was failing to see the connection that morning at Channel Nine, when Logan Murphy showed off his honorary gold shield in its Plexiglas case: *Friend of the Police.* "I've got one too," Colby had bragged, a brazen allusion to the very model which his anonymous artisan had used to fashion two perfect copies. "Passports to murder," Logan Murphy called them in his prime-time editorial on Channel Nine, canceling *Crime and Punishment* and apologizing to the citizenry at large.

If the goldsmith was the loose end, Elly Briggs, Joe Colby's mad "Countess," was the missing link. We never knew that Franklin Delano Hollowell had raped and nearly killed her. All we knew about the female Avenger(s) was what the behavioral scientists told us—that she harbored an overpowering, deeply personal motive, probably as a result of a life-altering trauma. Murderers are 90 percent male, and serial murderers even more so. Elly Briggs, therefore, was a rare, rare case, and she eluded us until the end.

While Elmo admonished himself for "damn fool mistakes," the other detectives celebrated what they saw as his success in finally putting down the two homicidal demons. And they kept badgering him for details—when did he begin to see it, what were the important clues, what led him at last to Colby's cave? Finally, Patterson suggested a "sitdown" to review the whole case in detail. His unspoken motive, I'm sure, was to provide therapy for Elmo, on the theory that getting him to talk might improve his dark mood. Thus it came to pass that, one rainy night, eight of us convened in Patterson's comfortable office, where flat boxes of Haitian art leaned against the walls and a fine bar had been laid along the window ledge. The only outsider was Juanita Daley Covington, Harry's bright and shining bride, and she was an insider now. I swore everyone to secrecy—I wanted to save the best stuff for my video.

We fixed drinks and settled into the soft gray leather. A few of the detectives thumbed their notebooks. Elmo stood near the window ledge, looking only slightly ill at ease, which was an improvement over recent days. When everything was quiet, Commander Patterson leaned back in his big judge's chair and spread his hands. "Mo," he said, "I guess the agenda is, what did you know and when did you know it? All of us can see some of the pieces, but you're the only one who can see the whole thing."

"And I was on the wrong side of the tapestry," Elmo shot back. My heart rate accelerated; surely Elmo wouldn't demean himself further before his fellow detectives. He took a healthy sip of bourbon, set the glass down and leaned on the window ledge.

"It started thirteen years ago, when Franklin Delano Hollowell raped Elly Briggs for six hours in her own bedroom. He tried to kill her—*would* have killed her if he hadn't been spooked by a slamming door. She was completely traumatized—she couldn't report it, couldn't seek therapy, couldn't talk to anyone about it. All she could do was brood, and make sketches of Hollowell's tattoos, and nurse fantasies of revenge. Then, about a year later, Franklin Hollowell assaulted Juanita's daughter Debbie, a terrible, terrible tragedy"—I peeked at Juanita, who was stone-faced, with a tight grip on Harry's hand—"but this time Harry put him down. Elly Briggs recognized Hollowell's picture in the paper and attended the trial every day, like a secret accuser. Hollowell was convicted and sentenced to death, and Elly Briggs thought her nightmare was over. But another nightmare was beginning, the appeals process, and through the years, Juanita, she's been agonizing along with you, secretly, over every new appeal, every stay of execution. Each year, she felt compelled to drive by her old house on the day she referred to as her anniversary. She'd park and just sit there for hours, reliving it like a penance. And as Isaacson and Lodge kept blocking the execution, they became as guilty in her mind as Hollowell himself. They were allies of a rapist and murderer, not allies of justice."

Juanita, still gripping Harry's hand, was nodding grimly. Elmo finished his bourbon and poured another, and I lit a cigarette, one of the six Marlboros I rationed myself daily. I had saved three for tonight.

"The years pass, the bitterness festers. But then she meets Joe Colby, love at first boink, and when Colby's wife dies of cancer, Elly Briggs sees a chance to start over. A new love, a new life. She even stops drawing the tattoos. But before the new life can begin, Boogie Brown destroys it by murdering Colby's children. After Boogie's mistrial, Colby is blind with rage, and his fury rekindles hers. The relationship becomes a partnership of hate. Their thirst for revenge consumes them, literally possesses them, like a demon. Colby calls it the ice-fire—part rage, part helplessness, part bloodlust. I've heard other victims say the same thing." He gazed off for a moment, then said softly, "I have felt it myself."

"We have too, Mo," Captain Patterson said, pointing to the wall: We Work for God. "In our way." The other detectives nodded silently, and my skin tingled, not from the bourbon.

Elmo seemed more comfortable now as he settled into the details. "So, down in that hole, they fan each other's flames. Before long, revenge against Hollowell and Boogie Brown isn't enough—they have to make Isaacson and Lodge feel the icefire, too. So Colby invents the Avengers."

"The Big Lie," Steve McDade mused. Next to Elmo, Steve had been the most self-critical of the detectives.

"It was like hiding something in plain view," Patterson said. "They were hiding right in front of us all the time."

For an instant, Elmo looked pained, his "damn fool mistakes" registering openly on his face. He took more bourbon, then said, "That was Colby's biggest worry—diverting suspicion. He agonized over it, he devised elaborate scenarios. Then came his great epiphany: First thought best thought. Randomness as a diversionary tactic."

"I don't understand," Kim Whitten said, frowning. "They just did stuff on a whim or whatever?"

"The whim was part of the plan. For example, take the kid who dropped the cemetery urn off the overpass. Duane Hickman. His murder was supposed to be a random killing to throw us off. Colby had listed all his diversionary targets—his red herrings—on three-by-five cards, and he just threw them up in the air. Hickman landed on top. He should have picked another one—Hickman wasn't even a pink herring. He was connected to Isaacson, he was connected to the Victims Group. But Colby's full of himself now, he's already gotten away with three murders, he's transfixed by *first thought best thought*—so he goes ahead with Hickman anyway. Elly Briggs berated him about it: 'First thought worst thought' "

"How do you know all this?" Harry Covington asked.

"He wrote it down."

In the desk drawers of Colby's bomb shelter, we found seven hundred typewritten pages—diary, confession, manifesto. Apparently, they planned to mail it to Elmo as they vanished to Costa Rica. That's most of what precedes this epilogue—Colby's pages—as edited and expanded and supplemented by Yours Truly. Hacking through Colby's preachy, delusional ramblings was hard going, like visiting an asylum day after day, but I kept slashing to get to the heart of the story. I invented nothing, not even the "Avenger" chapters (mere dramatizations taken from Colby's narrative), not even the sex scenes (Colby apparently recorded every erection). There was no need to invent—the real thing was dramatic and monstrous enough.

"How did they learn about weapons and explosives and all the technical stuff?" asked Tad Sullivan, the young detective who had infiltrated Colby's Victims Support Group. "They never showed up on any of the FBI lists."

Sullivan had struck another nerve, but Elmo pushed on. "After the funerals, when everyone thought Colby was traveling, *healing*, he was actually in a survivalist camp learning how to kill, how to create a false identity, how to build a bomb. He bought the weapons from the survivalist underground. Getting me to help them buy a shotgun was just another red herring—they were already Bonnie and Clyde. They bought the white van and the hatchback for cash. They stole license plates. They could modify the van with roof racks for skis and bicycles, chrome strips, lettering, magnetized panels. They perfected several disguises, including Colby as a woman and Elly Briggs as a black. They stockpiled the bomb shelter with enough food for a year. They camouflaged the old barn for the vehicles—we couldn't even see it from the air. They surreptitiously shot the long-lens photographs that they put in the mailings—including Cassie McDade and Julia Cromartie and Colby's mother and the cabdriver's son and Elly Briggs herself. They rehearsed everything, over and over and over and over."

Elmo paused for more bourbon, then turned to the window and looked out at the rain. We were quiet for a long time. Everyone seemed shaken by Elmo's recital of the cold meticulousness of death.

"Was it Burl's camp?" Kim asked finally.

"Burl helped me find it. Still some cop left in him."

"Four-Ball Burl," Harry said brightly. "Give him a gold shield, Cap! Friend of the Police! Friend of the Po-lice!"

"With a nutbeam on it!"

We eagerly took a break and bustled around the bar on the ledge. A few Burl Devine stories were told, and Patterson brought over fresh Texas fifths of Absolut and Jim Beam seven-year-old. "Guess nobody needs a shot glass," he laughed. We were deep into the second bag of ice.

"How many false IDs did they have?" someone asked when we resumed.

"Two," Elmo said, "excluding the gold shields. They searched tombstones for a boy and girl who died in infancy. They got birth certificates mailed to vacant houses where she could control the mail. They rented post office boxes but hardly used them. Then they did it all over again to set up their escape to Costa Rica."

Steve McDade, who was drinking bourbon laced with coffee, said, "You know what gets me the most? That very first morning, when it all started. Colby disguises himself as a low-life fruit picker, harasses people on the street, gets himself arrested, and then makes sure that his disguise flops so I'll spot him at headquarters—and the son of a bitch had just gunned down two women in cold blood! An hour before!" He looked off somewhere. "The Big Lie."

"You know what gets *me*?" Patterson slapped the arm of the judge's chair. "We let Colby sit in on everything! Right here in this office."

"Every fucking thing," Steve said bitterly. "We *invited* him to sit in, for God's sake, thought we were so goddamn smart co-opting the media. Talk about damn fool mistakes, Elmo— we're the biggest damn fools of all."

"Mo, just tell me one thing," Harry said. "How'd they get themselves invited to sit down at Nasty Brown's kitchen table, drinkin' coffee, and then pull out a forty-caliber and blast away? I know they said they were cops—"

"IAD women," Elmo said, "Colby in drag and Briggs in brownface. Flashed the gold shields. Internal Affairs officers investigating police misconduct against Boogie. Hush hush. Elly Briggs was superb at acting black—she fooled Nasty Brown, Beulah Crabtree, Paul Pitts, and James, the cab driver—and three of them are black themselves."

"Perfect," Harry said with a sneer. "IAD women investigating the dirty police who fucked Boogie over. Perfect."

"Their strength was putting victims at ease. 'When the lion fawns upon the lamb, the lamb will never cease to follow him.'

So Maggie Lodge and Ruth Isaacson open their doors to flowers. Nasty Brown to women IAD with gold shields. Duane Hickman to a free pizza. Paul Pitts gets in a van with a hot honey who knows his name. The posseman falls for the gold shields. Marvin Isaacson accepts a radio from Beulah Crabtree, a gift for her old friend Frankie Hollowell, and Isaacson delivers it himself. Judge Lodge gets out of his car when someone bumps him from behind. Pretext. Facade. George, how did Colby say it?"

I found it on my laptop. "Any uniform or nameplate allays suspicion. On a woman it is nearly foolproof."

Elmo poured another tumbler of bourbon. I could hear him tomorrow morning: 'The only cure for a hangover is death.' After a big slug, he started in again on Colby's and Briggs's dogged attention to detail, hurrying through each example as if it were an open wound. How they assumed every conversation was taped and played their parts religiously. How they acted out every call from every pay phone, knowing the cops would check phone records. How Colby wore two wigs at once, a black one over his natural gray hair, then a *gray* wig on top of the black one, convincing the witnesses at the trailer park that a *dark-haired* man had removed a gray wig. How Colby sometimes misspelled names, sometimes handprinted zip codes with the wrong hand, sometimes used a second typewriter—"just to get us chasing up trees."

I decided to make my own confession. "Talk about damn fool mistakes, I'm supposed to know something about videography—but I never suspected that the famous Avenger interview was a complete fake. There's enough damn fool mistakes to go around."

Elmo said, "Colby worked on that interview for days, playing both parts. Remember what he told us afterwards—that the Avenger wanted the interview broadcast in toto, and that was such a quaint expression, *in toto*, and he remembered how his father had used that same expression. It was a completely manufactured detail, like a hundred others. A thousand. In toto . . ." His voice trailed off.

"The devil is in the details," Patterson mused softly.

We drank for a while in another funk. At length, Juanita asked, "Elmo Finn, how'd you find that bomb shelter? How'd you even know to look for a bomb shelter?"

"It was just a hunch. Avengers had to have a protected base of operations somewhere. We had forty-year-old typing paper curling from moisture, and a forty-year-old typewriter, suggesting a basement or an outbuilding or something. George and I researched the bomb-shelter era, which led us to the head of Civil Defense in the Eisenhower days. Eighty-five years old, remembered everything and still had his old files. And that's where we found Warren Colby, Joe's father, duly recorded. A bomb shelter plus plenty of acreage."

"Jesus," Harry said. "Without that hunch—"

"There was evidence—I just didn't see it. Colby told me he once contemplated suicide lying on his own cemetery plot. Said he thought about blowing his head off, implying he had a gun. But George's time matrix showed he hadn't bought a gun yet. What gun was he talking about? Then I misidentified a Bulldog forty-four as a Ruger, and he corrected me—he knew it was Charter Arms. This was the guy who supposedly didn't know a revolver has no safety. But I didn't catch it."

Steve said matter-of-factly, "I didn't catch a bigger one. The rage thing."

Elmo grimaced. "The knife wounds to Nasty Brown's throat. Shooting the little boy, same thing. Colby had a motive for that level of violence. It seems so obvious now."

"That's why we took him to the goddamn murder scene!" Steve said, jumping up and pacing to the door and back. "We didn't suspect *Colby*, but since he'd been contacted once by Avengers, *or so we thought*, maybe he'd been contacted *twice*, maybe he knew something, maybe seeing the carnage . . ."

"What a pair of psychos," Harry said. "But I'll tell you this, horrible as it sounds, if Colby's kids had been my children . . ."

"You'd arrest the killer, Harry, not kill the innocents," Steve said. "But I know what you're saying. When I got that picture of Cassie in the mail . . . what would any of us do?"

What would any of us do? Elmo Finn, a purist and a perfectionist, had been forced to ask himself that question, and answer it. I had helped him answer it.

Harry went to the ledge and poured a glass of vodka, carefully adding a whisper of tonic. "Elmo, goddamnit, you can't blame yourself!"

Everyone knew Elmo had refused the $350,000 reward. But they didn't know he had convinced the governor to earmark the money for a Patterson-McDade Victims Fund, to be announced after he had left town.

"Elmo," Harry insisted, "you told us to warn everybody, and we warned everybody! Isaacson bought a gun. Lodge hired security but didn't use it. Paul Pitts just laughed at us. Ned Cromartie—hell, we thought he *was* an Avenger. At least take enough money for a month of golf. Make it two months—we need a break from you and Cecil B. Graves!"

"Three cheers for Elmo Finn!"

"Hear hear hear!" they stammered out, but with spirit.

"And Cecil B. Graves!"

"Two's enough!"

I feigned indignation, but I was pleased. I hoped this would bring Elmo around a little, but he merely smiled his enigmatic smile, which I had seen before.

Someone said, "They'll never convict 'em. Some scumbag lawyer'll get 'em off—life in the rubber hotel."

"They'll convict 'em. Vengeance is premeditation on its face. They knew it was wrong."

Elmo said, "I think Colby lied to Elly Briggs about Snot Boogie—said he shot him accidentally. He knew it was wrong. Even in his depravity, he knew it was wrong to shoot a three-year-old. Ergo, competent to stand trial." Elmo's face sagged again. " 'Men ne'er spend their fury on a child.' But they do."

"Mo, how'd you trace the George Orwell mask?"

"Colby's father-in-law was an English professor at the university. Dr. Lemontaine Kell, virtually a recluse now, whose daughter died of cancer and whose only two grandchildren were slaughtered. Always despised Joe Colby. He gave a *1984* costume party, very popular that year in academia. Told me where literary masks were sold—and the Orwell mask was a big seller in 1984. And Joe and Connie Colby came to the party." Elmo paused for a sip. "There were a lot of family photographs in his apartment. Joe Colby had been scissored out of every one." Most of the heads nodded; the murder police had seen more than a few altered family snapshots.

"What were his other mistakes, Mo," Harry asked, "besides knowing too much about guns?"

Elmo had thought plenty about this. "He knew the pizza delivered to Duane Hickman was 'pepperoni and sausage.' You held that back, Steve."

"He could have overheard it, all the times he was sitting right here."

"That's what I thought. Still, I should have noticed it. And they never bought the Doberman, they never took the shooting lessons. Should have noticed that. And when everybody else's alibis . . ." He tapped his forehead with his index finger. "A century ago, Conan Doyle had Holmes say that when everything else has been eliminated, that which remains, no matter how improbable, must be the truth."

Elmo Finn, the perfectionist. Only time would mute the meae culpae. I remembered a day when Elmo Finn, the perfectionist, after a lousy round at Grandfather Mountain, pulled into a pristine overlook on the Blue Ridge Parkway and proceeded to drive every ball in his bag off the mountain into the mists below. Then he methodically snapped every club over his knee, and flung the pieces off the mountain. He saved half the six-iron. I videotaped the whole thing.

We mused about Harry's phony suspension from the force. Elmo said, "I thought an embittered ex-detective might be able to coax something out of somebody. . . ." He looked off again. "More of his ploys worked than mine."

Juanita took Harry's glass and headed for the bar. Without a word, she stopped and hugged Elmo for a long time. He kissed her on the cheek.

We kept going until very late. Then Patterson got some uniforms to drive us home in squad cars. By that time, I had drunk myself sober, and I called my carnal friend, Angie, who whispered to me lustily. At some point, I think I heard Kim arrive in Finn's room, but I wasn't listening.

After Patterson's "sitdown," Elmo and I could have packed up and left, but we stayed around to help Bucky Webb, the prosecutor, prepare the case. Elmo would have performed any penance. Joe Colby himself was in isolation, refusing to talk, refusing pro bono legal help, refusing everything; until he could meet face-to-face with Elmo Finn. So, Elmo conceived a final ploy, and one afternoon Joe Colby found himself spirited to a special room one floor below the jail, containing a round table, three swivel chairs and a concealed video camera. Elmo and I were waiting.

Colby, wearing orange coveralls, grinned at us as the handcuffs were removed; a reckless, cocksure grin, as if this meeting were a victory. After the bailiff went out and the heavy door clanked shut, Colby poured a cup of coffee from the plastic carafe and took the empty chair.

"Unbreakable coffeepot—perfect for us nuthouse cases." He was still grinning, rocking slightly from side to side. I searched his face for signs of madness but saw none. He could have been anybody.

"Enough eyetalk, gentlemen, it is showtime. Showtime. I wish this room had a window. There's no windows in this goddamn place."

Elmo, looking bored, folded his hands in front of him. I opened my notebook to a blank page and clicked my pen. My own little herring—the camera was rolling.

"Why'd you hurt Elly?" Colby asked. "She's still in the hospital."

"No, she isn't. She tried to shoot us."

"Did Elly get off a shot?" Colby's grin brightened.

"No," Elmo said.

"Steve broke her arm."

"Both arms."

Colby frowned. "Why didn't you guys just knock on the door? We couldn't have escaped—there was no way out."

Elmo finger-shot his temple. I remembered his careful planning to lure Colby out of the bomb shelter and avoid a frontal assault.

"Hah! Like Hitler and Eva in the bunker." Colby's laugh was scornful. "It would have saved you a lot of paperwork."

"I wanted to watch you die."

"Hah! Hah! Sherlock Holmes is an avenger! Don't hold your breath, El-mo. How could you want to watch a poor nutcase die? I'm crazy, El-mo, don't you know?" His grin became a wild leer, but it was an act.

"As they do unto you," Elmo said.

Colby drained his coffee and poured another cup. I thought his hand shook slightly. Elmo sat motionless, his fingers interlaced, his eyes hooded and dark. The only sound was the hum of the heating plant, and I had been expecting that.

"So, Quixote and Sancho, Sherlock and Watson—where did I screw up? Show me the error of my ways. I congratulate you, but spare me the sermons—I happen to know you were both avengers yourselves."

Elmo's gaze remained dead-level, unyielding. I saw something in the gray eyes that I had seen only in Vietnam. He said, "If you had truly avenged your children, Colby, by going after Boogie Brown . . . but not innocent people."

"Innocent people die anyway, El-mo! My children were innocent! I had to make the system *feel*! Make the goddamn lawyers and judges *feel* the icefire! Does the word *copycat* ring a bell, El-mo? Victims are striking back! Your fucking system—that's the real jungle. Mr. Phoenix. Mr. Avenger." He was glaring, his eyes wide and wild. I wished I were behind the camera—stay tight, capture every bead of sweat.

Colby drank more coffee, and this time the tremor was unmistakable. "So—what was it—dumb luck?"

In a rapid monotone, Elmo reeled off Colby's missteps—knowing too much about guns, never taking the shotgun lessons nor buying the Doberman, knowing that Duane Hickman's lethal pizza was pepperoni and sausage, confessing too much about his graveyard visitations, yielding to Ned Cromartie's pleadings. Colby listened intently, frozen in the plastic chair.

Elmo said, "I thought you might show up at Ruth Isaacson's grave on her birthday, just to see Marvin grieving."

"I almost did, I almost did."

"We were there. Waiting for you." That was true—we had powerful lenses trained on the gravesite area from dawn to dusk, waiting and watching for *someone*.

"Hah, El-mo. That's what we thought your stupid community meetings were for—to lure the real Avengers into the open. Us lunatics are supposed to be drawn to horseshit like that, mingling with the survivors and the innocent. We saw through it."

Elmo's cold stare was noncommittal. But Colby was right—we had hidden cameras at every community meeting. That's what the meetings were for.

Colby leaned back smugly and locked his fingers behind his head. "Why'd you get all the librarians together? Hah! Thought we were consulting books on bombmaking!" His grin had become grotesque.

"Bomb shelters," Elmo said, but he was lying. Colby was right again.

"We never thought you suspected us, Sher-lock."

"How long have you been a crossdresser?"

"Hah! You mean my disguises. As a woman, I could do *so* much more. The gentler sex, don't you know, El-mo, so harmless, said the black widow." He leered arrogantly. Zoom in.

"You wear panties and pantyhose, Colby, you love to dress in drag. That's why sex with Connie deteriorated—she caught you wearing panties. She couldn't accept it."

"You're crazy." For an instant Colby put his hands on the table, fingertips together, then folded his arms across his chest.

"Connie told her lover all about it. She had a lover, Colby, while you pranced around in panties for Elly Briggs. His name is Logan Murphy. And he will testify in open court."

"Logan—you're lying! You—what a cheap—"

"Want proof, Colby? Connie had a pet name for your dick—Tyrannosaurus Rex. She even told Logan, who asked her if it was really that powerful. She said, no, it's really that extinct. She was laughing at you, Colby. She only stayed because of the kids."

Colby's face and neck reddened deeply, his lips working silently, his fingers clenched white against the orange sleeves of the coveralls. I snickered, then snickered again, perhaps overplaying my part.

Elmo said, "You're going to plead insanity, Colby, which is a defense used in only one of a hundred cases, and it fails in three-fourths of those. You've really got to be crazy to plead insanity, Colby."

Colby tried to sneer but didn't make it. He reached for the carafe, then pulled his hand back quickly, folding his arms again. I felt a flash of warm air, not by accident. Elmo's plan included turning up the heat in more ways than one.

"You knew that shooting the little boy was wrong, so you lied to Elly about it. Before and after the fact. Knowledge of right and wrong equals legal sanity. You've got a date with Old Sparky, and I'll be there."

Colby spluttered an unintelligible sound. His eyes were white with fury. Elmo leaned forward. "Elly didn't kill anyone. She'll testify against you."

"Elly—that's what you think. No chance."

"She's already sold you out, Colby—how did I know about Snot Boogie?"

"Not Elly. Not—"

"There's a lot you don't know about Elly. Remember all her jokes about making it with Ned? That was no fantasy, Colby. Ned wasn't walking dark streets every night."

Colby was breathing raggedly now. A look of incredulity and despair colored his face. I snickered again but I don't think it registered.

"You're . . . you don't understand, Finn . . . I thought *you* would understand, of all people. *You don't get it.*"

"Oh, I get it, Colby. Everybody gets it. *As they do unto you.* Your jungle, our system. The system prevails."

"Not yet. Not yet. I don't think so. Not yet."

Without warning, Elmo stood up. The bailiff opened the

heavy door too quickly and Elmo whisked out. I worried that Colby would spot our ploy.

"So," Colby said between loud breaths. "Where's Sher-lock going?"

"I never know," I said, riffling my notebook to a prepared page and slouching in my chair. The room was much warmer now. "I'm producing a video, Colby, for national TV. Elmo said to leave you out of the interviews, we've got all your goofy writings. What could you say that we don't know?"

"All you've got is . . . I could say plenty. I'm on national TV *now*, fuck your video."

"Fine. Fuck you."

"There's a lot you don't know."

"No, there isn't." I stared challengingly, my hand frozen on the notebook. Zoom in.

For the third or fourth time, he drained his empty cup. "She's lying. She's lying about everything. The wives—she did them. I just worked the camera."

"Prove it."

He gestured wildly. "She had the only motive for Lodge! Lodge was Hollowell's judge, not Boogie Brown's! I had never even heard of him! She said, 'I want you to rape them first so I can see their eyes, I want to see their eyes.' Give her a polygraph. They were the first two and she did them! She didn't even know how to work the camera!"

"She says you did everybody."

"Sure she does! You guys are so dumb! How'd you ever catch me—must have been Steve McDade."

I closed my notebook and propped my foot on the empty chair. In a confessional tone, I told him how all his ploys had fooled us, how the photograph of Steve's daughter, labeled *next*, had caused massive chaos, how the cops were mortified that they'd invited Colby into their midst, how all of us knew that if Colby hadn't tried to help his friend Ned, we wouldn't have caught him. Colby smiled and nodded, and we talked for a while. Gradually, despite the heat, the smug expression returned.

"There's still a lot we don't know, Joe," I said earnestly, "no matter what Elmo Finn says. Like how the little boy got shot."

"It was an accident. A stray shot. I didn't want to do the kid—I didn't even know he'd been hit."

"She says you shot him on purpose."

"Sure she does, she wants a deal! You guys, Jesus! You know what, Graves, you'd do exactly what I did, you'd avenge your children. Tell me this, for old times' sake: Did you and El-mo avenge his girlfriend? On the big day in September, the big fucking day? Just between us, yes or no."

"We weren't even charged."

"*Medieval*, they called it! *Medieval!* The only difference between you and me, Graves, is I got caught! Every victim wants revenge, and some of us go out and get it. Like you and me and Sher-lock!"

It was very hot and still in the room, and I thought I heard the camera, which was impossible. I made a scraping noise with my chair, just in case. I could feel drops of perspiration forming on my face.

"Colby, why didn't you just hire a gangbanger to knock off Boogie Brown in prison? Nobody would have even investigated."

He leaned toward me with a wild stare. "Death was too good for Boogie Brown! Death was too good!" He exhaled loudly. "He had to feel what he made me feel."

"So you shot the boy."

"I just aimed at the little nigger's mouth and squeezed."

Cut and print. I wondered if the prosecutors would use it, or even need it. Then, abruptly, wondrously, a dark weight seemed to lift from me, and I became slightly giddy. As I wiped my face with a handkerchief and pocketed my note-book, the heavy door boomed open. Our bailiff was spring-loaded to the cue position, but it didn't matter now. I walked out without a glance at Joe Colby.

A few mornings later, as Elmo and I were entering the courthouse, a gaunt, hollow-eyed woman suddenly stepped in front of us, blocking our path. Both of us reflexively reached inside our coats.

She said, "Mr. Finn, my name is Julia Cromartie."

I had seen her photograph but didn't recognize her. She was very thin, lines of anguish desecrating her face. She was trembling all over.

"Mr. Finn, I must . . . please—" She began coughing and continued for a full minute, almost doubled over, but finally gained control. She said, "Mr. Finn, I must know, I must know. Was Ned involved?"

Elmo gently took her hand in both of his. "He was not an Avenger, Mrs. Cromartie. He wanted revenge against the man who mutilated him, and Joe Colby arranged it. Joe Colby and Elly Briggs were the Avengers."

Her body slumped, and I thought she might collapse. I edged a little closer.

"I never knew him," she said softly, almost inaudibly, her eyes searching our faces as if perhaps we did. "I never knew any of them. I never . . . did Ned walk the streets at night with a gun?"

"I don't know," Elmo said, still holding her hand. "Colby says he did."

"Joe Colby, Joe Colby, Joe Colby!" She looked around wildly. "Did he kill Ned, Mr. Finn?"

After a pause, Elmo said, "Yes, he did, Mrs. Cromartie. He killed thirteen people. He killed Ned to keep him from talking to the police, even though Ned didn't know Colby was the real Avenger."

"Will he get off? Will he get off?"

"No. He won't get off."

"Were Ned and Elly . . . oh God." Her voice broke and tears welled in her sunken eyes. I offered her a handkerchief, but she didn't take it.

"I don't know, Mrs. Cromartie."

She closed her eyes. "Will he get off, Mr. Finn?"

"No. No. This is not a jungle yet."

"Oh, yes, it is, Mr. Finn. Oh, yes—it is a jungle." She looked defiantly at each of us. "I wish I could kill him."

We stood in our tracks for a while. People going in and out of the courthouse began to notice us. Then Elmo relaxed his grip and Julia Cromartie walked past us toward the street. I was afraid she might fall, but her step was firm.

Two things happened before Elmo and I departed. Captain Patterson threw a private party at the Thunderbolt for the murder cops and certain special guests—Burl Devine, who was nutbeaming in all directions; the radiant Juanita Daley Covington in a rainbow dress; John Ewell, who had gained a few pounds and was accompanied by a bouncy nurse from Presbyterian Hospital; and Logan Murphy and Janie Thomas, recently engaged to be married. Everyone cheered when Patterson presented Elmo an "expense" check for $50,000. Not even Elmo the purist could refuse it, and he didn't.

Then they rolled out something huge in a frame. It was an enormous aerial photograph of a jungle—impenetrable, forbidding. There were inscriptions in the two bottom corners. The first said, "Foul deeds will rise, Though all the earth o'erwhelm them, To men's eyes." Guess who. In the other corner were these words: "Cheers to our friend Elmo Finn, He fought the jungle and he did win." It was signed "The System," followed by the names of Commander Avery Patterson and his homicide detectives. I had never seen Elmo Finn become emotional in public, and I didn't see it then. Almost.

Then came Logan Murphy's grand gesture. He knew about our Holy Days, the Masters Golf Tournament in the flowering first week of April, when the dogwood and azalea illumine Bobby Jones's masterpiece. Augusta National was our shrine, and the Masters was the toughest ticket in sports. As we drank Bollinger's champagne in Logan's office before our flight, he reached in a drawer of his oval desk and tossed Elmo an envelope. Inside were two Masters badges with clubhouse privileges and a Monday tee time. He had arranged for us to stay over and play the course ourselves, when the pins would be the same as in Sunday's final round. Elmo and I became borderline delirious, then crossed the border, switched to a later flight and put a serious dent in the Bolly supply toasting Logan and CBS and Bobby Jones and MacKenzie and Palmer and Nicklaus and Crenshaw and Amen Corner and Sarazen's double eagle and we switched flights yet again.

Finally, we flew away, exchanging the locus of death for the locus of life along the soft shores of the Gulf. Elmo was still having trouble with his "damn fool mistakes," and nothing I said helped. Both of us needed time for the well to fill up again. So began our days and nights on Longboat Key, according to God's master plan: thirty-six in the daytime and twosomes in the dark. Sandra was there for Elmo, just as he had gone to her in times of trouble, and Angie, carting her portable brokerage firm in a tidy briefcase, was there for me. By day, Sandra practiced her leaps and whirls around the pool, Angie bought and sold and hedged, and Shakespeare and I dueled over fifty-dollar Nassaus, back side doubled. Then we mated back up and got through the darkness as heaven intended.

Even the accursed menagerie was almost bearable. Dr. Watson, the retarded bulldog, was taking something for his gas and sat motionless in the shade for long stretches, like a cast-iron lawn dog. I had visions of bronzing him. Macduff, the cross-eyed orange cat, had a fit of overgrooming, licked off all his belly fur and had to be fitted with a Hannibal the Cannibal mask. Perfect for the little deviate. And Falstaff, the imperial cockamamie, was preening and practicing, "All the world's a stage blah blah," but he'd never get the blah blah. I sipped ice-cold Bombay martinis and said it wrong just to watch his feathers.

As the well inexorably filled up, I tallied the balance sheet:

Joe Colby and Elly Briggs behind bars forever, if not executed. Encroachment of the jungle impeded. Elmo Finn extolled by everyone except himself. The good citizens of Avery Patterson's exhausted city rising up to reclaim their system (although As They Do Unto You bumper stickers were still in evidence). Top-dollar bids streaming in for my Avengers video, which meant we could stick to God's plan a little longer. And sweet, sweet Augusta beckoning in the spring. All in all, pretty good omens—bright days ahead!

I can tell you about omens. Forget omens.